Other Books by Sherrie Hansen

Night and Day
Daybreak

Maple Valley Trilogy:
Book 1: Stormy Weather
Book 2: Water Lily
Book 3: Merry Go Round

Love Notes

Wildflowers of Scotland Novels:
Thistle Down *(Prequel Novella)*
Book 1: Wild Rose
Book 2: Blue Belle
Book 3: Shy Violet
Book 4: Sweet William
Book 5: Golden Rod

Seaside

Daisy

Bonnie,
To quilts
and the grannies,
who stitch them,
Sherrie
Hansen

by

Sherrie Hansen

Published by Blue Belle Books

Saint Ansgar, Iowa

Blue Belle Books

www.BlueBelleBooks.com

PO Box 205

St. Ansgar, Iowa 50472

Cover Design: Sherrie Hansen

Cover Photo: Sherrie Hansen

Manufactured in the United States of America

ISBN: 9781699846025

DEDICATION

To my husband, Mark, and his enthusiasm for traveling the world with me, with much appreciation for his patience with me as I write, edit, and perfect each book.

ACKNOWLEDGEMENTS

To Ben Caron and Will Bartz, two gifted musicians who held a Community Songwriting Project Showcase in my hometown. Their mentoring inspired me to write and debut an original song, Seaside Daisy's Shanty. Their encouragement and sharing of their gifts is much appreciated!

1

Daisy Fitzpatrick flipped down the kickstand of her bicycle, untwisted the handles of the bag that held her granny's dear, hand-stitched, wool quilt, and counted it a blessing that Granny Siobhan wasn't alive to see what the foxes had done to her pride and joy.

She stood straight and tall. The Wild Atlantic Way might be a hard foe to tame, but it was no match for a Fitzpatrick with her mind made up. She'd re-staked her claim to Granny's sea shanty and made it clear to the fox family that they were no longer welcome. As fate would have it, she'd known of a recently emptied sea cave that had made a perfect shelter for the cubs.

She reached for the handle of the bright yellow door that led to Dingle Dry Cleaners and pulled it halfway open.

"Serves the girl right!" A voice that sounded suspiciously like her Great-Auntie Ailene's greeted her ears.

What girl? What poor, unfortunate lass were they bashing now? She inched the door open a little further, but not far enough to trigger the bell.

"Daisy always did have to learn things the hard way."

Daisy's ears started to burn and a spot near her right temple began to throb. She tried to think of some other Daisy the ladies might be talking about, but unless someone new had moved to town in the few months she'd been gone, it had to be her they were chewing on.

"You can thank the Good Lord Siobhan isn't here to see the

mess Daisy has gotten herself into. It near broke the poor woman's heart when Daisy scorned her good Irish upbringing and stopped going to mass."

"And then again, when she started spouting off about never getting married and having children because she wanted the freedom to pursue her dreams."

"And look where it's gotten her now."

Daisy's heart was already so tender. She could feel it wilting to near nothing with each new word that was said against her.

"From what I understand, her little shop was doing well enough. The bits and bobs she made from sea glass and driftwood were quite unique. I'm told the tourists loved them."

Thank you, Aunt Sheelagh. At least one of the diabolical old biddies believed in her.

"Although, for something that was supposed to be the girl's life work and passion, she was certainly quick to toss it aside when she found the gold."

Sigh. So even Aunt Sheelagh wasn't a fan – at least, not a loyal one. She took a deep breath and resolved to fling the door open and rush in unfazed just as soon as there was a lull in the conversation. Although it would serve them right if they realized she'd heard every word. Of course, knowing them, they'd find a way to twist things around, forego repenting of the sin of gossiping, and find her guilty of eavesdropping.

"That's what gold does to people. The luck of the Irish, my foot. If the girl had kept going to mass, she'd know that money is the root of all evil."

"What do you expect given the lax upbringing Siobhan gave the girl? T'would have been better if she'd ne'er found the gold."

Right. Like any of them would have turned their backs on the treasure trove she'd unearthed. Fools. What Irishman didn't dream of finding a pot of gold at the end of a rainbow? It was the stuff legends were made of. It was inconceivable to think that someone would walk away after being so lucky as to find a stash of gold coins in an ancient sea cave on their property.

Or at least, what they'd thought was their property.

"Well, I pity the poor lass. There was a day when I thought I'd found my pot of gold, only to have it wrenched away from me by that sweet-talking Lolita-"

She heard a different voice jump into the fray. "I'm right here,

Ailene. You only thought Colin was your pot of gold. Everyone else on the Dingle Peninsula could see that we were the perfect match."

Auntie Ailene's sharp voice cut through the ruckus. "Goodness, gracious, Lolita. The man's been dead for nigh on forty years and didn't bring either one of you much luck if you want the truth."

The room erupted in a tirade of chitchat. At least they were off her. And unless she wanted the extra time and expense of a car hire and driving to the cleaners in Killarney, she had little choice but to face the firing squad. Daisy squared her shoulders and marched through the door.

#

Cavan Donaghue signed his fifth rental agreement of the morning, lifted a blue Raleigh ten speed and a yellow CycleOps racer from the rack, and reminded the French couple to ride on the left, with the traffic, contrary to what their instincts would tell them. His business had boomed ever since he'd moved to his new location, where his front door opened up to the Wild Atlantic Way itself.

The smells of homemade soda bread, cherry bakewells, Irish stew and brown bread from the bakery next door - plus carrot or lemon cake, depending on the day - lured the customers in. The sparkling new, bright yellow and blue window display he'd created when he'd remodeled the place three months earlier did the rest.

"How's about you, Cavan? What's the craic?"

He looked up and smiled as Rory, an old friend and frequent customer, came through the door spinning the front wheel of his fancy titanium Colnago.

"Flat?"

"Piece of glass. Got the tyre and the inner tube."

"Ouch." He took the wheel gingerly as Rory pointed to a jutting piece of what was probably the remnants of a bottle of Guinness. "That's what happens when a bottle of Irish Stout goes up against a glass of Italian Chianti."

Rory smiled.

"I can fix it while you wait unless I'm besieged by another round of tourists."

"I'm in no hurry."

"You could pop in for a bowl of Maeve's Irish Stew while I'm working."

"But I've hardly seen you since you left the old neighborhood."

His old shop had been in a primarily residential area just a block from Rory's townhouse. Before the move, Rory had stopped in almost every afternoon.

"So your risky business venture has paid off for you, has it?"

"I'm very happy with the way things have been going. My expenses are near twice what they were, but my rental business has skyrocketed, and sales and repairs have almost tripled."

Rory had no financial worries, but he wasn't so rich or far-removed that he'd forgotten what it was like to live on a shoestring or dance the delicate balance between business and bankruptcy.

Cavan grabbed a couple of tyre levers and positioned them so he could pry the tyre from the wheel.

"I'm delighted for you, man. Aren't you glad you signed a five year lease now that you've made a success of the place?"

"And here I was worried about what would happen if I didn't make a go of it."

"But now that you have, your extended lease is gold in the bank."

"For sure. Now that I've made the transition, I'm glad Daisy insisted on a long term lease. I can't imagine having to leave here now that I've worked this hard and put so much of myself into redoing the place. I like living upstairs, too. There's a great view of the harbor, and the sunrises are phenomenal. Even the clatter from the pubs suits me well. The music and the voices, the clinking of glasses and an occasional bird song are a mighty fine mix when it comes down to it."

He went to the wall of tyres and chose one of the right size that had a similar tread.

Rory grinned. "Listen to you now. All you need is some pretty colleen to give you a backrub and ease your sore muscles at the end of the day and you'll be set for life."

"Well, at least for five years."

#

Daisy whooshed through the door of the dry cleaners like she hadn't been standing there listening to her relatives and supposed friends talk about her for the last five minutes. She smiled brilliantly and tried to ooze confidence and nonchalance and charm. She had nothing to be ashamed of. She'd had every reason to believe the gold was on her property – and that her former boyfriend had really, truly loved her.

She went right to the counter, like she hadn't heard her Aunt Ailene's voice and had no clue she was there. Maybe they wouldn't notice her and she could get in and out without having to pretend she was happy to see her or engage in fake sweet talk.

"Daisy! How nice to see you!"

No such luck.

"Hi, Auntie Ailene. Auntie Sheelagh. What brings you out on such a fine day as this? I would think you'd be home putting your gladiola bulbs in the garden. First time we've had sun in a week."

Aunt Sheelagh lifted her chin and sniffed the air. "What is that smell?"

Daisy moved her granny's quilt from her left arm to her right and tried to use her body to block the odor of fox urine that was wafting out from the fabric. "I don't smell anything." She lifted her foot and twisted it this way and that. "I just walked through the park. Maybe I stepped in something."

"Isn't that my sister's favorite crazy quilt? The one she made from our da and grandda's wool suits? Oh, the memories that are wrapped up in those bits and pieces of fabric!"

Daisy put her foot down, smiled bravely and tried to build a mental shield around the quilt to diffuse the fumes. "What? I'm just dropping off some dry cleaning. You know – airing out the home place since I've moved back in."

"But I'm sure that's the quilt your granny loved so much. Siobhan was so proud of all the pretty embroidery work she did around the edges. It took her hours. She even won an award for it at the town festival one year! I can't recall what she won but I remember she said it was the second luckiest day of her life. I never did figure out what she meant by that. I suppose the luckiest was the day she met Xavier."

"Humph," Auntie Sheelagh snorted. "None of the rest of the family thought so. That unsavory gypsy was Siobhan's ruination."

Auntie Ailene coughed. "Now, now, Sheelagh. Xavier claimed to be a Celtiberian, and he was a staunch Catholic. We had no reason to doubt him."

What difference did it make? Her grandda had been dead for decades. It was days like this that Daisy wanted to send a sample of her DNA to Ancestry.com to prove once and for all that she was adopted, and no relation whatsoever to Aunties Sheelagh or Ailene.

"Anyway, the quilt smells awful." Auntie Sheelagh wrinkled her nose and made a gagging noise. "Like a cat has been using it for a litter box – but worse. The smell is so strong it's making me feel faint."

Daisy was feeling a bit woozy herself. "You know, it's a shame the old sea shanty sat empty for so long. I was already in my apartment over the shop when Granny died, and no one else wanted to live there."

"Next." The drycleaner's voice cut through the clatter and Daisy found herself at the front of the queue.

"I – um – have a quilt that needs to be dry cleaned."

The drycleaner raised his eyebrows and swiped at his nose. "I'm sorry, we don't accept – ah –"

"But it's wool," Daisy said. "I can't wash it. It needs to be dry cleaned."

"Have you tried airing it out?"

"Um. Yes." She lowered her voice to a whisper. "For three or four days. Please. You've got to help me."

"There are products designed to help with odors. I could give you a referral. I might even have a coupon."

She scanned the room. People were holding their noses and a few were making choking noises.

"I cannot help you," the drycleaner said. "I'm going to have to ask you to leave before the clean clothes start to take on the odor of your quilt."

"But," Daisy stammered. "Maybe if I took it with me now, I could make an appointment for the exact time you're able to clean it, and then I could bring it by and–"

"Perhaps the drycleaner in Killarney would be interested in helping you." The man looked totally unsympathetic.

"Hey, Daisy. What's the craic?" The friendly vibes from Cavan's voice surrounded her like a soft quilt – a clean quilt that smelled of fresh summer breezes and brisk sea air.

"Cavan." She watched as he sized up the situation.

"C'mon, Daisy. Let's get out of here." Cavan shifted the bulky wool sweater he was holding to his other arm, took her elbow and led her out of the drycleaners.

Customers parted like she was Moses and her stinky old quilt was a staff. When they reached the street, Cavan gingerly took the quilt from her and started to walk.

"My bicycle is right here."

He took the quilt and slid it into the plastic trash bag she'd used to haul it into town.

"So I've been hearing rumors that you were back for a visit." Cavan leaned against the side of the building. "What's going on?"

"It's a long story. But thank you so much! You're my hero. I mean, my brain knew they were kicking me out, but my feet were rooted to the ground like a tree growing in solid rock out by the Atlantic."

"Where did the quilt come from? Why didn't you take it to the drycleaner in Killarney instead of driving all the way down here?"

"You don't know?"

Cavan leaned down, pinched her bike tyres, ran his fingers along the rim of her back tyre where it was starting to crack. "Know what? And where's your car? If you're going to be riding this old bicycle around, you need to bring it into the shop so I can check it over. Or maybe you should look at new ones. This one's got major problems."

Daisy made a face. He really didn't know that she'd lost her house and her car and her new life, nor that the gold was gone, nor that she was penniless or next thing to homeless, nor that she was a person of interest in a murder investigation?

Cavan looked up at her with curious eyes, not judging, not condemning, not suspecting her of anything. For a second, she was tempted to play him. I mean, how wonderful to have one person in her life that she could be with without feeling totally humiliated, pitied or scorned.

"Daisy? Are you okay?"

She couldn't do it. Cavan was not only her tenant but her friend. But how to convey everything that had happened since they'd last spoken?

2

Daisy took a deep breath, sucked in as much fresh air as her lungs would hold and let the smell of sea air and saltwater replace the dank, musty smell of the fox-infested sea shanty she now called home.

Cavan put his hand on her arm. "Last time I saw you, you were on the top o' the world and sitting pretty in a sparkling new Mercedes convertible. Now, you're riding a rusty old bicycle with worn tyres and carrying around a raggedy quilt that stinks to the high heavens. And you look more than a wee bit depressed. What's the craic?"

"Enough about me! How are you doing? Has business been good at the bike shop?" She would never wish failure on a nice man like Cavan, but the simple fact of the matter was that he was living in her old apartment and using her old arts and crafts shop for his bicycle sales and repair work. If he was doing well, then so be it. But if for some reason, he wasn't happy with his new location, she would love to have her old life back. That's all she was thinking.

"Couldn't be better," Cavan said. "Business has tripled since I moved the shop to the new location. There's so much foot traffic. I think the main difference is that when I was on a side street, people only found me if they were already thinking of renting a bicycle and specifically searched for a rental company. Now, tourists see the sign, and think, oh, what a great idea! We should rent some bikes!"

"So they just pop in unannounced then?"

"Yes. The new location is very conducive to spur of the moment decisions, especially when the weather is good. It's perfect for me."

Perfect, huh? No wiggle room there. Cavan sounded content and more enthusiastic than she'd ever heard him. If he'd been even a wee bit unhappy she might have been able to talk him into giving up his lease so she could move back in.

"Speaking of business, I need to pop back into the store to take care of the customers who just walked in. Can you wait a few minutes while I get them signed up and off on their ride?"

"Sure. Don't worry. I won't bring the quilt in."

#

Daisy leaned against the front of the bike shop and realized, for the first time in quite some months, that her old life had been pretty good, all things considered. The shop had been in the perfect location, and the apartment above had been sunny, cute and comfortable. She'd had a great thing going. She never would have considered moving if she hadn't struck gold.

"Hello?" Are you Daisy Fitzpatrick?"

Daisy looked at the woman. No one she remembered knowing. "Who's asking?"

"Maxine Caithness. I'm a reporter with the Dublin Herald. I was told you might be willing to talk to me about the gold that you found and then lost."

"I've already given quite a few interviews about that topic. So, no. I don't think so."

"I've driven a long way. I would appreciate it if you could give me a few minutes of your time. If you don't want to talk about the gold, we could chat about the priest who was murdered just a few yards from your sea shanty."

Daisy looked around to make sure no one was within earshot. "Um, I don't think that would be a good idea."

"I don't see what it could hurt." The reporter's pout looked so childlike that Daisy wanted to scream.

"Listen. Last time I spoke to a reporter, it cost me over a million euros. So – no. I don't think so."

Maxine looked not only petulant but devastated. "I promise I'll put a favorable slant on your involvement. I mean, all those people who were mad at you because you bought things from them using money that wasn't really yours, could be brought around to the point of forgiving you if they know you're trying to help the authorities catch the priest killer."

"I don't need to be forgiven. I did not do anything wrong." Her mouth gaped open. The gall of this person...

"But the people you purchased your mansion from, and all the shops that you bought your furniture from, and the home improvement stores where you got materials to upgrade your house – surely they all lost money."

She was shaking. "And this is the way you try to convince me to give you an interview?" She was incredulous. And pissed. "So not going to happen."

Maxine grinned. "Ah. But it is happening. You're talking to me aren't you?"

Her head was so full of steam she felt like it might pop off.

"I mean, it's all pretty simple." The reporter – Maxine – twisted a loop of her long hair between two fingers. "If you give me an interview, I'll give you control over your quotes and the general content of the article. If you don't, I'll be forced to make things up based on my own vivid imagination. What I write may not be completely accurate, but we both know you don't have enough money to hire an attorney and sue me. So you may as well cooperate."

Daisy turned on her heel and started to stalk away. It was like something out of the movies, really. Is this how celebrities or the president felt when they were being harassed and under constant scrutiny? She even felt a small stir of sympathy for the British royal family and their legendary skirmishes with the paparazzi.

And then she tripped. She hit the ground and her hand skidded across the pavement. She felt the pain of tender flesh tearing and wondered how long it would be before she could hold a paintbrush in her hand. She kept sliding and felt a sharp rock against her finger, then the force of her weight gouging it into her skin. Her momentum was as strong as her anger had been, like a boulder rolling downhill, bouncing over the edge of a cliff and rolling down to the sea only to crash into a wave. She hated this!

She finally got herself halfway righted and sat there on the pavement with her legs crossed, resisting the urge to bawl her eyes out. She could only hope Cavan's business kept him long enough that he wouldn't see her covered in bloody scrapes and debris from the road.

The girl from the paper was snapping shots with her mobile and doing nothing to help her up.

Eejit.

What next? She'd held her head high through all the indignities that had befallen her. She'd been both humbled and humiliated. Through it all, she'd stayed calm and never once shed a tear. Now, they were leaking from her eyes and running down her chin, and coming out of her nose. There was water everywhere and she could only wish it was so deep that she would float down to the Wild Atlantic Way and sail away.

Finally, Maxine reached out her hand and said, "Can I help?"

"No!"

Maxine took a step back.

"Oh, no."

Her Aunt Sheelagh walked out the door of the drycleaners, marched over to Daisy and launched another attack.

"Well, Daisy. I hope you're happy about what happened in there because I for one am beyond embarrassed. Your granny would roll over in her grave if she could see what you've done to her favorite quilt."

"I didn't do anything to her quilt except rescue it from the shanty and try to get it cleaned!"

Ouch! Had she torn the skin off her earlobe? It felt like a midge was biting her.

"You're such a screw-up, Daisy. You never do anything the way you're supposed to. I don't approve of anything you've ever done in your life. Your mother and father would be so disappointed in you."

Daisy's mouth opened and closed. Her throat started to feel clogged up and for a second, she thought she might really cry.

With a shock, Daisy realized that the words she'd heard were coming from her own head, and not Aunt Sheelagh's mouth. The things Sheelagh was saying probably weren't half as bad as what Daisy had imagined. Or maybe they were.

Not only that, but Cavan had reappeared. He looked a bit dazed. At least Maxine seemed to have gone.

She saw Cavan take her aunt's dry cleaning and say, "Why don't

I carry those things to your car for you? It's a good reminder that I need to get the rest of my winter woolens cleaned so they'll be fresh and ready to wear come fall. You're wise to think of it now. But they do look heavy."

Cavan was such a nice man. He was only one of the things she'd missed about her old life even before she'd lost her new one.

Cavan disappeared with her aunt. Daisy crawled a few feet until she could sag against the building behind her bicycle. She would get this all sorted. What choice did she have? As soon as she got the sea shanty cleaned out and made more suitable for living, she could start collecting seashells and pebbles and sea glass so she could build up her inventory again. Of course, she'd have to hunt for a new place to sell her wares and find a way to spread the word that she was reopening in a new location.

"Hey. Aren't you the one who killed the priest?"

Her heart leaped into her throat. She lowered her head and turned her face away from the crowd of teenagers who didn't have anything better to do than taunt her. Thank goodness Cavan hadn't still been standing there.

Thankfully, the throng kept moving. They were disappearing around the corner by the time Cavan returned.

He stuck his hands in his pockets. "You look pretty sore." He held out his hand to help her up. "Your aunt said you've moved into your granny's sea shanty."

She winced and tried to hold on to the one shred of pride she still possessed. "Yes. The house in Killarney was just so huge. The heat and electricity alone were higher than my whole house payment in Dingle. I was just rattling around in that big old barn all by myself – and for what reason?"

"I thought you had a boyfriend."

"Well, I did. But Aodhan, well, we're not dating any longer, so my social life was kind of dwindling anyway." She blinked her eyes and tried to come across as perky and upbeat. Cavan looked skeptically on.

"So I thought, why not spend the summer down by the sea at Granny's, enjoy the Wild Atlantic Way, get back to my roots. You know. I always loved it there."

"Right," Cavan said. "Daisy? I've known you for too long. I can tell when you're feeding me a line of crap."

Daisy gave him a look. "And here I was just thinking what a

nice man you've always been."

"I am a nice man. And you've always been a terrible liar."

"So you're not going to let me-"

"I'm not trying to hurt you, Daisy. I want to help. How can I help if you won't tell me what's wrong?"

She looked around to make sure no one else was within earshot. Why, she had no idea. Cavan was probably one of the few people in town who hadn't already heard the news.

She swallowed. Hard. "It's gone. The money. The gold. My car. My new life in Killarney. It's all gone.

"What? But how is that possible?"

"Turns out the gold I found was on my neighbor's land instead of Granny's. Remember that interview I did with the reporter from the Killarney newspaper? Well, he invited a telly crew down from Dublin to do a feature on me and they wanted to film me on the beach in front of the sea cave where I found the treasure chest. There was a distinctive rock in the background of the video clip, and that's when a cousin of the priest realized that the gold was found on the priest's land and not on my grandmother's land. I mean, if the cave was just two feet to the west, I'd still be rich and living in my house in Killarney and none of this would ever have happened."

A tickle of ice cold air swooped down and wrapped itself around her neck. Granted it was only May, but it should be starting to warm up by now, shouldn't it? She slapped at her earlobe. Again, it felt like a midge bite, except that it hadn't been warm enough for them to come out.

She scratched the soft skin behind her ear and felt a tear slip from her eye. "How I wish I'd never said a word about the gold. No one ever would have known."

Cavan grimaced as realization dawned on him. "So this priest you mentioned. He's not the priest who went missing a couple of weeks ago – Father McLeary, the one everybody's been looking for, is he?"

She gulped. "I'm sorry to say they're not looking for him any more. They found him dead inside the next little sea shanty to the west of the one where my granny and I lived."

"What was the priest doing down there?"

"According to the police, he owned the shanty and was living down there off and on so he could have a little privacy. He knew

about my gold long before I found it. Well, his gold. Whatever."
She rolled her eyes.

Cavan looked worried. "In all the times I've hiked along the beach, I've never seen a priest – or anyone else – anywhere near that old shanty.

"Well, supposedly, he missed the monastic life and found the rectory to be too hectic because of all the people coming and going. He was evidently a bit of a recluse and very secretive about the fact that he owned land on the coast, so when he went missing, no one knew where to look for him."

Cavan looked deep in thought, and she assumed he was trying to process the information dump she'd just laid on him.

Cavan said, "His parish must have been frantic when he suddenly didn't show up to officiate one Sunday morning. Didn't he disappear a good month ago?"

"I guess so. Of course, I never heard a thing about it since I was up in Killarney. And I never knew the man. I left the Catholic church the second I was confirmed. I mean, my mother was Protestant and once I had a choice, it seemed easier to be a Methodist than to feel guilty all the time about things I hadn't even done. I didn't know anything about any of it until the police came to my house in Killarney and forced me to go down to the station with them. A few days later, I came home to a padlock on my front door and then, suddenly, my bank account was frozen, and everything I'd bought with the gold was being repossessed."

She stopped short of telling Cavan she'd been named as a suspect or as she preferred to think of it, a person of interest, in the murder of the priest. No need to totally disillusion the man.

"So do you want to grab a bite to eat? There's a new bistro on Dingle Avenue that makes a great seafood chowder."

"I'd better not," she said. "I should go home and get cleaned up." Right, in the shower the shanty didn't have or an icy cold tide pool. At least the wind off the Atlantic would dry her off quickly once her teeth had stopped chattering from her freezing cold dip.

Cavan smiled just a little. "If you're afraid someone's going to steal your granny's quilt while you're having dinner, I can say with one hundred percent certainty that there's no need to worry."

"Ha ha."

"You can use the bathroom upstairs in my loft to clean that scrape off while I'm locking up the shop."

She hesitated. 'His loft' sounded odd. She still thought of it as hers. But it did have running water. Clean water. Hot water.

"My treat," Cavan said. "You look like you could use a warm bowl of soup."

She was hungry, and there was nothing to eat at home.

"Sure. As long as I get home in time to make a fire before it gets dark."

3

A few minutes later, Daisy met Cavan at the bottom of the stairs. 'Her loft' looked a bit too sparse and masculine for her tastes, but she'd have wondered about Cavan if the place still had the whimsical look she'd decorated with when she lived there.

"How are things going out at the shanty then?" Cavan held the door while they exited the back way to the alley. "Do you have enough peat or do you need me to cut a new supply?"

"Thanks. I'm staying plenty cozy for now, but I guess I'll need more for next winter."

See, that was another thing she liked about Cavan. The guys she'd known in Killarney couldn't even imagine a house without a furnace. They wouldn't have the slightest notion how to cut peat or lay out a fire. And they wouldn't know a bog if it bit them.

Cavan had been raised the same way she was. He was handy and practical, and knew how to fix things and fend for himself if the need arose. He was definitely one of the good guys. Too bad he wasn't – she was about to write him off as not being her type – but then, she looked at him.

She'd always thought of Cavan as being skinny and nondescript. When had he gotten so buff and muscular? She couldn't imagine him spending hours at the gym like her friends in Killarney did. He was very tan – not an easy thing to accomplish this time of year when the air was barely warm enough to tolerate being outside and the wind was usually blowing at gale force. He must be bicycling or jogging or kayaking or doing something outside.

She gave Cavan a blank look and screeched her thoughts back to more important matters. She wondered if Cavan knew how to inspect a chimney and if there was any way he would consider getting up on her granny's rickety old ladder to make sure there wasn't a squirrel's nest inside the shaft. She didn't mind the smell of a peat fire – part of her even liked it in a nostalgic kind of way – but she didn't relish the thought of the smoke not being able to escape should the chimney be plugged.

She nodded and they walked side by side up the hill to Dingle Avenue and then up the hill again and down a few steps to the bistro. Cavan stood to the side and held the door open for her.

A waitress tipped her head in the direction of a little round window table for two flanked by upholstered wing back chairs. She was polite enough not to say anything about Daisy's bedraggled appearance. Her hands held two oval plates, one stacked high with a sandwich that looked to be stuffed with turkey, bacon, tomatoes, and possibly avocado. The other had a steaming bowl of seafood chowder with two shrimp wrapped in some sort of pastry on top. It looked and smelled heavenly.

Cavan pulled out a chair for her and helped her get snuggled up to the table once she'd sat down.

"So do you have a plan?" Cavan took a seat and took off his jacket.

"Not really," Daisy glanced at the menu and thought about the days when she had enough money to order lobster without thinking twice about it. She remembered how fun it was to order whatever she wanted from the menu, including one of each dessert if she so pleased. One night at a pub in Killarney, she'd treated her whole crowd of friends to what they'd called a dessert orgy.

But that was all a dream, a memory of things past. She was back in Dingle now, up to her elbows in her old life, except she'd cast aside her old life when she found the gold and moved to Killarney.

She'd tried very hard not to slip into the grass is greener syndrome. Being rich and living in a turn-of-the-century mansion in Killarney had been pretty wonderful, but so had her old life in Dingle, now that she thought about it. Her circumstances had changed so drastically. Everything was such a confused jumble that she didn't know what to think about anything.

"So let me ask you this, Cavan." She toyed with the thick cloth napkin and folded it and pleated it and twisted it a bit for good measure. "If there was a way to lower your rent by 25% by giving up the display window and the north wall of the front room, would you be at all interested?"

"Aw, Daisy. That's a horrible position to put me in. The front display is the thing that draws the customers in the door, and the north wall is the first thing they see once they're inside."

She grimaced sheepishly. "So what about half of the display window and the east wall?"

"I know what you're thinking, Daisy. The thing is, the type of people who are drawn to bicycle shops just aren't the same kind of people who want to look at arts and crafts and bits and bobs from the sea. I've seen your artwork and it's creative and beautiful and unique, but speaking as a man, there is no way I would voluntarily set foot in a store filled with cutesy bric-a-brac even if the sign said there was a bike hire inside."

"So what about this? No window space. The west wall. And a small placard underneath the bike hire sign saying arts and crafts."

"It would send the wrong message. It would confuse my customers and drive off my clientele."

"But-"

"Bike shops smell like rubber inner tubes and new tyres. I know you. My bicycles would drive you crazy. You'd be fine with it for about a week before you'd be wanting to diffuse essential oils like Joy and Stress Away and decorate the place up with fluffy white clouds and rainbows and shamrocks. And you'd make garlands out of seashells and drape fisherman's netting over my bike racks."

"But my arts and crafts would give the ladies something to look at while their husbands are deciding which bicycles they want to rent. Or buy."

"Nice try, but it doesn't work that way. My customers come into the shop looking to rent a bike feeling happy and enthusiastic. Should their wives suddenly start seeing stuff they want to buy, the men would get irritated and tense, and start envisioning how empty their wallets are going to be by the time they get out of the place. Eventually, their jaws would clamp down and they'd leave without renting anything."

"Happy wife, happy life?"

"Sad bike shop owner."

The waitress came to take their order and Cavan ordered two

bowls of Dingle's best seafood chowder with brown bread. "If soup is still okay with you." He raised his eyebrows at her.

"Sounds perfect."

"Good. At least we can agree about that much."

They stared at each other across the table.

She finally broke the silence. "You can't blame me for trying."

"I understand. I really do. You rented your place to me assuming that your new start in Killarney would be a permanent thing. You went after what you wanted and didn't look back. Now, you've lost everything you had, and you want the comfort and security of the familiar."

"I guess what they say about not being able to go back is true. But if that's the case, what am I supposed to do?" She pursed her lips and looked at Cavan across the table, looking solid and reliable and like he would never let her down. Except that he was as stubborn as she was and there was no way he was going to give up the lease he had signed and move back to his old apartment and his old bike shop location so she could have her apartment and her shop back.

Cavan eyed her skeptically. "You know I'll do anything I can to help get you settled into your granny's sea shanty and figure out what to do with your life from here on out, right?"

"Anything except rip your lease to shreds and move out."

"Yup. Anything but that."

The waitress brought their soup and they stopped talking until they'd spooned every last ladle full from their bowls. That was another good thing about Cavan. He was the kind of man you could spend time with without feeling like you had to be cute or entertaining. You could relax and feel comfortable with Cavan. Daisy didn't know what it was like to have a big brother because she'd never had one, but she thought Cavan might be the kind of man who would make the best big brother ever.

"So tell me this," Cavan said. "Why did you leave Dingle and move to Killarney in the first place?"

She just looked at him. What kind of question was that? "Because I could?"

"I'm serious. I've heard some people win the lottery and don't change much of anything about their lives because they're happy with the way things are. They might buy a bigger car or build an addition on their house, but basically, they don't want to change things too much because they had it pretty good before they came into the money."

"They liked their lives." She paused. "So you're asking me if I rented you my shop and moved to Killarney because I hated my life here in Dingle."

"Yes," Cavan said. "Because it you weren't happy here, you shouldn't come back or you'll make yourself even more miserable. If it was your dream to move to Killarney and live in a big mansion and make new friends, then you should find a way to do it even if the gold is gone." He smiled. "Except I'd ask you to please not raise my rent."

She smiled back and took the opportunity to study his face. He was so cute and honest and intent on helping her.

Cavan held her gaze. "I'm serious. Even if you have to start out by renting a small room in one of those big mansions like the one you used to own and sell your artwork at street fairs, if that's what you want, then you should go for it. Or maybe you don't want to make things anymore. Then figure out what it is that you want to do and find a way to make it happen."

"How did you get to be so smart?" The truth was, Cavan was making her uncomfortable. He was making her think. She'd been going through the motions and ignoring her emotions for days, and now, Cavan was forcing her to own up to the truth and examine her feelings, and she just wasn't ready.

She forced a laugh and it came out dry and bitter sounding even to her own ears. "I don't know what I feel – about anything. Oh, there's hurt, and disappointment, and this feeling of being cheated. It's like taking certain things for granted – like the tide coming in night and day, like clockwork, until one day, it doesn't, and you can't figure out what the hell happened because the tides are supposed to be reliable, and people are supposed to tell you the truth, and not lie to you."

She clamped her hand over her lips, mortified at the words that had come out of her mouth – her soul. "Sorry. So much for a light dinner between friends."

"Yeah. That ship kind of sailed when you tried to get me to tear up my lease and move out of your building."

"Oh. Right. Sorry."

Cavan reached across the table and took her hand, rough and dinged up as it was. His was a little scratchy, too, and she noticed that the little lines in his skin were tinged in black. Working hands.

She smiled. "Could we forget about our troubles for a wee bit and share a sticky toffee pudding?"

Cavan squeezed her hand. "I'd like that."

4

Cavan counted four empty spoke holes on the rim and inserted a new spoke, then picked up the next spoke and inserted it into the hub in its proper space. It was methodical work and anyone who could count to four could do it, but he found a certain satisfaction and pride in creating the geometric design of a wheel. He'd spent the whole morning trying to balance his checkbook and filing VAT tax reports for the government. He was glad his business was doing so well, but the mound of paperwork that went along with the increase in business was the bane of his existence.

The catch side of having more money in his account was that the reason it was there was because he'd been so busy, which meant he had no time to spend any of it. When he'd been in his old location, he'd only made it through the lean times by refusing to spend a cent, stretching out any surplus that he might have from one month to cover him in the next.

A tall, cocky looking Englishman came through the door chatting with an even taller mate with a Harris Tweed jacket with leather elbow patches and a flat wool hat.

"Two 29 inch Titanium bicycles with extra large frames for the afternoon, please," the taller of the two gents said without even glancing his way.

His companion also ignored Cavan but said to his friend, "Should I let Royal Birkdale know that we may not be able to make our tee time on Tuesday evening? I'm told the ferry company is notorious for cancelling the crossing if the waves are a bit too high. And the drive through west Wales can be slow going if it's foggy or wet – which it usually is."

"Yes. Although not nearly as foggy and wet as the Wild Atlantic Way."

The men laughed in unison.

"I have extra large frames available, but not in titanium."

The men were still not paying attention to him and evidently didn't hear him over their laughter.

A middle-aged couple opened the door and the chime jingled as they came through.

One of the Englishmen removed his cap and ran his fingers through a crop of thick blond hair. "So if we cancel, we definitely don't get to play."

"But if we risk it, there's at least a twenty percent chance we can make it in time to tee off," his companion said. "And with the way you drive, we can safely cut the predicted time of travel by at least a third."

"Why, thank you."

The couple was now waiting in line behind the Englishmen. The woman looked a bit younger than the man, and had strawberry blond hair with tinges of grey.

The Englishman's loud voice boomed through the shop. "How much does it cost to play Royal Birkdale these days? Two hundred fifty pounds? Three hundred?"

"A small price to pay if we make it as planned, and no great loss if we can't get there in time."

"Now if we were talking Turnberry, or Old Course, St. Andrews, we might have to rethink our plan."

"I have extra large frames in steel, or regular frames in titanium. Would you prefer-"

Once more, the men laughed jovially.

He sighed, took an order pad and a rental agreement and walked around the counter to the couple. "Rental?"

They nodded their assent. Or maybe they said yes. The two Englishmen were being so loud that he couldn't have heard them if they had.

He leaned in closer. Both the man and the woman were tall and fair. Swedes? "Extra large frames? I have seven speeds ready to go."

"Perfect," the woman said, and smiled.

"As long as there's no extra charge for the tall bikes," the man said.

"Sign right here." He pointed at the price and the man handed him a credit card. He went behind the counter and ran the card, then handed the credit card machine to the man – Anders Westerlund. He'd been right. Either Swedish or Danish.

"The bikes are in back. If you'd like to come through with me, Anders, we'll fetch them both at once so you can be on your way."

Anders followed him through the open door to the back room. The Englishmen took no note and continued to blather on about golf courses where it cost more to play one round than he'd pay for his entire lot of groceries for the entire summer.

Of course, he'd have to adjust his budget a little if he kept doing things like spontaneously treating Daisy to seafood chowder and sticky toffee pudding at cozy little cafes. Next time, she'd have to be content with Irish stew and brown bread at the bakery next door. They had a few small tables in front of the store where you could watch the seagulls and listen to the waves crashing against the breakwater.

Anders thanked him for the prompt service and shook his hand before he and his wife rode off on their bikes. He'd offered to adjust their seats, but they had insisted they fit like a glove.

Cavan went inside and returned to his post behind the counter. The men continued to talk for another minute or two before acknowledging him.

"Were those our bikes?" The taller of the two men handed him a Carte Blanche.

"No. Those were for the couple who left with them."

"Will ours be out soon?"

"As soon as you tell me if titanium frames with regular wheels are acceptable."

"I thought you said you had extra large frames."

"Yes. In steel. But they're gone now."

"What the-"

"If I adjust the seats on the regulars they'll ride just fine. And they're titanium, which is what you requested."

"I requested extra large titanium."

"Which I'm sorry to say, once again, I don't have."

"No need to get cocky."

"Respectfully speaking, sir, I'm just trying to set you up with the bicycles that most closely match your specifications. If you're not happy with the selection here in Dingle, there's a bike hire in Killarney."

See, this was why Cavan hated people with money.

The companion spoke. "But Killarney is over an hour away."

"Fine," the taller gent said. "We'll take whatever you have. They'd better be in top-notch condition."

"You have my personal guarantee. They were just serviced yesterday."

"Small comfort since we don't know you from Adam. You shopkeepers in tourist towns never have cared much for customer service, have you? I mean, why bother? You're never going to see us again, or any of the other poor sots that come through the door. Every day brings a new set of tourists, willing to pay whatever you charge no matter the poor quality you bestow."

Cavan was only six foot, but he stood as straight as he could. Wasn't it enough that he'd lost his father to money? Did he have to continue to suffer at the hands of those who used wealth as an excuse to mistreat the rest of the world?

"I've been serving the locals on the Dingle Peninsula and offering quality goods for a fair price since I was sixteen years old. And, if you care to see what tourists from all over the world think of me and my work, you can look me up on Trip Advisor or see how many five star ratings we have on our Facebook page."

The man looked down his nose at him and said, "You have no idea who you're speaking to, do you?"

No he didn't, nor did he care. His father had thought he was just as important as this man did, which was the reason he chose wealth over his wife and wee son and left to travel the world. Money corrupted. His father probably still had fancy accommodations, servants, and a mistress in every major port. Meanwhile, his mother had raised him on her own with nary a half-pence to her name, and eventually remarried a potato farmer, which meant she forfeited her alimony, to eek out a living with the man she loved, a man who loved her and treated her like a lady despite his substandard means.

Cavan looked the man square in the eye. "I've suddenly remembered that I have customers coming in twenty minutes who've signed an online pre-lease and paid in advance. I'm sorry, but my last two bikes are spoken for."

The pair left in a huff. Fine by Cavan. As far as he was concerned, money was the root of all evil just like the Bible said. Money corrupted everything it touched.

Good thing fate had spared Daisy of her gold before it completely ruined her.

In his opinion, finding the pot of gold at the end of the rainbow was hardly good luck – it was a curse.

5

Granny Siobhan Fitzpatrick shook the dust from her half-materialized skirt, hitched her petticoat up to her shins, and picked her way around the rocks jutting up through the sand on the beach. The waves crashed on the bigger rocks a little further out while shiny pools of water stayed behind, gleaming in the sunlight. It was one of those golden moments she'd always taken for granted when she was alive.

"Any luck getting through to her today?" Captain Scully Donaghue's scruffy sea uniform was nay only faded from a hundred years of sunshine; it bore witness to the vestiges of the storm that had brought his ship down and crashed it against the rocks again and again until it was nay but smithereens.

"Nay. When I whisper in the lass's ear, Daisy thinks she has a rash tickling, or a cramp in her earlobe, or that the bugs be biting."

The captain had been dead for several decades longer than she and had much more experience at making contact with living souls. "I could start in on Cavan again and see if he'll open up to the possibility of hearing a message from the great beyond."

"Daisy's always been a wee bit dense. But nay worries. I'll find a way to get through to the lass. Now that she's moved back to my house, I feel closer to her than ever."

"I know ye love yer granddaughter, but I fear that if Daisy finds

27

the rest of the gold, she'll only spend it on herself just like she did when she found the stash in your neighbor's cave. My great-great grandson, Cavan, hates money. If he was to find the gold, he'd start looking into the history books, figure out that it came from my ship, and convince Daisy to give it to the families of the men who were lost in the shipwreck."

Granny stubbed her toe on a rock and yelped out loud. "Cavan won't have any say in the matter. The gold is on Fitzpatrick land and ye know the rules."

"Aye. Finders keepers, losers weepers. Like I haven't heard you say it a million times in the past half century. And might I point out that if you'd turned the gold over to the authorities or even the church to distribute to the families of the men who perished at sea, a lot of good would 'ave already been done and we would nay be in the pickle we're in right now. That gold is helping no one buried in that sea cave under years of silt and sand."

"I left them a treasure map! I had nay idea I'd pass so unexpectedly, or that when I tried to tell them about the gold when I was on my death bed that they'd chalk it up to the mad ravings of an old woman. Dementia, my foot! I tried to tell them, they just would nay listen."

"Ye'd had a stroke, old woman. Ye might have thought ye were telling them where the treasure was hidden, but all they probably heard was blah, blah, blah."

"Ha! Ye've been hanging around Cavan for too long. You're even talking like a teenager. Begorah!" Granny stubbed a toe on the other foot.

"Did ye see that?" Captain Donaghue peered through his eyepiece. "Those beachcombers didn't hear a thing when you cried out, but the birds sunning themselves on the rocks all jumped and took off flying."

"Ah. Perhaps we can capitalize on that wee bit o' information. Of course, our footprints are visible, too, if they'd only look." Granny lifted her skirts even higher and waded out into the water. How she longed to douse herself in the waves, wash away winter's grime and lethargy.

"They've seen them. They just assume they're footprints that belong to other beachcombers who walked the beach earlier in the day."

"I'm just exhausted." Granny wished the water was just a wee bit warmer – and it would be soon. The Wild Atlantic Way would be friendlier and quieter once the season came into its own. Until then…

"I know what you mean. I've been whispering in Cavan's ear since he was born. The sad thing is, he was more receptive to me when he was two than he is now."

"I had such bright hopes for Daisy when she was little. She's so artistic and creative. She can see beauty in ugly old rocks that would slide right by most people. I knew if she could take those rocks and paint them and arrange them in ways that people respond to, I knew she could take my gold and do absolutely wondrous things with it."

The sea captain kicked at a long, half-dried piece of seaweed and sighed. "If only you'd told her where you had it hidden before you died. She and Cavan were friends – maybe together, they'd have found a way to use it to make something truly beautiful."

Granny hung her head. "It just all happened so fast. Everyone says the years fly by, but it's so hard to see it going on when you're in the middle of living."

"I wouldn't know."

Granny couldn't blame him for being bitter. Scully'd had a lovely wife and two young children at home when he perished at sea through no fault of his own.

The sea captain said, "When Cavan was a teenager he would read stories about ghosts and haunted houses all the time. There was a time that I thought for sure that I'd get through to him. He believed in ghosts. He used to tell his friends about me and brag about how brave I was when my ship went down. It warmed my soul in a way I can nay begin to explain."

Granny cleared her throat. "It must have been very special considering you never even got to meet the lad."

"Aye. I was dead years before he was born."

"We'll find a way." Granny reached back and patted the Captain's arm. And then, she dipped her hand into the waves, cupped a handful of water, and splashed the living daylights out of the man.

#

Daisy walked along the shoreline on either side of the sea

shanty to see what the tide had brought in. The whole quilt thing had been a huge fiasco, and the emotional toll had set her back a bit. So had talking to Cavan and finding out that he had no interest in finding a different location for his bike shop or even sharing her old shop with her. Her eyes scanned for sea glass, star fish, pretty shells, rocks that she could paint, and flat pebbles that she could shape into people, cottages, four leaf clovers – of course - and sailboats and lighthouses – and if possible, bicycles.

Her best selling painted rocks and pebble art had always been traditional Irish themes like rainbows, sheep, fairies, mermaids and Irish cottages on scenic beaches. But if she was going to get a foot in with Cavan, she needed to create a new line of bicycle art. She'd already found one idea on Pinterest – a bicycle made with two old buttons, one for each tyre, connected by twisted wire to make the seat, pedals and handlebars. She'd found Granny's button box in the shanty filled with all kinds of treasures.

If she could find some rocks round enough to be wheels, or maybe some abalone, she could create a series of bicycle themed pebble art.

It wasn't ideal, but if she could convince Cavan to hang a few of her pieces amongst the bicycle tyres, chains, baskets, toe clips and repair kits already hanging on the walls of his shop, she could get a little exposure and hopefully sell a few pieces, too. She could paint bicycles on rocks just as well as rainbows and shamrocks. If she was clever enough, she could paint a bicycle in a field of shamrocks or a bicycle with a rainbow in the background. Or maybe even a fairy riding a bicycle.

She smiled and picked up a piece of green sea glass. See? It was going to be a lucky day after all.

Her pockets were full by the time the sun was high in the sky and her stomach was rumbling. She was hungry for potato pie but the kitchen in the shanty was still a mess and she was too hungry to have to spend time cooking something with multiple steps even if they did lead to a depth of flavors. She needed a quick already roasted chicken sandwich made with pre-cooked bacon and a slice of tomato and a few fresh spinach leaves that came pre-washed.

She quick-footed it back to the shanty, grabbed an old towel from the clean clothes pile and went outside to wipe the sea gull poop off the picnic table.

She'd just taken a bite of her sandwich, which could have used a little garlic aioli, when a stranger walked up, pulled something out of his pocket, and flashed a badge in her face. The sun glinted so sharply off the silver metal that it almost blinded her.

"Daisy Fitzpatrick?"

"Yes."

"I'm here to ask you a few questions about your neighbor."

"Right. The mysterious monk." She took another bite of her sandwich. If she was going to be interrogated, it might as well be on a full stomach.

"So when was the last time you saw your neighbor, prior to discovering that he was dead?"

"Um. Never?" She grabbed a paper towel and wiped her mouth. "I've been living in Killarney. And before that, I lived above my shop in Dingle. I came out here once in awhile to make sure everything was okay, but obviously not often enough, because it would seem a litter of foxes moved in and made a litter box out of my granny's favorite quilt. If the priest was there during any of this, I sure didn't know it."

"But you were down here on the day you discovered the gold, and several days thereafter, when you stood guard over the gold, photographed the gold, and eventually, moved it to the bank."

"Should I be calling my solicitor to be here while you're asking me questions?"

"Not unless you have something to hide."

"I have no secrets." And if she was completely honest, no money to pay a solicitor.

"Fine. I'm told by your friends that you came to the beach at least twice a week to look for beach treasures." He glanced at the rocks and the stash of sea glass that she'd spread out on the other end of the table to dry in the sun.

"That was when I lived in Dingle. Once I moved to Killarney and closed the shop, I stopped making things to sell. So there was no reason to come down here and comb the beach."

"But your friends in Killarney said you had a two-tiered coffee table with glass on top that showed off a huge rock collection."

"Well, sure, but those were old rocks that I picked up when I was a child."

"But your friend said the collection kept growing each time he was at your home."

Aodhan. He was the only one of her so-called male friends who had spent any amount of time at her home. Some boyfriend he'd turned out to be. Hadn't he hurt her enough already without ratting her out to the police?

Each time the policeman shoved another personal tidbit that only could have come from Aodhan in her face, the more ticked she got.

"Well, sure. I came down to Granny's shanty once in awhile. And since I wasn't making things with the rocks I found, my favorites pile might have gradually gotten a little bigger."

The officer looked dubious. "All of this behavior suggests that you've spent a considerable amount of time on this beach and in the caves surrounding your neighbor's property in the past few weeks even though you were living in Killarney."

"Well, I always spent a little time here. I still had ties to Dingle. As far as being near his property – I may have inadvertently crossed the property line since I was confused about what was mine and what was his, but I never went anywhere near the priest's shanty."

"The footprints would suggest the opposite."

"They're not mine. I can guarantee it."

The officer closed his notebook and clipped his pen in the binding. "That's all the questions I have for now."

For now? She watched his back fade into the sandy palate of the highlands that ringed the shore.

6

"Daisy?" Cavan pounded on the door of Daisy's sea shanty and hoped she was awake. Her mobile – anybody's mobile for that matter – was almost useless down by the sea. He hated to wake her up, but he had news to share, and he was too excited to wait until that night when the bike shop closed.

"What? Who is it? If ye're the policeman who was here yesterday, or a friend o' his, ye're no friend o' mine."

Daisy could lay the brogue on thick as could be when she wanted to. He could have sworn he was hearing Daisy's Granny Siobhan's voice if he hadn't known for a fact that she'd been dead for half a decade.

"It's me, Daisy. Cavan. I need to talk to you about something."

"Cavan Donaghue? I've a good mind to send my very large dog, Brutus, out to run you off this property right this minute."

"You don't have a dog."

"I didn't have a dog last time ye saw me. How do ye know what I have now?"

"I don't hear him barking."

"Her. And don't let her good manners and fine training lull ye into thinking she's not extremely territorial and very protective of me."

"You named a girl dog Brutus?"

"Her former owner didn't know how to tell a boy dog from a girl dog."

He rolled his eyes. "C'mon, Daisy. I've got some news about the gold. I'm sorry I didn't call, but you don't have a telephone. How am I supposed to get in touch with you?"

"Just give me a second."

He heard a clatter of what sounded like plates and mugs clinking in a porcelain sink. What was she doing in there?

Finally, the door opened and Daisy stepped out. She had on a pair of faded purple and black sweat pants and a big necked sweater in washed out shades of purple. Her hair was tousled and sticking up in a couple of places and her skin was flushed pink and had creases on one side like she'd just woken up and crawled out of bed.

Her bed.

"So, tell me your news." Daisy smiled faintly, like she wasn't sure if she should invite him in or chase him away.

"I – um. I-"

She crinkled up her eyebrows and looked confused.

"I – um – did some research on ship wrecks along the Wild Atlantic Way to try and figure out where the gold coins in your treasure chest came from."

Now she looked really confused. "Because?"

"Because I know how important it is to you. Because you need money to pay your bills and get back on your feet financially. Because there may be more gold, and if we can find out where the coins came from and how they got into the cave, we might be able to find the rest of the treasure."

"May be? Might? You woke me up for that?"

"Yes! Did you know that my great-grandfather was a sea captain? And that his ship crashed on the rocks off the Dingle Peninsula in 1903?"

"No." Daisy looked like she wished she was still back in bed.

"The official historical account says the Sunbeam was carrying a load of flour, but people have speculated for years that there was gold aboard when the ship went down. Lots of gold."

Now he had her. He could see the sparkle in her eyes.

"Were they smuggling it? What were they doing with that much gold if they'd already picked up the flour? And who pays for flour with gold anyway?"

"No one. They had the gold because they'd had a run in with a pirate ship and taken the gold so they could return it to its rightful owners."

"Rightful owners?" Daisy's face fell.

"Legend has it that after defeating the pirates, they were on their way home with the gold when the storm hit. They were fighting with everything they were worth to navigate through the gale when the pirates, who had regrouped and repaired their ship, boarded their schooner and tried to retake the gold."

"But they were fighting the storm."

"The wheelmaster and the helmsman were so busy fighting off the attack that the ship started floundering in the water. By the time the pirates were defeated once again, the ship had taken on so much water and was listing so badly that they never recovered control."

Daisy looked thoughtful. "When did all this happen?"

"1903. The shipwreck washed ashore near Roseebeigh Beach."

"Is that the one across from Inch Beach?"

"Aye."

"So what makes you think there's more gold?"

Cavan thought for a few minutes. "Call it a gut instinct. It's like someone keeps whispering in my ear that there's more out there."

Daisy laughed. "So if this voice from beyond tells you where the rest of the gold is, let me know!"

"That's why I'm here," Cavan said.

"You're serious."

"I am. The feeling is too real to ignore."

She shook her head.

"But you have to promise that at least part of the gold will be returned to the rightful owners. It's what my great-grandfather would have wanted."

"You're nuts, Cavan. No offense, but it's not like the gold can talk. Who knows where the pirates got the gold? They could have robbed rich Englishmen, or taken it from the Spaniards, or found it hidden on some deserted island. How would we ever begin to trace it after all this time? It happened over a hundred years ago. Local legends can be interesting, but there's no way to corroborate any of this. You have a hunch, and I respect that, but if - if I find any more gold, I'm going to use it to dig myself out of the hole I'm in. There's no way I'm going to spread it around to a bunch of people

I don't know just because they might have had some connection to the gold over a century ago."

He felt a surge of disappointment. Hadn't Daisy learned that money didn't bring you happiness?

He was about to backpedal, and he knew it, but he had his reasons for wanting this to end well. "I'm not saying that we can't spend any of the money on ourselves, just that some of it could go to charity – as a way to honor your granny and my great-grandfather."

Daisy's eyes shot fire. "My granny raised me on a lick and a promise. If she hid a stash of gold away and kept it secret for decades, she did it because she wanted to leave me some sort of legacy. Me. Because she loved me. Something I've had precious little of extended to me in my life."

He stepped toward her. "I didn't mean to imply that-"

"And I don't need you making me feel guilty about what I did with the gold I thought was mine, or what I would do with any additional gold I may or may not find. I've got Auntie Sheelagh and Auntie Ailene and half the town of Dingle to do that."

"No one's trying to make you feel guilty. But the way I see it, there were people who died on that ship. The least we could do – if we find more gold – is to try to trace the ancestors of the men who perished."

Daisy glared at him. "Of which you're one." She scowled at him. "I thought you were different, Cavan."

"But-"

She stepped into the shanty and closed the door.

He'd have felt even worse if she'd slammed it, but the sound of the latch sliding slowly against its slot, like he'd caused her infinite sadness with his visit – broke his heart.

Maybe Daisy was right. Who was he trying to help – Daisy? Himself? Strangers without faces to whom he could be some sort of hero?

A shiver of guilt ran through him, top to bottom. What would he do with the gold if he found it? Would he even tell Daisy? The only thing he knew for sure was that there was more gold, somewhere. Very probably on Daisy's land. He could feel it with every bone in his body. It made no sense given the way he felt about money, but it was like he was a divining rod and the gold was water. It was calling out to him, pulling every fiber of his being toward it.

#

Captain Donaghue did a happy jig around the shanty. "I told ye we'd get through to my grandson long before that stubborn lass o' yours would listen to anything we might have to say."

"Aye. Well, you were right about that. But look at her now – your grandson has made her cry!"

"As well should be. He's got the right idea, giving the gold back to the ones from whom it was stolen, and if that's not possible, then the families of the men who lost their lives trying to save it from the pirates."

"Are you saying that my Daisy is selfish? Because if ye are, then ye've crossed a boundary, and I'll not have it!"

"Boundaries?" The sea captain snorted. "I'm long dead and can go anywhere I please. I have my youth, my strength, and my sharp wits - three things even the grave canna take from me."

Granny nodded. "Aye. Ye've had the advantage from the start. Yer essence is stronger than mine. I'll give ye that. But my Daisy is a smart girl. She'll put two and two together. And she knows these sea caves better than anyone. Why, after her ma and da died, she stayed with me for months and spent hours exploring these old caves."

The sea captain scratched his head. "So why did she never find the gold back then?"

"The storms hid them from us. That's why so little of the gold was ever used even though I had plenty o' need for it. I knew full well that the sea would give back what it had taken one day, and so it was with the storms of 2014. Of course, if I'd really needed the gold before then, I would have gotten someone to move the boulders blocking the entrance and dug through the drifts of sand with my bare hands to get at it. But I always had enough to get by. If only I'd told her about the gold before I died, all would be well."

"Well, I say all will be well once again when Cavan finds the gold and gives it back to those to whom it belongs."

"Cavan, Cavan, Cavan. It's my Daisy who'll save the day, and I'm nay just sayin' it because I love her."

"Shhhh!" The sea captain shushed the old woman. "I want to hear what's on Daisy's mind now that she's alone."

#

Daisy scurried down the path to the sea, hanging on to the sea grasses to stabilize her rapid descent. She kicked at a rock in the sand and slid the last few feet to the sea floor.

"Ouch!" She landed with a bump. She'd wanted to walk off her frustration, but today, it seemed even the seaside wasn't on her side.

That Cavan was the most infuriating man she'd ever met. The nerve of him – implying that she was selfish and unwilling to share the gold with those who deserved to have it! She deserved it just as much as anyone! Descendants, deschmendants. She'd lost her parents when she was young. She'd been left a penniless orphan with only her old granny to look after her. Didn't that make her as gold-worthy as anyone?

Not that it mattered. Cavan was delusional if he thought there was more gold on her property. Even if - by some stretch - he was right, and they found more gold, he was crazy if he thought she would give it away to a bunch of pirates' spawn.

Cavan was a great bicycle repairman, a good friend, and a fair tenant, but when it came to gold, he had a blind spot bar none. Sure, people didn't need a lot of money to survive in this world, but it sure made things easier, reduced a boatload of stress, and made life a lot more fun. What was wrong with that?

She rounded the corner of another of the hundreds of sea caves, their mouths wide open to the Atlantic. She slapped at her ear. Why in damnation were the midges so fierce this year? It was way too early for them to be out.

The feeling that something was biting her earlobe continued until she was well past the cave. What was it with these bugs? Honestly, she was so over living by the sea. Beachcombing for an hour or two a couple of times a week was one thing, but the constant wind blowing off the ocean was quite another. Having sand everywhere – including the silverware drawer – heaven only knew how it got in there – was driving her crazy. And not having indoor plumbing was going to be the death of her. How had Granny ever managed it all?

A part of her loved the old shanty with its thick walls and small windows. The dirt floor and the smell of a peat fire in the hearth made her heart pitter patter with warm, fuzzy memories of her parents and her childhood.

It wouldn't be half bad, living on the edge of the world, if she could build an addition on the side of the shanty that looked out at the sea. The first thing she'd do would be to install a humongous, triple-insulated glass window so she could actually see the sea. The second would be to put in running water so she could have one of those double showers with a rain head, and a heated towel rack, maybe even a bidet. The kitchen would keep its traditional look, but underneath the vintage accoutrements would be state of the art appliances and top-notch fixtures. She could see every last inch of it in her mind's eye.

She was almost home when a man dressed in khakis, an expensive rugby shirt, and Dockers stepped out from behind a rocky outcrop sheathed in sand and sea grass.

"Can I help you?" She said it instinctively, although her heart had started pounding and every hair on her body stood at attention. Her voice came out sounding as anxious and on guard as she felt.

"Sorry. Didn't mean to startle you." The man extended his hand. "I'm Cavan's friend, Rory."

Okay. So this was no chance meet up. He obviously knew who she was and that he was at a spot where he would likely encounter her. Her skin prickled.

"Is everything all right? Is Cavan okay?" Irritated as she felt toward Cavan right now, she wished him no harm. She could think of no other reason this Rory would be creeping around her shanty, looking for her.

"Oh. No. Everything's fine." He looked flustered, like he'd suddenly realized he should have had a story in hand to explain what he was doing on her property. "Just having a little walkabout to take a look at Father O'Leary's shanty. Everyone in the parish is talking about it and wondering what kind of secret life he was leading out here."

Her eyes narrowed. So he was curious about the priest and not her. For whatever reason, she didn't believe him.

She replied, "I haven't been round much since I had moved to Killarney, but in all the years he'd evidently been coming to his shanty, I never once saw him."

"That's what Cavan said."

So they'd been talking about her, and the murder investigation.

"Well, it's nice to meet you." Could he tell how insincere she was?

"Likewise. Sorry if I frightened you."

Right. She wasn't the only one who was being insincere.

She resumed her trek home, looking over her shoulder now and again to make sure she'd have no more surprises.

What a discouraging day. No one trusted her. She was an oddity in her own town, just like always. Her only friend thought she was selfish. Her worthless boyfriend, Aodhan, had dumped her. The only living beings who wanted to have anything to do with her where a legion of midges determined to have her earlobes for dinner. Ouch!

Couldn't Cavan understand why she'd wanted a better life for herself? Without the gold she'd thought was Granny's, there was no way in a million years she was ever going to be able to afford to do anything to improve the shanty. The rent money she got from Cavan barely covered her utilities, upkeep and mortgage on her old shop and apartment in Dingle. She could become a street vendor, but she'd have to invest in portable tables, a tent, and a collapsible shelving system she could use to display her artwork. She'd need a van to lug it around from town to town and a credit card swiper and permits and who knew what else. She'd be lucky if she broke even.

She was going to have to sell her granny's land and move out of the shanty and let someone else's dream come true. She hadn't owned her place in Dingle long enough to accumulate any equity. The shanty was the only asset she had left.

"Ouch!" This time, the pain felt less like an insect bite and more like someone with sharp, ragged fingernails pinching her ear. Enough with the midges. Or maybe it was fleas. The fox family had probably infested the whole house! And that quilt! Every time she went near the thing, a dozen fleas probably jumped onto her skin, looking for a new host. The embroidery around the patches would provide the perfect hiding place, and the organic debris from the foxes that lingered would nurture any number of larvae. She'd read once that a female flea consumed fifteen times its body weight in blood every day.

This had to stop!

She ran out the shanty door and started the trek back down to the sea. She was in such a panicked state that she barely noticed the sunset or the ribbons of pink, lavender, peach and gold in the western sky. The water would be barely warm enough for a dip, but she knew the whereabouts of a tide pool that caught the afternoon and evening sun.

"What?"

A guy with ratty jeans and a crusty, short-sleeved shirt that showed off arms covered in tattoos walked toward her. He didn't look all that different from a thousand other men she'd seen, but something about him gave her the creeps. The closer he got, the more she felt the sensation of her hair rising on the back of her neck.

What was it with random men showing up at her door all of the sudden? And where was Brutus when she really needed her?

The man was heading straight for her, walking in a direct line to the spot where she was standing. His was no random stroll on the beach. He clearly had her in his sights.

She thought about turning around, avoiding a confrontation and going back to the safety of the shanty, where for all he knew, there really was a Brutus.

He waved. She froze like she was a fish in the mouth of a sea eagle. She might be able to squirm or flop her way to safety but it was a moot point because she was so frozen with fear that she couldn't move.

7

The man finally stopped, but not until he was so close that she could see a tattooed snake rippling on his neck as he spoke.

Did she imagine a hissing sound when he said, "Aren't you the one who found the secret treasure?"

She wanted to dissolve into a million grains of sand. She never should have done that interview on the telly.

"Darcie Sneem." The man reached out his hand.

She took it, for lack of a better plan. Now that she thought about it, she certainly didn't want to make a run for the shanty and lead him right to where she lived. Although if he knew who she was, he'd probably already figured out where she lived. The thought sent chills down her spine.

She withdrew her hand and tried to calm her nerves before she started shaking.

Darcie. A descendant of the dark one. The words echoed inside her head as loudly as though they'd been spoken by someone standing right beside her. The voice was so real, so convincing, that she looked around to see if someone else was there. It wasn't her who had spoken, but it was a female voice. And God help her, unless this Sneem character was a wickedly good ventriloquist and a female impersonator on top of that, the voice had to have come from heaven itself. Or, was she losing her mind?

"So what brings you to the Wild Atlantic Way, ah, Mr. is it Sneem? If it's the gold you're looking for, I can guarantee you it's long gone. Unfortunately." She managed to laugh.

"I found your story to be very interesting," Darcie Sneem said.

"That it is, I guess." She gulped. "It's been quite the roller coaster ride." My gosh, she was glad she hadn't made it to the tidal pool. What if she'd been stripped down to her birthday suit to take a bath when this creep had shown up?

"One of my ancestors was a famous buccaneer," Sneem said.

Something was biting her again. Probably another leftover fox flea drawing blood even as she spoke. She swatted at her ear.

"Be careful, Daisy," said a female voice. The son of a pirate gave no indication that he had heard anything. What was going on?

"I, um, need to get something down by the beach – I – um – a friend is waiting for me."

"I see," the buccaneer-of-old's relative said.

And indeed, he seemed to see right through her. The look he gave her left her feeling like he had sliced her through with a saber. Famous buccaneer, my foot, she thought. Call it what you will, romanticize it and rationalize it to heck, but they were still greedy, killing, thieving, scourge of the seven seas, pirates.

And then he left. His long legs took him away as quickly as he'd come. He hadn't said goodbye. She hoped that didn't mean she'd be seeing him again.

She stood still for a few more minutes, waiting to see if she would hear the woman's voice once more, if it would tell her what to do, or where to go, because she sure didn't know.

Nothing. There was no way she could go down to the tidal pool and take her flea-ridden clothes off. Not now. When she was sure Sneem had gone, she turned and made her way back to the shanty. She had some moist, antiseptic towelettes back at home that she could use to give herself a wipe down once she was safely inside with the door locked. Her and the fleas, all cozy-like in the cottage, bedded down for the night.

Yikes, Sneem gave her the creeps. So did the voice she'd heard. At least the voice didn't seem to have wicked intentions.

#

"Did you see that?" Granny danced around the front of the

cave where the gold was hidden. "She heard me!"

"She certainly seemed to."

"Begora! I knew I'd get through to her eventually!"

The sea captain looked thoughtful. "Maybe your power to communicate with Daisy intensifies when the lass is in danger."

"That could be. The important thing is, we've made some headway today."

"Aye! Now that I've got Cavan's ear, we can keep using him to alert Daisy to the fact that there's more gold."

"Right under her nose, it is." Granny held out her hands and invited the sea captain to join her in a jig.

A few minutes later he was grabbing at his toes and huffing a bit, too. "I haven't had so much fun in a long while."

"That's all fine and well," Granny Siobhan said. "But things took a serious bent today, too."

"Aye. We need to keep our eyes on Darcie Sneem."

"That's the first order of business," Granny said. "The second is to get Daisy to take a closer look at the quilt. The sooner she realizes I stitched a treasure map into the four corners and put a huge 'X' in the center square to mark the spot where the gold is buried, the sooner this story will end, and happily-ever-after at that!"

"After what those foxes did to it, ye'll be lucky if she doesn't throw the quilt into the trash."

"Nay. My Daisy may be a bit misguided at times-"

"Like when she went out with that dolt of a boyfriend, Aodhan."

"Right, but she's a quick learner. She'll nay make the same mistake twice. You'll see. She knows how to put two and two together. You'll see."

"If she's smart, she'll set her sights on Cavan, the finest man there e'er was if I do say so me self."

Granny gave the sea captain a good once over. The man was not only pleasing to the eye, but handsome is as handsome does. She'd always been fortunate enough to keep her youthful vitality about her. She'd turned the head of more than one younger lad. Captain Donaghue might have died at a far younger age than she, but she was fit as a fiddle, and she intended to give him a run for his money, even if it was in the afterlife.

#

Cavan removed the wheel from the bicycle and used a lever to break the bead that sealed the tyre to the rim.

He was just lifting the tube from the tyre when the door opened. A tall man entered and the bells jangled behind him. He had long hair with a red scarf twisted around his man bun. The man didn't look like a cyclist – now he wouldn't have been surprised to find out the man owned a Harley Davidson - but he tried not to judge. He had nothing against people who preferred motorcycles to bicycles.

He turned his back to the wall so he could survey the remaining three walls of the shop. "Can I help you?"

"You're the owner?"

"That's right." His heart quickened. What was wrong with him? He'd never once had a feeling of dread when faced with a potential buyer. For some reason, this guy set him on edge. "What can I do for you?"

"Nay worries. I'm not here to sell you anything."

The thought had never occurred to him. Sure, he had salesmen stop by once in awhile trying to convince him that their brand of tyres was better than the one he already carried. But they were dressed nice, fresh from the shower, and looking to make a good impression. This guy smelled like he'd been on the road or camping out for at least a week.

"Can I get you a rental bike?" He didn't have a bicycle in tow, so Cavan assumed he wasn't in for a repair.

"Just wondering if you know that girl who found the gold. The one who lives in the shanty down by the sea?"

"No." Cavan's gut instinct was not to tell the guy anything about Daisy. But he obviously knew who she was and had probably found out she owned his building. "Yes. I mean, she's my landlord."

"I hear she's interested in selling the place."

"Really." Cavan froze. "Do you mean this building or her shanty by the sea?"

The man laughed. "I'd never be happy in town. Especially not one crawling with tourists." He laughed again, rolled his eyes, and shook himself like the very thought of living in Dingle gave him goosebumps. "I meant the sea shanty and the land she owns along the Wild Atlantic Way."

"I hadn't heard anything about her selling either place. I guess you'd have to ask her." He panicked at the thought of the man tracking down Daisy at her isolated shanty – if he hadn't already. He got so cold he almost felt clammy. "If you'd like, I'd be happy to get in touch with her and tell her you're interested in her land. Do you have a card?"

"Naw." The man picked up a chain hanging on one of the walls and made a show of stretching it almost to the point of breaking. He flexed his muscles and popped his abs into view. "I'll just drop by to see her next time I'm in the area."

"Well, she's not around much these days, but I'll make sure to inform her of your interest next time I see her."

"So what about you?"

"What about me?" Cavan asked.

"Do you think there's more gold still hidden somewhere in the cliffs? Gold that she's nay told anyone about?" The man gave him another look – this one chilled him to the core.

It was as though this guy could see through him. Of course he believed there was more gold, but no, he did not think it was anything Daisy knew about.

"I'm not sure what you're inferring, but if Daisy knew where there was more gold, I'm certain she would have told the authorities about it."

"Not if she was smart." The man half growled.

"But if she still has gold, she wouldn't be forced to eke out a living at the old sea shanty."

"Unless she's trying to throw them off her scent until the whole thing blows over so she can start to use it, bit by bit."

Cavan relaxed a little at that. It was pretty funny that this guy thought anybody in southwestern Ireland was ever going to forget about the gold. He obviously wasn't from Dingle.

"So where are you from, and why are you thinking to move to the Wild Atlantic Way if you don't like tourists?"

The man looked at him as though he was the odd one, and didn't reply.

The bells on the door jingled merrily once more and Rory entered the shop, eyeing the other man suspiciously.

Cavan turned to him. "You'll be wanting your bike. I'm happy to say I have your tune-up finished."

"As soon as you're free."

By the time Cavan finished helping Rory, the man who'd been hunting for Daisy was gone. He went to the window and looked out, but saw no trace of him anywhere.

8

Daisy shivered in her timbers and thanked the Good Lord that her shanty was woven together with stone and plaster in addition to the bits and bobs of driftwood that Granny had used to build her house. It wasn't that cold outside – the weather was finally warming a wee bit – but she couldn't escape the chill she'd felt since Darcie Sneem had infringed on her space.

She still hadn't had a bath, and her ears were itching like crazy. Damnable fleas! She could almost hear them nibbling inside her ears, chomping away on her dead skin and penetrating the healthy skin to suck her blood. She was going to lose her mind if they didn't quiet down!

She heard the knock on the door just as she was drifting off to sleep.

"Daisy? Daisy? It's me. Cavan."

She sighed and leaned against the door. "We've got to stop meeting like this."

"I'm worried about you, Daisy. There was a man asking all kinds of questions about you at the bike shop."

"I know. Darcie Sneem, most likely. Did he tell you he's a descendant of the pirates who had the gold?"

"Let me in, Daisy."

"I hope you have a bone for Brutus."

"I'll win her over, I promise."

See, that was why she loved Cavan. He respected her enough to humor her, play along with her, and soothe her when she was upset. He understood her quirky sense of humor. And he seemed to have a sense about when she needed company.

She opened the door. She hadn't even realized the wind was howling. That was one of the perks of living in a house with tiny windows and walls that were almost three feet thick. She closed the door and held out her arms to Cavan. "Thanks for coming."

"I wanted to make sure you were okay." He held her tight.

"I should warn you that I probably have fleas. And since you're much more substantial than I am, they're probably leaping over to your side even as we speak."

He kept hugging her. "Brutus?"

"No. The fox family. After all, they used Granny's quilt as a nest, or maybe as a bathroom, or maybe both. What difference do a few bloodsucking, parasitical houseguests make?"

"I see." He drew back a little and gazed deep into her eyes, seemingly to look at her. At least she hoped that was it, and not that he didn't want to get fleas.

Cavan reached for her hair and wound a curl around one of his fingers. "Your Granny would think it's pretty special that you still want to save her quilt, even after all that."

"I hope she knows. The quilt is very special to me." She slapped at her ear. "Ouch!"

Cavan smiled. "My ma always told me that the bugs liked me because I was so sweet."

"Yeah. Well, Granny never once told me I was sweet. Spunky. Feisty. Cute and sassy, if I remember right. But never sweet."

"I think you're sweet."

"Granny used to do this play on words. She said, 'Other people will tell you to keep looking up because you never know when you'll see a rainbow. But I'm telling you to keep your head down and your eyes wide open because you never know when you'll stumble upon a pot of gold.'"

"Wow." Cavan led her to the sofa, slung his arm over the back cushion and pulled her close. "Do you think Granny knew about the gold?"

"She certainly didn't live like a rich person. If she knew about the treasure chest, she was pretty frugal about doling it out."

"It makes a person wonder though. It almost seems like she was leaving you hints about how to find it one day."

"But if she wanted me to have it – if she was saving it for me, wouldn't she have told me about it, or left me a buried treasure map, or a secret safe deposit box with a mysterious key or a note or something?"

Cavan looked around the room. "Maybe she did. Have you looked?"

"Why would I? I didn't know there was any gold hidden until I stumbled onto the treasure chest."

"You found the gold, but then you found out it was your neighbor's gold."

"And then, I lost it."

"Well, you didn't exactly lose it."

"No. I had to give it back."

Cavan smiled, and squeezed her shoulders a little tighter. "Which was only fair, since it wasn't your gold to begin with."

"Finder's-"

"Don't even say it." Cavan got up and walked over to the hearth. "What if your Granny and her neighbor were together and found the gold at the same time? The only fair thing to do would have been to split it. He well could have buried his in a sea cave on his property and your Granny, the same thing."

She stood up and joined Cavan in front of the fire. "Where do you get these wild ideas? Is there some little ghost sitting on your shoulder, whispering things in your ear?"

They both laughed at the idea. It felt good. She offered to make Cavan a cup o' hot chocolate, and started a pot boiling on the cook stove. They talked theories and possibilities for over an hour before Cavan finally said, "Let's go for a walk."

"It's kind of late."

"It'll be light for another hour. It sounds like the wind has gone down."

Why not? She poked her head out the door and it had in fact turned out to be a nice evening. The sun was low over the Atlantic, shining over the water until it glowed like molten gold. Life hadn't been too kind to her as of late, and it felt good to have a friend. Why not?

#

It was a good night for eavesdropping. Darcie smiled. He'd gotten just what he wanted. Cavan and Daisy both believed there was another pot of gold still waiting go be found.

He eased away from the window. It wouldn't do to have the two lovebirds stumbling upon him when they left to go for their walk. The wind was no longer blowing at gale force, but it was still making enough of a whistle and clatter to explain away the crunch of his shoes on the random seashell or loose twig as he made his escape. It was not yet dark, but he doubted they would notice his tracks with the low light. By morning, the wind would have wiped the sand smooth.

He was a few meters from the house when he stumbled over a quilt strung between two chairs. The smell that rose up from it filled his nostrils with a feral stench so strong he almost passed out. Thankfully, the next gust of wind blew it away.

Stupid, sentimental lass. Clinging to her granny's memories when she ought to be out with a pick ax and shovel, digging for gold. It would serve her right when Darcie Sneem found it instead of her. Pirates always prevailed.

#

Daisy dug through her granny's button box looking for two big buttons of the same size that she could use for the front and back tyres of another bicycle. If Cavan wouldn't let her use part of the shop for displaying her artwork, then she was going to get a permit and set up a table in front of the building.

She found the buttons and marked where they would go on the rock, then used her paint brushes to draw handlebars, a frame, pedals and a basket filled with flowers. She made about a dozen, each one as unique as the buttons she'd paired. When these were done, she planned to make more bicycles by slicing wine corks into circles to use for wheels.

When she was finished, she painted five more rocks with a primitive style rainbow as a background and a bike in the foreground. Her style was loose, with indistinct edges. She hoped they would be popular. She'd always prided herself on the fact that she didn't care if people liked her work, or even her, but she needed money – she needed to make a lot of money very quickly and that meant bowing to current fads and popular culture.

The truth was, ever since her rich and famous cohorts and her worthless boyfriend had dumped her because she was no longer as well-off as they were, she desperately craved approval.

She looked at the finished bicycles and smiled. Lovely, if she did say so herself. Which was fine, since no one else would. Even if Cavan loved them to the moon and back, he'd never admit it. Happy wife, bummed husband, sad bike hire shopkeeper indeed.

Speaking of vibes, she'd been thinking about this Sneem guy. She was slightly ashamed that she'd judged him so harshly, primarily because of the clothes he was wearing and the way he looked. She hated it when people did that. Honestly, she'd been hanging around her disapproving old great-aunts for too long. She hoped she got a second chance so she could get to know Darcie better before she wrote him off. Of all the people she'd been in contact with since she moved back to Dingle, he was the only one who'd seemed truly interested in her, her property, and her life. There was Cavan of course, but Cavan was like family. He'd known her since she was a kid. And, she was his landlord. He had to be nice to her.

She'd always liked to live dangerously.

A simple friendship with Sneem would be a walk on the wild side, for sure, but sometimes the nicest gifts came wrapped in the least conventional packaging. And if Darcie was up to something, what better way to keep an eye on what he was up to than to stick to him like glue?

She was just settling in and starting to relax when one of the bloodsucking larvae bit her ear again. Damn fleas. Lucky for them she couldn't afford to hire an exterminator.

\#

Cavan couldn't believe that Daisy had actually agreed to meet Darcie for dinner. Couldn't she tell that the guy was trouble? He slammed the bicycle wheel down on the countertop so hard that the axle scratched the counter and the rim almost bent.

"What's the craic?" Rory walked in with a wheel under his arm.

"Don't mind me. What happened now?" He took the wheel from Rory and tried not to let his displeasure show. "Another flat tyre?"

"Seems like there's glass everywhere."

"You're a glass magnet. If you'd stop hanging around bars all the time, you wouldn't be so likely to run over broken glass."

"Having a pint is my only social outlet. To me, it's worth the price of a few new tyres."

"Well maybe you should learn to fix them yourself then."

"Ouch." Rory gave him a dirty look. "Thanks for appreciating my business, friend."

Cavan sighed. "Sorry. Bad day." Bad night. Bad life, at least right now.

He carefully removed the glass, marked the spot and took the tyre off the wheel.

"At least it didn't go through to the inner tube this time," Rory said.

"Yeah."

"So what's bugging you?"

Rory knew him too well.

"Daisy."

"She still trying to get you to move out so she can reclaim her old life?"

"I don't know. Maybe. I think she's given up on the idea for now, but with her, you never really know."

Rory rolled his eyes. "Women. They don't back down. What they do is pretend you've won, and then the second you let your guard down, they pounce and rip you apart until you admit defeat."

"So I've got that to look forward to then."

"What? Are you guys a thing now?"

"No. No. I mean, we've gotten a lot closer since she moved back to Dingle, but it's not like that. In fact, she's kind of intrigued by that guy who was in the shop the other day. I think he's a jerk, but she must see something in him. I don't know."

"You're kidding." Rory watched him as he roughed up the spot where the patch would go. "You're really that into her?"

"I've always liked Daisy."

Rory scowled. "So she's a nice woman. Is it wise to get tangled up with someone who's a suspect in a murder investigation?"

"Daisy is no murderer!"

"Have you never read a detective novel? The one you least suspect is always guilty."

"If we hold by that theory, maybe it was you who killed the priest, Rory."

He smeared the adhesive over the hole and blew on it to help it dry.

Rory snorted. "Cavan, you're a nice guy and you're definitely going to find the right woman one day, but if this Daisy was going to like you that way, wouldn't it have happened already? I mean, you claim you guys have always treated each other like a brother and sister. Unless something has really changed, and I don't mean a little flare of jealousy because she's got the hots for some other guy..."

Cavan sighed and placed the patch onto the tacky glue. Rory was right. About everything. If Daisy had been interested in him, she never would have moved to Killarney in the first place – or found herself a rich boyfriend, or turned her back on Dingle. Even now, she was only back in town because she had no choice.

"Hey, you should stop by O'Flaherty's. The new barmaid is totally wicked, and she has a nice personality, too."

"So why aren't you into her if she's so fair?"

"I've been on a few dates with her sister."

"You're kidding." His mind started to spin. Rory had good judgment. He'd always respected his choices, and if Rory knew this girl's family and thought the sister was nice, it was worth checking out. He felt a tinge of guilt. But why?

He directed his attention back to Rory's tyre, pressing firmly so the patch would stick. "So, I'll promise to go down to O'Flaherty's one night later this week if you'll let me keep your bike for a day or two so I can check out the cables and do a little preemptive maintenance on the brakes and the frame."

9

Daisy made her bed, straightened up the kitchen and cleared off the table so she could work at some new crafts. She wished she could be working outside but it was raining. The sun was trying to peek out. Maybe there'd even be a rainbow.

"No!" With a start, she realized that Granny's quilt was out in the rain. She'd been so careful of covering it up or putting it under a tarp when it might get wet, but she'd been tired the night before and the forecast hadn't said anything about rain, and... Crap. Just crap.

She ran outside and grabbed the quilt, dodging raindrops as she ran. It was pouring! What was she going to do? What if it was already ruined? What if it had shrunk or the colors had bled or the old stitching melted away? She grabbed the quilt and ran toward the door. If she put it in a plastic bag or covered it with a tarp now that it was wet, it would be a mass of mold by the next day. Once the sun came out, she could lay it out on the picnic table and let it air dry. But until then, she was going to have to spread it out somewhere inside the shanty.

She grabbed the door latch, swung the heavy wood door open and rushed back inside, the quilt gathered up in her arms. "I'm so sorry, Granny." Her eyes and cheeks were already wet from the rain. May as well have a good cry while she was at it.

She grabbed some trash bags, folded them out to full size and laid them out on her bed. The quilt came next. Despite her efforts to air it out, the quilt still smelled of fox urine, and now, on top of that, it smelled like a wet dog. What choice did she have? After all her efforts to save it, she couldn't abandon it to the elements now.

For the first time, as she spread the quilt flat, she looked at some of the handiwork. She ran her fingers over a field of seaside daisies with light lavender petals and yellow centers on a background of spring green wool. Had Granny stitched them into the fabric in honor of a new granddaughter, after she'd been born, or had her mother named her Daisy because she'd been inspired by the delicate colors of the quilt block?

A foot or two over, she found Granny's initials. The letters were formed in a sweeping cursive so old world that it looked almost foreign. More daisies, tiny ones, embellished the ends of each letter.

A few squares over, there was a line drawing of the sea shanty, outlined in deep blue to match the paint on the outside. It looked like a child had drawn it, and she remembered being fascinated by it when she was small. The roof was filled in with tiny threads to resemble thatch. The door was low and the windows small, just like it was in reality. She smiled. This was why she would never part with Granny's quilt.

A few inches over from the shanty there was a well and a horse tank with a few shiny haypennies gleaming up from the water, also just like they would have in real life. A few inches from there, she traced some bluffs with a path winding through the center, and then, a cluster of sand dunes, and then a formation of rocks, followed by a sand colored patch of wool with tufts of green sea grass embroidered here and there.

She followed the design from corner to corner like she was reading a picture book. It was almost like a map, illustrated with all the landmarks she knew and loved. There was even a compass marking the directions, a few inches to the right, flanked by a patch of blue wool with curly, peaked stitches placed at regular intervals to resemble waves. A little further out, a schooner with billowing white sails bobbed in the sea of blue.

The embroidery threads were patchy and faded, disappearing altogether in spots, but it was amazing! The quilt definitely told a story. Something about the threads being wet made them stand out a little more than usual. She glanced to the block in the very center of the quilt and touched the faint threads gingerly. Were the brown threads and tan markings supposed to represent a sea cave? Was that an X? The threads were so faint it was hard to tell. Did the X have something to do with her Grandda Xavier? Could his initials have been etched into the quilt at some point?

"Daisy?" She heard Darcie's booming voice first and the knock a second later.

Daisy stood and went to the door to open it so Darcie could get out of the rain. He was soaking wet.

She greeted him and ran to get a towel so he could dry himself.

He chitchatted for a moment, apologized for showing up looking such a wreck and then said, "What's that smell?"

He stepped a few feet further into the room. "What do we got here?"

"The answer to both questions is Granny's quilt."

"Ah. Well, I'm not a fan o' the smell, but the quilt itself looks to be quite the treasure." His eyes scanned the design and for a few minutes, he said nothing.

She was surprised to find out that he was a connoisseur of quilts, or handiwork of any kind, for that matter. It didn't exactly fit his bad boy, biker persona. But then, he'd told her previously how beautiful he found her artwork and what a good eye she had for colors and design.

"I assume getting it wet wasn't what ye planned to do. Have ye thought of having it dry cleaned?" His eyes were still on the quilt, as though mesmerized.

Granny would be so pleased with the way he was admiring it. And it was very striking now that it was wet. It was as though someone had pressed the contrast button on a digital camera to make the colors and handiwork pop. It had looked so faded and washed out in the sunlight that even she had never really noticed how bright and detailed the designs were. The embroidery was exquisite.

"I took it to the dry cleaners in Dingle, and they refused to give it a go because of the – um – odor."

"Snooty lot, Dingle. I've got errands in Killarney first thing next week. I could take it with me, drop it off at the cleaners in the morning, and probably pick it up again before I leave town."

"Well, um- What a nice thing for you to offer." There it was – again. Something was biting her earlobe. "That would be grand. It would be so wonderful to have it taken care of. But no thank you." What? She had been ready to say no – yes! She meant yes! What was going on? Ouch. She could have sworn something much bigger than a flea was biting her neck.

Darcie looked puzzled. "If you're worried about it getting splattered on the trip to and fro, ye needn't. I promise the quilt would be carefully wrapped to protect it."

"I'm sure it would be. Okay. Sure. No." What? She tried to speak the word yes and found it stuck in her throat due to a sharp pain and the sudden need to cough.

"Wouldn't you like to have it cleaned so you could enjoy the colors and warmth of the quilt without having it smell like – like – whatever happened to it?"

"I would, it's just that - no thank you." Good grief! Why couldn't she say the word yes and accept his offer? "You're very gracious to offer, but I guess it's just something I need to do myself."

Darcie looked as mystified as she felt.

"I – um – plan to be in Killarney next week, so I might as well take care of it then." It was a bold lie, but she couldn't think of any other excuse to offer.

"But you don't have a car, do you? Maybe we could combine errands and go together?"

"No. I mean, I already have a ride lined up. But, thank you." It would seem she no longer had a brain of her own. Her tongue was tied and would not form the words that she wanted to say.

"Well, it's your choice." He thought for a moment. "You seem jittery about the prospect of parting with it even for a few hours. If you'd like, I could photograph it for you so you have a permanent record of what it looks like today – just in case something should ever happen to it. I have a good camera on my iPhone."

"Sure. That would be a great idea." Her throat felt like it was starting to swell. She started to choke. She reached for a glass of water. Darcie was already snapping photos. He seemed particularly intrigued by the area she'd just been looking at.

"Of course I'm worried – especially now that the fabric has gotten so wet. I hope the colors don't start to run."

Darcie snapped a couple more photos. "It's amazingly smooth for such an old quilt. It would be a shame if the squares shrank – worse yet if some did and some didn't. The design would be ruined."

"Yes. Thanks for photographing it, just in case."

"Sure." Darcie took a couple of close-ups of the area where

Xavier's initial was, then took a step back and started to fiddle with his camera. "That's odd."

"What?" Daisy cleared her throat, which still hurt and felt like it was half-clogged with gunk.

"My phone camera. It's acting just like it always does when I take pictures, but nothing's showing up in the photo gallery."

"That's odd."

"Completely black, like someone is standing directly in front of the lens, blocking the shots."

"Weird."

He tried again, and seconds later, reported that the same thing had happened. "I guess I'll have to take it to the Apple Store when I'm in Killarney."

"Don't worry about the quilt. We can always take photos of it another time."

Now, she was itching. She scratched at her neck and decided she must be mildly allergic to fleas or whatever was biting her. "You never did say why you stopped by?"

"I was going to see if you wanted to go walking along the shore. Then I got caught in the downpour – of which there was no sign when I left home. I figured your place was the closest spot to get out of the rain."

"Funny you should say that – that's exactly how I found the gold."

"Really."

"I was out walking and it started to sleet – a cold, icy wind was blowing – so I ducked into the nearest sea cave and there, staring me in the face, was a chest of gold coins."

"Wow – sounds meant to be."

"Before I had to give it back, I would have said the same thing."

"And that was because? I know you've mentioned it before but it's still kind of confusing."

"It was on the neighbor's land, not Granny's as I'd assumed. I mean, who knows how many eons it's been since the beach was last surveyed, but those were the findings."

"Did you ever think of disputing the decision? For all you know, the surveyor was paid off by some descendant of the priest. You did say he was a priest, didn't you?"

"Yes, but I had no idea that he was a man of the cloth, or even that anyone was staying there. Father O'Leary was evidently very reclusive, and came out to his place by the sea to escape his bustling parish life."

Darcie had a funny look on his face. She supposed speaking of the dead – especially a priest who'd been murdered – was enough to make some people squeamish.

The pinching, biting, poking started up again and she clutched her neck.

"I guess I should be going." Darcie turned and peeked out the window. "The rain seems to have slowed to a drizzle, which may be as good as it gets."

"Right. I guess they don't call it the Wild Atlantic Way for nothing."

"I'll take another look at my photo files and send you some pictures of the quilt if I can figure out where they're hiding. Once I get to someplace that has Wi-Fi I can use the help app to check it out."

"Thanks, Darcie. I appreciate your help."

#

Darcie tried to patch the pieces of the quilt puzzle together in his mind's eye. If he was interpreting the map correctly – and he felt absolutely sure that's what it was – he believed the gold should be right about here.

He could hardly squelch his excitement as he knelt to the sand and pulled aside the stones blocking the entrance to the sea cave. He gave his phone a sharp rap and waited for the flashlight to come on. When that didn't work, he located the app and set the flashlight to shine on a high beam. Nothing. It was getting too dark to see. He tried one more time. What was wrong with his mobile now? Two systems malfunctioning on the same night? It was like the thing was possessed.

He looked out to the sea and was met with utter darkness. The path leading from the beach back up to the bluffs was not much better. He was going to have to give up his search for the moment, but the darkness would only deter him for a few hours.

Daisy didn't have a clue that her precious, odiferous quilt was a treasure map, the clue to everything. By this time tomorrow, the gold would be uncovered and he would be a millionaire!

He had to come up with a contingency plan. Had Daisy's friend

Cavan seen the quilt, really seen it? Nothing was certain. He thought about bedding down on the sand and sleeping right there on the beach to stake his claim, but he knew the tide would be coming in eventually, and the whole area most likely would be under water.

He would come back first thing in the morning. If he was able to uncover the gold and smuggle it out without Daisy knowing about it, then fine. If she found the gold before he did or discovered he'd found the gold, he'd get her to marry him and sign a new will, leaving the money to him. Ha! If she didn't make a good wife, perhaps he'd have to find a way to make sure she died at a young age, maybe have her conveniently slip on a wet rock and fall off a cliff.

He laughed. Crazy. What did he care as long as he had the gold?

Seriously though, if he was proud of one thing, it was the fact that he'd thought to get to know Daisy before the new gold was discovered because now, she would always believe he loved her before she came into the money. After all, she was currently destitute, and he had still shown interest in her.

He stepped around another cluster of rocks in the growing darkness. Daisy – what a twit. She didn't even realize the old quilt had a treasure map sewn into it. Talk about clueless.

Her loss. His gain. The map had led him right to the sea cave. Now, he just had to confirm that the gold was hidden inside and get it out of there fast, before Daisy put two and two together, or someone not so dumb as she was saw the quilt and pieced things together – no pun intended.

10

Cavan gave Daisy a disgusted stare. "Look. All I know is that Darcie is bad news. I don't know how I know it, I just do."

"What has Darcie ever done to you that would make you think such horrible things about him? He's been nothing but kind to me, complimentary of my artwork, and supportive of what I've been through. If you have some proof of these so called evil intentions of his, then I'd be more than happy to listen to what you have to say."

Cavan paced back and forth from one end of the room to the other. "You should not be inviting him into your home or going on walks on deserted beaches with someone you know absolutely nothing about. It wouldn't be wise under the best of circumstances, but factor in the gold, the notoriety you've gained from being in all the papers and on the telly, your neighbor turning up dead, and a murderer on the loose, it's completely insane!"

Daisy looked a little less sassy and a lot more somber – for about five seconds. Then she looked as pissed as hell. "So who am I supposed to go to for comfort then? Or just to talk? My great-aunts to whom I'm an embarrassment, a screw-up, and a fool for being taken in by a wee bit o' gold? My neighbors? Oh, wait. I don't have any. My ma and da? Oh, right, they're dead. My friends? Oh yeah. I didn't have any in Dingle because all I ever did was work on my art and make doodads to sell and work some more and sleep, because I was the odd one out, probably because I'm not married and don't have kids and go to the wrong church, or maybe just because people don't like me. Who knows? And the new friends I made in Killarney? Gone, right along with the gold. So you tell me how I'm supposed to get through this and who I'm supposed to go to for advice and camaraderie, and maybe even a quick hug once in awhile, and I'll do it." Daisy looked like she was going to cry.

"You've got me, Daisy. You always have. You still do."

Her mobile jingled merrily with the cheery Celtic melody that would soon be disconnected if she didn't find a way to make some money. If she did manage to keep her phone, she wouldn't be able to afford any fancy ringtones. She reached into her pocket and flicked the button to answer.

"Daisy Fitzpatrick."

"Maurice here from A-1 Collection Agency. I need to talk to you about a stack of unpaid bills on the furnishings you purchased in Killarney some months ago and a Mercedes that was recently repossessed."

She clicked to disconnect and turned the ringer off. Drat. She wished more than anyone that she had the funds to make good on her old debts so she could put the past entirely behind her, but there was no way she could help the man when all she had was pocket change.

Cavan looked on with a big question mark on his face.

Her lower lip started to quiver and she took a step back. "Listen Cavan, I appreciate you and all you've done for me more than you know, but you have my old life. And I'm mad because I can't have it back! And I resent the hell out of you because you're happy and thriving while I've made such a mess out of things. I can't go back. I know that, but it doesn't make it any easier to be around you!"

He reached out his hands and walked toward her until she was wrapped up in his arms. "How can I be happy when I know how sad you are? Or when I'm so worried about you that I can't even sleep at night?"

"Don't you dare put that on me, Cavan Donaghue! I will not take responsibility for your issues on top of my own."

"Then I'll give up the bicycle repair shop. I'll find another location. I'll move out of your loft and stop standing in your way. You can have your old life back if that's what it takes to get you to stop hanging out with Darcie."

She looked shocked. She didn't say a word. Just looked at him. "You'd do that? For me?"

"Well, it's not my first choice. To be frank, it's my last choice. But yes, I would do it if I have to. That's how much I care about you, Daisy."

She looked elated for – not even a second. And then her face fell. "Don't worry. I won't ask you to-. I mean, I couldn't live with myself if you had to give up your dream and sacrifice everything you've worked so hard for."

"And I couldn't live with myself if something happened to you because I was too stubborn to put first things first."

"I'm a first thing?"

"Of course you are. Would I be here if you weren't?"

She kissed him on the cheek. "So if Darcie is really as dangerous as you say, I can't just tell him to get lost. Who knows what he would do?"

"Maybe you can start being really super unpleasant to be around until things get so tense that he stops wanting to hang out with you."

She smiled at that. "Not gonna work. He's pretty into me right now. Besides, if Granny's quilt didn't scare him off, nothing will."

Cavan tried to think of another way. If he was right and Darcie was "into" Daisy because he thought there was more gold hidden somewhere on Granny's land, then nothing would make him leave short of him finding the gold and disappearing with it – and doing who knew what to Daisy once he didn't need her anymore.

"Let me think on it," he finally said. "But until we come up with a plan, promise me you won't be alone with him."

"I don't know how I can do that, Cavan. I can't pretend I'm not home or that I don't hear him at the door. He shows up unannounced – of course, there's no way to get a hold of me when I'm down by the sea since there's no phone reception."

"And no way for you to get a hold of anyone if you should find yourself in trouble," Cavan reminded her.

"Then what would you have me do?"

"Move in with me. I don't think he'll bother you when you're here in town, or around me. Especially since the harbor police are right across the road."

"You'd let me do that?"

"Yes. Should I be worried?"

"You're not afraid of-"

"Should I be?"

She sighed. "I guess as far as worries go, Darcie is a far bigger concern."

"Exactly."

"I'll have to go back to the shanty and get my clothes and toiletries."

"We can go together once I close down the shop. I have two riders still out. Once they return their bikes, we can head down to the sea."

"And you're okay if I bring Granny's quilt?"

"Has the smell gotten any better?"

"Not really. But it hasn't gotten any worse."

"Can't you leave it at the shanty?"

"No." She shook her head. "I'm not sure why, but I've grown very attached to the old thing. It's like it's the key to some vast puzzle I've been charged with solving."

"Well, maybe we can string it out on the clothes line outside the porch window. That way you can see it, but no one can get to it, and we can't smell it."

"Unless the windows are open."

He laughed. "We'll figure it out."

Daisy smiled for the first time since she'd walked into the shop. "I guess we will. But I have to tell you, Darcie loves that old quilt as much as I do. He even photographed it for me last week – or tried to anyway. I really think he was trying to be thoughtful. You know, in case something ever happened to it, so I'd at least have the memory of what Granny's stitching looked like."

Hmm. That sounded odd. But then, when it came down to it, everything about Darcie was a wee bit off. Cavan made a note in his head to take a closer look at the quilt once they got to the shanty to see if he could figure it out.

#

Two hours later, when the last of Cavan's bikes were put to bed, Cavan hooked up a Burley to the back of his bike so he and Daisy could pedal down to the shanty and bring back a few of her things. He'd figured out a long time ago that just because he didn't have a baby to put in the back of the carrier didn't mean that it wasn't a useful thing to have. He'd carted his sleeping bag and camping gear in it when he wanted to sleep under the stars and used it to bring supplies home from the grocery or hardware store. The best thing was that when the tourists saw the Burley, they assumed he had a baby in tow and gave him an extra wide berth.

They left the bikes where the path ended and the rocks got closer together. They walked the last few yards to the shanty in silence.

"I've really liked living out here," Daisy said. "It made me feel closer to Granny and my dad in particular, since he grew up here."

"It's a shame to leave the place just when the weather's starting to get a wee bit brighter."

"Right. Maybe the whole thing will get sorted so I can move back in time to enjoy the summer months."

#

Begora! How could anyone be so dense? Granny kicked the door of her sea shanty and yelped in pain. 'Twas as solid as the day Xavier had first hung it from its hinges. And speaking of Xavier – what was wrong with that granddaughter of hers? Had she nay heard of the expression, X marks the spot? Why in the Good Lord's name had she suddenly equated X with Xavier?

The evil Sneem had pieced together the fact that the quilt was a treasure map showing exactly where the gold was hidden in seconds. Daisy still thought the markings she'd stitched into the quilt were naught but a random pastoral scene. Did Daisy think she'd had nay else to do but sit around all day, stitching for hours for the mere pleasure of creating something idyllic?

Of course that's what Daisy had thought – because that's what she did. Ye'd think now that Daisy had lived in the shanty for a couple of months, she'd be aware of the fact that it took every second of the day and every whit of energy a woman had to haul water for showering, cooking and cleaning, cook food the old fashioned way over the fire, scrub your clothes clean on a wash board, wring 'em out and hang them out, along with yer linens, wash yer dishes by hand, and do the million other things required of a homemaker. And Daisy could buy produce and fetch her chickens already butchered at the grocery! And, she had no dirty diapers to change or launder, and no children or livestock to chase after or keep out o' trouble.

Ye'd think with all that spare time on her hands, Daisy could solve the simple mystery she'd woven into the quilt.

It irked her no end to think that a pirate's spawn was more keen than her own granddaughter. Thank goodness that Darcie fellow had nay seen the last two quilt squares that held the final directions for finding the gold. Of course, unless Daisy figured it out pretty darn quick, it wouldn't matter. Darcie would find it eventually by process of elimination.

And what if Daisy did find it? Or even her friend, Cavan? Once they went into any of the caves, Darcie would be on them like a tick that would nay release its grip. Granny had no doubt that if need be, Darcie would kill both of them to get at the gold. It was a touchy situation, alright, and dangerous now that a pirate was involved.

Part of her wished she and her neighbor had ne'er found the gold. It had already reeked havoc on Daisy's life, and now, if Daisy found what was left of the gold, it could cost her her life.

Granny got the shivers just thinking about that. She was still quaking in her boots when the sea captain showed up. What had she started anyway? Was Daisy doomed either way?

"What's got ye so upset, Siobhan?" The sea captain shimmered in the sunlight. He only ever half-materialized as it was, but in the bright sunlight, he was little more than a wisp.

"It's that evil spawn of a pirate who's ingratiated himself to me Daisy. I'm afraid he'll kill her and maybe your great-grandson, too, if they find the gold before he does."

The sea captain did nay look as concerned as she felt. What was wrong with the man? Did he nay care if his own kin lived or died?

"Well, by all rights, the gold probably does belong to the pirates. Some of them shed their blood over it, just like my men did." The captain snorted. "They've certainly more claim to it than yer Daisy."

"Begora! If ye do nay stop it with that bleeding heart of yers, I'm going to scream. Those pirates almost certainly stole the gold from kindly folks who were sailing to America to start their lives anew. You and I both had kin on the boats that sailed the seas back in those days. In some cases, the pirates took more than those kindly souls' gold. They took their women, their daughters, and sometimes their lives. By whose standards should those randy scourge of the seas get any of the gold?"

"Fine. But ye know as well as I do that the gold still would nay go to Daisy as succession rights go."

"Listen to yer fancy lingo now, Captain Donaghue. If ye had been successful in recapturing the gold, wouldn't ye have returned it to the families of the folks who lost it to the pirates? That'd be Daisy just as much as anybody."

"Yes, I would have! It's what ye should have done decades ago when ye first found the gold. And if ye had, Daisy and Cavan would nay be in danger now!"

Granny stomped her foot. "Easy for ye to say! I'd just lost my sweet Xavier, but because we'd ne'er formally wed, I was left to raise our child with no help from anyone. What would you have had me do?"

"Notify the authorities and let them sort it out," he said smugly.

"I give up on ye then. Ye've not an ounce of compassion for they who deserve it, but you've got plenty of energy to fret about the poor pirates who lost their lives while they were out marauding. I'll never."

"Nay. Ye're the one who does nay understand. If ye had seen what I saw after the ship broke apart... men drowning, bodies washing ashore up and down the coast, word spreading that there were dead to be identified and families rushing down to beach, praying they would nay find one of their own. It was cruel and heartbreaking."

"Especially for ye," Granny said.

"Of course! I blamed myself. Still carry the guilt of it, though I swear there was nothing I could have done except to nay try to rescue the gold in the first place. I swear those coins have a curse on them."

"If I had seen what happened back in 1903, known the people who had lost their husbands and fathers, maybe I would have turned the gold in to be divided amongst them. But by the time I found it, more than a generation had passed, people had remade their own fortunes, or moved on, or remarried. They'd put the past behind them, and so did I!"

"Well, when ye put it that way..."

"Ye know what the law says as well as I do – if it washes up on your land, it be yours. It's the luck of the draw, and as I was penniless at the time, I took it as divine intervention that the storm uncovered what it did, in my sea cave."

The sea captain grimaced and said, "The Good Lord does have a way of calming down and riling up the sea to suit his own purposes, does He nay? Unless a pirate ship comes along and takes matters into their own hands, wreaking havoc all around."

"Ye're generous to say so, Captain, having lost yer own life in the storm." She tried to pat his arm before she remembered he was a ghost – and so were she. "We've got to stop fighting now and put what's left o' our minds together to sort this out before someone else ends up dead."

"Aye!" The captain raised an arm. "For Cavan and Daisy!"

"For Cavan and Daisy."

11

Darcie moved another rock and tried to peer into the sea cave. This had to be the place. He'd gone over the map on Daisy's granny's quilt a hundred times. The X marked the spot and this sea cave was plainly at the exact spot pictured. The only variables to take into consideration were the storms that battered the Wild Atlantic Way every few years. There had been a lot of storms since Daisy's granny had stitched this quilt.

The picture of the cave's opening on the quilt didn't look at all like what he was looking at in the here and now. Of course, the stitching was primitive and sparsely illustrated but the real difference was obviously the work of the wind and the waves. Storms routinely rolled in huge boulders. High tides and aggressive waves battered the shoreline and cleaned out caves like a giant vacuum cleaner.

A beach where he camped once or twice a year had always been comprised of tiny, one quarter inch pebbles that were as shiny and smooth as though they'd been through a rock tumbler. Then one year, when he'd returned after a big storm, the entire face of the beach had changed. The tiny pebbles were gone, and in their place were jagged rocks that were ten or twelve centimeters across tossed in pockets of fine sand. He'd rechecked his map and tried to gather his bearings. When everything checked out – he'd been absolutely sure that he was on the right beach – it all looked completely different. In the end, he'd repacked his bike and looked for a different spot to camp. The allure had been gone.

So was he looking for the gold in the right sea cave or not? He rolled a large boulder to the side, crouched in front of the opening and wiggled his flashlight between two remaining boulders in the hope that he could see deeper into the cave.

No gleam of gold that he could see. But he wasn't ready to give up yet.

That's when he saw Daisy and that friend of hers from the bike shop up on the ridge where the sea shanty was, loading up the baskets on the bicycles they were riding with what looked to be large bags of something.

His heart jumped into his chest. Could it be-? Surely they hadn't found the gold somewhere else while he'd been digging in the wrong spot? If they had coins, they certainly wouldn't be trying to transport them out by bicycle, would they? That Cavan was an odd sort of gent, but he must have a car, didn't he?

His brain raced into high gear. He wanted to know what was going on with Daisy, but if he happened by now, what excuse would he give for being in the area once again? Any lie he might concoct could blow up in his face if they'd already seen him lurking down by the caves.

Drat.

He got out his binoculars and peered up at the top of the cliffs. Was that the quilt they were refolding and arranging on top of the bike trailer? Probably taking it to the dry cleaners like she'd said she was going to. Thankfully he'd gotten a good look at it when he'd had the chance.

He laughed. Dumb little twit, Daisy. The one good thing to come out of this was that he doubted he would have to kill her after all. She was so stupid she'd probably never even notice the treasure map. He'd have the gold and be long gone before she ever figured it out.

Now Cavan. That was another matter entirely.

#

Daisy pedaled as fast as she could and still couldn't keep up with Cavan. He probably rode every day this time of year, probably had a stationary exercise bike in his loft, probably been riding it all winter. She'd ridden into Dingle a few times since she'd been back at the shanty, but she'd taken her time and stopped at a nice midway point to pick up pebbles and look for sea glass. Every stretch of beach held its own set of treasures and she knew them all well. She pedaled on for another half mile or so, distracted by thoughts of pottery shards and driftwood, sea glass and flat pebbles.

Her legs felt like they were going to go into a massive cramp. Probably because she was so tense about moving into Cavan's loft. Number one, it was going to be weird going back to her old home – her loft – when it really wasn't hers any longer. Her mind filled with images of a sort of twisted déjà vu. Would she instinctively start rearranging furniture until it was set up the way she'd had it? She assumed Cavan had some sort of futon or guest sleeper somewhere where she'd make her bed – maybe out on the porch. That would suit her. She could open the windows and get a good cross breeze going, smell the sea air, hear the gulls screeching – all things she'd missed when she was in that bunker of a shanty.

What if the angst of being home in a place that was no longer her home led her to sleepwalk? What if she subconsciously went to her old bedroom and climbed into Cavan's bed by mistake? Anxiety gripped her like a vise, and her legs pumped furiously. She could hardly breathe! What had she been thinking when she'd agreed to move in with Cavan? Had she finally lost her mind?

That made her smile, because when she was a wee lass, her mother used to say, "You drive me crazy!" to which her da always replied, "For some of us, it's not a very long trip."

"Cavan?" Her voice came out in a mere croak. "Cavan?" The wind stole her voice this time, even though she fancied it a little louder. It was blowing against them, which was one of the reasons she was so out of breath.

She never knew if he'd heard her or was just being kind, but he circled round. Bless him.

"Ready for a break?" Cavan came to a stop and balanced on one leg while she got stopped.

"I didn't realize how out-of-shape I've gotten."

"It looks like you've been busy making more bits and bobs to sell."

"Oh, right." She never should have let Cavan in the shanty until she'd hidden all the bicycle arts and crafts she'd been working on. "Yes. Those." She didn't try to explain herself away because really, what could she say? It was pretty obvious she'd taken Cavan's 'no' as a firm 'we'll see, maybe when I see how wonderful your bicycle art looks.'

See, that was the problem with Cavan. He knew her too well. She couldn't pull the wool over his eyes about anything. Not that she wanted to keep the truth from him, but with a stranger, you could apply filters to what information you disseminated and when.

Cavan cleared his throat. "I'm sure if we put our heads together we can find a place to display a few of your bicycle related items."

"Really?" Her tattletale eyes must have given her away because what she saw in Cavan's eyes was a mixture of compassion and – pity.

She looked away. "It's okay. I'm thinking of opening an Etsy account and selling my art online. I mean, I've only been hurting myself by limiting sales to the handful of people who visit Dingle every year."

"Handful?"

"Yes – our tourists are a drop in the bucket compared to the gazillion people who will see my work on the internet."

"Okay." Cavan looked to the left. She followed his eyes and saw the sea glimmering with the pink and purple skies of the sunset.

"I'm glad you're making things again. I'm sorry you're having to go through all of this, but I'm glad you're painting."

"Well, I was stupid to give it up. I had a huge studio in the house in Killarney with windows on three sides. The light was just about perfect and it had this wonderful tile floor and the original wood trim. I looked out into the middle of a huge tree. It was covered in beautiful pink blossoms the day I had to move out."

"Daisy, I'm really sorry about all the crap you've had to put up with."

"It's not like I was all that attached to it or anything. I never once got out my paints the whole time I lived there."

Cavan gave her a look. "Still - getting your hopes up, having the courage to start a new life, and then having it wrenched away from you, your dream crumbling away to nothing... I can't even begin to know how that must feel."

Daisy mounted her bicycle and started to pedal away from Cavan as fast as she could. It wasn't like he wasn't going to catch up with her, but she wanted as much space between them as she could get for a few seconds anyway.

The sun was casting a surreal glow over the sand dunes, making long shadows behind every rock and each pebble.

Why was this happening to her? She just wanted to have a place to call home, someone to love her, and maybe a little of the respect she'd lost when she moved to Killarney and given her heart to Aodhan. How could she have been such a fool as to give herself to the sort of man who would ever only love Rich Daisy?

Cavan stayed behind her for the rest of the trip. She didn't know if his lagging behind was supposed to be some sort of silent statement that he had her back, or if he was worried she would tip over and die before they got back to Dingle.

She was bone-tired by the time she made it to her used-to-be-home. She dismounted and waited for Cavan to unlock the door. Daylight was fading and so were her spirits and her energy levels.

Cavan was acting as dispirited as she felt.

"C'mon in."

She trudged up the stairs behind him with her satchel of clothes.

"Daisy?"

"Yes?"

"I'm glad you're here."

"You are?" Lord, she hated feeling so vulnerable. So needy.

Cavan sniffed the air. "We're going to have to take care of the quilt tonight or the loft will smell so bad by morning that we'll have to abandon the place."

"I agree." She was so tired, but Cavan was right.

"You said you had a clothes line strung out the window?"

"Aye. It's on a pulley. I'll crank it in just as soon as I find the clothes pins."

She took the quilt from its bag and unfolded it carefully so that Cavan could string it out on the line. She cocked her head and took the corner in her hands.

"Is that a treasure map?" Cavan was looking at the quilt from a spot a few feet behind her.

"I was just thinking the same thing. I've always thought it was just a pretty scene stitched in as a centerpiece."

"But there's an X to mark the spot." Cavan touched the square with the X in his hands. "It could mark another sea cave. I still think there's more gold somewhere on your granny's land."

"I know you do." She let her eyes fly over the design. "What's this?" She pointed to the right hand corner of the quilt.

"Another X." Cavan twisted his neck and his eyes followed a path that led from the X to what looked like a steep cliff overlooking the sea. "Are there any more patches with clues?"

Clues. It almost made sense. She'd never thought that the design might reveal some sort of secret. "I'll check the other corners."

"It's another X." Cavan traced the outside edge of the quilt from corner to corner. "Each corner has an X."

"It looks like each one is a continuation of the last." She craned her neck. "But in what order are we supposed to be viewing them?"

Cavan said, "I'm not sure." He thought for a minute. "Did you say Darcie photographed the quilt?"

"Yes, but he was having some sort of trouble with his camera." Her heart sank. "Do you think he realized it was a map?"

"I would tend to think so."

"I blew it again, didn't I?"

Cavan started to refold the quilt. "Not if he didn't see the corner blocks. I'm sure they're part of the puzzle."

"I only remember him taking pictures of the center part."

"I hope you're right." Cavan started to clip the quilt to the line. "If the quilt leads us to another treasure trove – this one on your land, not your neighbors, I'll be very happy for you. But I still don't want it smelling up my loft."

"I understand. Now that I know it might be a map, let me get my own photos of the four corners and the center to see if I can figure out how the pieces fit together."

"Good idea." Cavan took the quilt down again and stretched the fabric out on the dining room table, a concession that must have irked him greatly, while she snapped her shots. Then, he refolded it and hung it on the line. "You'll have a record in case a sea eagle smells it, mistakes it for prey and carries it off in the night."

"Right." She smiled in spite of her misgivings. Maybe staying a few nights with Cavan wouldn't be so bad after all.

12

Cavan was up early the next morning in hopes that he could use the shower and get to work before Daisy was awake. He kind of missed his privacy already and wanted to make sure he was dressed in case he ran into Daisy. He hadn't really wanted a roommate, but this seemed not only necessary, but the right thing to do.

He was tinkering on rental bicycles that needed a little extra maintenance from time to time when he saw Rory at the door. He hadn't unlocked the front door yet since it was still a half hour until opening.

"What's the craic? You're here awfully early." He greeted his friend.

Rory smiled. "I could ask you the same question."

"I've been behind ever since 'Ride Dingle'. Seems like suddenly, all the members of the Dingle Cycling Club have discovered the shop. I'm not complaining, mind you. It's a thrill to have nearly more business than I can handle, but I'm finding I really have to keep at it night and day to stay ahead of the demand."

"Yeah. I figured you'd be here working. I hate to bother you, but if my bike is done, I'd like to pay you and take it with me so I have it for the weekend."

"Sure." He went to the back room and rolled out Rory's bike. "I had to go down to the sea shanty with Daisy last night after closing so I didn't get as much done on it as I'd hoped, but I can finish it up another time."

"So Daisy was sniffing around again, eh?"

"She's not trying to get me to move out of the shop if that's what ye're thinking." But his mind flashed to the stacks and stacks of bicycle themed arts and craft projects that Daisy had underway at the shanty. She was certainly planning something to do with his space.

"So what is she up to?" Rory asked as though he could read his mind.

"Well, she's staying here for a few days until we get this thing with Darcie Sneem sorted out."

"You're kidding. You let her move in with you?"

"She needed a place to stay. That guy is dangerous. I couldn't just stand by and leave her at his mercy. If you had seen what I saw or had the conversation I did, you'd have done the same thing."

Rory rolled his eyes. "Listen. I know you have a soft heart. You're a caretaker. That's probably what makes you so good at what you do. But you have your own life, and your own set of problems. It's not your job to take care of Daisy Fitzpatrick or save her sea shanty or be her bodyguard."

"It's not that I feel like I have to do anything." But he did. He remembered the feelings he'd been having since this whole mess started and the sensations and premonitions, constantly hovering over him that there was more gold, and that Daisy was in danger, that there was more at stake here than anyone realized and that it was somehow his responsibility to get to the bottom of it and make it all okay.

"Really," he said. "I'm only doing any of this because I want to."

"Fine," Rory said. "All I ask is that you do me one favor and think about the story I'm going to tell you next time you have the urge to do something drastic for Daisy."

He almost said sure without even thinking. Rory was no dummy. He'd always respected his advice. But he held his tongue.

"So are you going to tell me the story or not?"

Rory looked over his shoulder. "So I know this guy and he fell in love with this cute chick who was a little far out. You know what I mean?"

"No. What? Was she into drugs or something?"

"Not exactly, although she probably would have gone down

that road eventually. This girl would do anything to get a rush."

"Like dangerous stuff?"

"More kinky than dangerous. She claimed she was heteroflexible or some sort of non-binary, multi-partnered pansexual or polysexual something or other, which is one of the things that drew him to her, but-"

"Also one of the things that scared the heck out of him?"

"Yeah. You could say that." Rory made a face.

"So what happened?"

"Well, this friend of mine had it so bad that he would have done anything for her, and done anything to be with her. So things are going really well, and they're talking about getting married and all of the sudden she morphs and decides she only likes women."

"So what did she do? Dump him for another girl?" For the life of him, he couldn't see what any of this had to do with him.

"Not exactly. But she was supposedly in love with this guy, or would have been if only he was a woman." Rory looked over his shoulder again. His voice dropped a few decibels. "So my friend knows he's going to lose her unless he becomes a woman."

"You're kidding me."

"No."

"So what did he do? Start taking female hormones or something?"

"Yes, and had a sex change operation."

Cavan could feel his eyes snapping wide open and then narrowing to slits. "And you're telling me this because you think I'd cut off my dick if Daisy wanted me to?"

"You said it, I didn't."

"You are so sick, Rory. For gosh sake. Just stop it. I don't even want to think about something so vile."

"Daisy's already got her claws into you, man. Just be careful and think before you act. With your head."

"Lord, have mercy," Cavan said. "And watch your voice. Daisy's upstairs. Who knows what she can hear up there."

"You don't know?"

"How would I know? The only time people are talking down here is when I'm down here with them."

"You've never run upstairs to use the bathroom while there are people down here talking?"

"No."

"Well, you should," Rory said.

"Just take your bike and go, Rory. You've done yer duty as a friend and given me more than enough to think about."

Rory grinned. "I hope so."

"Just get out o' here. I know where to find you when I want my money."

"Are we still on for O'Flaherty's?"

"Not this week. I want to stick around in case Daisy needs me." He said it mostly to mess with Rory's head. But sadly, or for whatever it was worth, it was God's truth.

#

Daisy motioned for Cavan to join her at the kitchen table.

"I think I've got it sorted now that I've had time to study the photographs we took."

"Tell me. I'm waiting on two riders and then I can close up shop."

"Well, at first I assumed I needed to track the corners in a clockwise direction, and the only question was which corner to start with. I looked at the X in the center of the quilt – the one I assumed was Xavier's initial, and found that the right leg of the X was a little longer. It was almost like it was pointing in the direction of the lower right corner. So I followed the corners around in a clockwise direction and tried to imagine where the pictures would lead."

"And? Do you think you have an idea what the final destination is?"

"If I'm right in my calculations, it would have been off Granny's land."

"Oh."

"Then I noticed that the Xs were in spots in each corner. In each case, the tail of the X more or less pointed to the next corner I was supposed to go to. It would be just like Granny to make things a little more complicated so there would be a mystery to solve."

"So you cracked her code?" Cavan's face lit up.

"I think I did. Of course, the true test will be to actually walk the land and see where we end up. But I can picture it in my mind pretty clearly, and I think we'll find the sea cave where the last X marks the spot on the far south edge of Granny's land just under the bluff that's shaped like a horseshoe."

Her mobile rumbled in her pocket. Not the best timing, but she thought she should check it out. She'd put out a few online feelers at craft shops and art cooperatives. She could only hope one of them would contact her soon.

"Hello?"

"Is this Daisy Fitzpatrick?"

"May I help you?"

"This is Maurice from A-1 Collection Agency and I'm calling to set up a payment plan to take care of your debts from MacAllister Furniture and Meeks Mercedes Dealership."

"Um, I'm sorry, but you must have the wrong number."

Cavan, who didn't have a clue who she was talking to, looked like he was proud enough to pop his buttons. "You're sure Darcie didn't photograph the corner pieces?"

She clicked off the phone and quickly turned off the ringer, anticipating that Maurice would call back in a second or two. Yup. There he was.

She tried to remember what Cavan had said. Gosh, that Maurice knew how to get her good and rattled. "Um, I don't think he did. And remember, I'm not even sure any of the photos that he took actually showed up in his camera files. But we're still going to have to be very careful when we start poking around in the vicinity of where we think the gold might be."

"Right. I'm worried about what he'll do if we find the gold and try to keep it from him."

She hesitated. "I don't want to believe that Darcie would harm us, but I trust your instincts."

"Let's go for a walk tonight – make a big circle around the area where you think the map directs us. If we walk randomly, just so you can get the lay of the land, I don't think he'd catch on that we were doing anything out of the ordinary."

"If we stick to the beach, I can look for pebbles and sea glass like I always do so he doesn't get suspicious – if he's even around."

"He'll be there." Cavan looked so serious it scared her. "We can't even mention the map or the quilt or gold when we're out walking. Not a word. We'll have to act completely natural, like we're just out for a stroll and enjoying the fresh air."

"Got it."

"Daisy? Are you sure there are no more clues anywhere? Isn't it possible that if your Granny had a flair for mystery, she quilted a pillow to match the quilt with the final X on it?"

"I hope not. I don't recall ever seeing anything like that, but then, I never paid attention to the stitching on the quilt until now."

She felt so funny thinking about the fact that for almost three decades, she'd looked at the quilt and seen something sweet, nostalgic, and colorful. That was it. She'd totally missed the quilt's nuances and hidden gems – the map, the beauty and precision of the stitches themselves and the amazing design. She'd always known she hadn't gotten her artistic talent from strangers, but she'd taken so much for granted – about Granny, the sea shanty, her whole life. She'd missed out on so much because she'd only looked on the surface of the situation.

Daisy had always considered herself a curious person, with eyes that saw past the obvious to the creative, the unique, the special aspects of anything, whether it be a plain pebble, an ordinary seashell, a completely normal chunk of driftwood. She looked at things and saw beauty where no one else did. That's what Granny had always said.

Now, Cavan was looking at her with a newfound respect, and she was learning all kinds of things about seeing a familiar situation from a different point of view. She found herself wondering what else she was missing out on. She'd certainly taken her Granny for granted, and before that, her shop and her customers. If she hadn't, she wouldn't have cast them aside the second she'd unearthed a pot of gold.

Past history, she chided herself. Nothing she could do about it now. But then, she looked at Cavan. He was still looking at her with a mixture of excitement and appreciation and – was she imagining it, or was there a hint of tenderness in his eyes that hadn't been there before?

She'd expected him to be enthusiastic about the prospect of finding more buried treasure. Who wouldn't be? But the rest – she didn't want to take Cavan for granted anymore, to look through him without really seeing him like she'd always done before.

Cavan had been a part of her life for so long that she'd never really looked at him, never really seen the man he'd become.

Cavan said, "I think I heard the door chimes sounding. Probably my last customers returning their bicycles."

She turned to say something, but he was already halfway down the stairs.

13

Cavan dashed down the stairs and rounded the corner, hurriedly weaving his way through the workroom in the back of the shop and into the display area. He could see the head of a tall gent on the other side of a bicycle mount that held the bikes upright on one wheel.

If he remembered right, the couple that had rented his last set of bikes was Italian, with dark brown hair.

This gent had jet black hair, and he looked to be alone.

Darcie. His heart quickened and his built-in defense system armed itself. Not that his gut instincts would protect Daisy or him if it came to that.

"Can I help you?" He tried to project an air of uncertainty, like, 'Haven't we met somewhere before?', or 'I know you look familiar, but I can't quite place you.' Best to act nonchalant, like he and Daisy hadn't just been talking about the quilt and the gold and Darcie himself.

"Darcie Sneem. I'm a friend of Daisy's."

He tried to keep his face from belying his feelings. "Sure. Right. What can I do for you?"

"I saw the two of you together last night."

"Oh, right." He acted like he hardly remembered. Or at least, he hoped he did. "Yes. We went for a bike ride just before sundown."

Darcie eyed him, his black eyes poking holes in him like he was a barrel of whiskey and Darcie, a sharp sword. "If Daisy came home last night, it was very late. I haven't seen her this morning either."

He didn't want to speak too quickly. Overconfidence could sound unnaturally flip. "If she was out late, she's probably sleeping in. You know women."

If Darcie asked him point blank if he knew where Daisy was, he was in trouble. He was fairly good at putting together the occasional quick comeback or double entendre, but he was pretty horrible when it came to outright lying.

He looked up at the wall opposite the counter where he'd hung a pair of Daisy's wire bicycles, which flanked a fairly large piece of driftwood with a Daisy original painting of two bicyclers riding into the sunset. He'd bought them because she needed the money. He wasn't selling them, but he had promised her that if anyone inquired about her artwork, he'd give them one of her cards and a good recommendation.

Darcie turned as he followed Cavan's glance to the far wall. He sighed. See? This is what happened when a person tried to fudge on the truth. Even if he did try to lie, he could get caught in the web all too easily. There were a million connections between him and Daisy if one started looking, and he got the distinct impression that Darcie already had.

It sickened him to think that Darcie might have followed them home last night. What if he'd snooped around back and seen Daisy's Granny's quilt dangling from the clothes line behind the loft, or even heard his and Daisy's voices before he'd gotten downstairs?

He had to find out what people could hear from the street or in the shop when people were talking upstairs.

Darcie was pulling on a bicycle chain just like he'd done last time he was in the shop.

"Ciao! We're back!" The door chimes and the greeting rang out in unison.

"Excuse me," Cavan said to Darcie, resisting the urge to hug the Italians, who had very probably saved his butt.

Darcie gave him a look, but left. Probably didn't want to be seen.

A chill ran down his spine.

He took the first bike from the Italian man. He heard a pipe creaking, a blast of water, and droplets hitting his shower pan in the loft upstairs. Well, that answered one question.

#

Daisy looked around at the four walls of her old apartment and felt more hemmed in than she had in her entire life. Her fingers were itching to pick up a paint brush. She'd loved her loft when she'd lived there alone. She'd done some of her best work there. But there was no way she could spread out her paints and canvases and stacks of rocks and driftwood from one end of Cavan's place to the other like she used to. She stood and paced the familiar floors. Being where she used to live and work, but not being able to do what she wanted made her feel like she was in a cage with a padlock.

The bathroom door creaked and Cavan came out with wet hair and a towel wrapped around his waist.

"Sorry," he said. "I didn't think you'd be up."

"Just feeling a bit restless." It should be her who was apologizing.

He headed to his bedroom – her old bedroom – opened the door, and closed it behind himself.

She needed to create something! This forced protective custody to which Cavan had inadvertently bound her was driving her crazy. She knew he was trying to help, but...

The door to the bedroom opened and Cavan stepped out, still looking a bit damp but fully clothed. "I guess we need to talk."

She sighed. "This isn't working, is it?"

"We both know the situation has its drawbacks, but given the fact that Darcie is out there creeping around-"

"But we don't know that his intentions are evil, or that he plans to harm me."

"He's actively looking for the gold. He came here and specifically admitted that he's been watching your comings and goings."

She looked out the front window at the sea and wanted to cry. "It did scare me that he came here looking for me, and that he may have heard what we said about the gold."

"Exactly. You need to stay where you're safe. I'm not even sure you're safe here! Maybe you should be contacting some of your friends in Killarney to see if you can stay with one of them until this whole investigation blows over."

"Right. I'm sure Aodhan would be all excited to have his now destitute former girlfriend hanging around Killarney, ruining his image."

"If anyone's damaged Aodhan's reputation, it's him, dumping you the way he did. Besides, who cares what he thinks? What's important is that you're safe – and happy."

"Oh, Cavan. I'm not unhappy, but I have to be able to do something or I'm going to go mad. I can't paint or work on building up my inventory unless I bring all of my supplies in from the shanty, and we both know that's not going to work."

"So, what's the answer?"

She walked around to the other end of the table. "Don't you think it would be a good idea for me to maintain a presence of some sort out at the shanty? Just to put the fear in to Darcie? If neither of us is ever out there, who's to say he won't find the gold and cart it off without us ever finding out about it?"

Cavan's eyes narrowed. "I see your point, but Darcie's not afraid of you or me or anybody as far as I can tell."

"But if I was to paint at the picnic table at the shanty during the day – different times every day, so he never quite knew when I'd be about, wouldn't that be some sort of a deterrent?"

"But would you be safe? I'm nervous about you being alone out there. And if you go through with your plan, you know he'd figure out very quickly that you're staying here."

"If he deduces that I'm staying here because we're on to him, it could be dangerous for both of us."

Cavan pursed his lips. "Unless he thinks we're a couple and that we have moved in together."

She tried to find a flaw in Cavan's logic and couldn't. "He might accept that."

"It wouldn't take much," Cavan said. "When we're out walking at the beach, we could hold hands at least part of the time, act a little cozy and so on."

"Is there an alternative? Could I wear a costume when I'm heading back and forth to the shanty? Sneak out the back?"

Cavan frowned. "He'd know it was you as soon as you got out there and started painting."

"True. But is pretending we're a couple fair to you? Wasn't your friend, Rory, trying to set you up with his girlfriend's sister? That's not going to go over very well if word gets around town that we're together."

Cavan grimaced. "I can't imagine your aunts, Sheelagh and Ailene, would be very happy either."

Daisy brushed her hand in the air. "They already think we're doing it anyway."

Cavan laughed. She did, too, but she thought he still looked more than a little uncomfortable.

She felt it, too. If there had been absolutely no attraction between them, this might have all worked, but as things stood, it was entirely too complicated. She in no way wanted to hold Cavan back from pursuing a relationship with Rory's girlfriend's sister, but the thought of him with another woman bothered her on more than one level.

Cavan was watching her. She glanced up, met his eyes for a second, and looked down, trying not to blush.

She didn't know if it made her feel better or worse that Cavan didn't know this woman at all. Even the thought of getting involved with someone she barely knew filled her with trepidation. No wonder after the way things had turned out with Aodhan. Then again, how would anyone ever get to know anybody if they didn't start somewhere? Sure, there were risks, but what good thing was without them?

It also bothered her that Cavan's potential girlfriend only wanted to get to know him because she was lonely and wanted companionship or romance. This other woman didn't have a clue what a wonderful man Cavan was.

But Daisy did.

#

The clatter of cooks dishing up food and waitresses clearing tables lent a comforting backdrop to the discussion at the table nearest the kitchen at Maeve's.

Cavan dipped his brown bread into a steaming hot bowl of Irish stew, then looked at Rory and his girlfriend, Lisette, and frowned. "It's obvious you want to say something. So go ahead and say it."

"You didn't like what I had to say the other day," Rory

countered.

He leaned close and spoke in a whisper. "With apologies to the ladies in the room, you were talking about some freak who cut off his dick for a woman."

Rory had the good graces to look chagrined. "Yeah. Sorry about that. I was just trying to get you to see reason."

"There was nothing reasonable about that story. So if that's where you're going with this, you can forget it."

Rory sighed. "Fine. So I shouldn't have gone there. But what I'm going to say now makes perfect sense if you stop to think about it."

Cavan crossed his arms and then uncrossed them so he could have another spoonful of soup. "Fine."

Rory looked him in the eyes. "I know Daisy means a lot to you. I'm not trying to hurt your feelings, or even to talk bad about her. But the thing is, if she was into you, she never would have left Dingle and moved to Killarney in the first place."

Lisette cleared her throat and took a long drink of flavored water.

Cavan weighed Rory's words for a minute. "It's not like I'd given Daisy any reason to stay. I barely saw her back then. We'd grown apart. And it's not like she left the country or moved to China or something."

Rory looked serious. "But her first choice was to get away from Dingle and start her life over again somewhere else. The only reason she's back here now is because she didn't have a choice. I mean, if she were to get interested in you now – as more than a friend, wouldn't you always wonder if you were her second choice, and that if a better opportunity came along, she'd be gone again?"

Cavan steeled himself against the barrage of questions – and emotions – that were racing through his mind. He tried to think of a smart-sounding comeback, but his mind was too tied up with probabilities and possibilities.

"Listen. Nothing's happened with Daisy yet, and nothing likely ever will. I know you're worried about me, but there's no sense in getting all worked up about some vaguely remote occurrence."

"But with her right there in your apartment, things are bound to come to a head eventually." Rory evidently got the message that his words weren't exactly welcome. He shrugged. "You can't say I didn't try."

"Thanks, anyway. I mean, I know you're just trying to look out for me."

Rory looked down at his sandwich and then gave Lisette a look. "I hope it all works out. If you change your mind and want to give things a go with Mandy, you know where to find her."

"I fully intend to look Mandy up." He nodded at Lisette and hoped she wasn't going to repeat everything that she'd heard to her sister. "Maybe later on, when things have calmed down and the priest's murderer has been found."

Rory raised his eyebrows at Lisette in a silent question, scraped out his bowl with a flourish and left twenty five Euros on the table. They both said their goodbyes and left him to think.

Cavan was no expert on romance, and he really didn't have time to ponder its intricacies at the present, but he had to wonder if it would be better with someone you'd just met, or someone you'd known since childhood? Was getting romantic with someone you knew that well and treated like a sister even possible?

He could risk wrecking his friendship with Daisy if he suddenly decided he wanted more from their relationship. He didn't want that. But if he was afraid to take a risk, he might miss out on what could be the best thing to ever happen to him.

14

Daisy ran her hands over the smooth surface of the white rock and painted a curvaceous blue streak that would become the basis of a mermaid's tail. She moved on to the next one in her pile and repeated the motion, and then the next, and the next. Her mermaids were her best selling rock design and she'd need a lot of them before the end of the summer.

She looked up at the deep blue sky and the puffy white clouds and the turquoise blue sea fanning the horizon. Granny's picnic table was her favorite spot to work. From her lookout perched high on the cliffs above the Atlantic, she would almost imagine mermaids frolicking off the shoreline.

When she was done, she painted angel's wings on a set of darker rocks that would offset the pale pastels of the heavenly hosts, and then, also on medium dark rocks, some fluffy white curls that would eventually become sheep.

After she'd painted the first color of the arc of a rainbow, a cherry red on a dozen light-colored rocks, her mermaid tails were dry enough that she could paint a second streak and part of the tail.

She raised her hands and stretched her arms in the air. She would have liked to have gone for a walk – either to pick up a few more rocks or to start to search for the mysterious spot marked by an X on Granny's quilt. But she'd promised Cavan that she wouldn't risk running into or inadvertently leading Darcie to the treasure. It was one thing to encounter him in the relative safety of her home turf, and another in a deserted sea cave along a 'steep, inhospitable shoreline.' Cavan's words, not hers. Until now – even now – she'd always felt completely safe and perfectly at home along the Wild Atlantic Way. But she did want to respect Cavan's wishes, especially when he'd been so kind as to invite her into his home so he could make sure she stayed safe.

Her cherry red arc was now dry enough to lay a peachy orange one beneath it. When she was done, she mixed a little of the leftover coral tone with some iridescent gold paint and worked on the pot of gold at the end of the rainbow. The irony did not escape her.

While she had some of the sparkly gold on her brush, she added a little aquamarine blue and painted some shiny scales on her mermaid tails. She washed out her brush. Next came black feet and noses on her little lambs. By then, she was ready for a real stretch.

She had just stood when she saw a man walking toward her from the east. As he grew closer, she could see that he was in uniform.

"Daisy Fitzpatrick?"

"Yes?"

"Lieutenant Donaldson, Chief Investigator in charge of the Case of the Disappearing Priest, which has recently been upgraded to an official murder investigation."

"Sir." She took the time to look at the badge he flashed. She wanted to be careful this time around.

"If you don't mind, I'd like to ask you a few questions pertaining to your neighbor."

"Is that all right, since I don't have a solicitor?"

He looked at her. "Do ye need a solicitor?"

"No."

"Then let's have a seat."

She sat back down and motioned for him to do the same. "I wouldn't rub against the rocks quite yet. The combination of sun and wind dries the paint fairly quickly but you can't even be too safe."

She doused her paint brushes in a tin filled with water and took another one to dip in yellow for the next stripe in the rainbow, then added a few flecks in her pots of gold to make them shine just like real gold.

If it bothered the policeman, he didn't say anything.

"Do you recall when you last saw your neighbor?"

"I've no clue. Every once in a blue moon, I'd see his back as he entered his shanty carrying an armful of wood. I don't know why, but he always burned driftwood and scrub brush in his fireplace instead of peat. The only reason I knew is because it has such a different smell. I could always tell when someone was there because I'd smell a wood fire burning. I use peat, so the difference was very noticeable. And welcome. But I'd no idea he was a priest."

"So he never came over to introduce himself or borrow a cup of sugar or invite you to a neighborhood barbeque?"

"No. I never met him."

"Did he ever have visitors?"

"None that I saw."

"Any of his mail ever get delivered here by accident? Postal service ever ask if they could leave a package here for him to pick up?"

"No. Sorry. He probably picked up his mail in town or had it delivered to the rectory, don't you think?"

"I'm just here to check out every possibility."

Daisy looked across the moor to the sea. "One of the things I've always loved about Granny's shanty is how isolated it is."

The detective looked down at his notes. "What about after you found the gold? Did your neighbor ever talk to you or correspond with you about the possibility of the gold being on his land instead of yours?"

"No! I told you I never met him, and I didn't know who he was. Do you think if I had known that the gold was on his land that I would have given up my shop and bought a new house and spent all of this cash, knowing that I might have to go to jail one day if I didn't pay it back?" She slammed her hand on the table a little too hard. The water jar she used to soak her used brushes tipped over and water ran everywhere.

The detective jumped up from his seat to avoid a waterfall of murky, dark pink.

"Sorry." She grabbed some paper towels and tried to sop it up. "Listen. I've got nothing to contribute to this investigation. I don't know anything that could possibly be of help to you."

"Sometimes people don't think they have any pertinent information until something I say jars a memory or a recollection."

Fat chance, she wanted to say. His questions were mediocre at best and certainly not deep enough to make her think about anything, say nothing about anything significant or subconscious. "Maybe a different set of questions might help me to think of something I'd forgotten."

He gave her a funny look. Really, she was just trying to be helpful.

"So what about the goings on since you've been back in Dingle? Have you met any new people?"

"Well, there's Rory, Cavan's friend. Cavan leases my building for his bike shop. We've known each other since we were young. Anyway, Rory has this fancy bike that Cavan likes to work on. I don't think Rory likes me all that well, maybe not at all, but that's fine with me. I've never had any friends in Dingle to speak of." Her mind flitted to the time she'd spent in Killarney. She'd been happy there. People had welcomed her, accepted her. And then an image of Aodhan zinged into her brain. She hated to admit that Aodhan had only loved her for her money, but it was pretty obvious that she'd been of no value to Aodhan once her gold was gone.

The wind scudded over her shoulders and she wished she had thought to wear a jacket. It was so sheltered and quiet in Dingle Town compared to the shore, with its notoriously wild winds and changeable weather. Not that it bothered her. It was what she'd grown up with. Granny's shanty was so close to the ocean, whereas in Dingle harbor, the breezes were far more gentle, and the waves more shallow and weak.

"Have you seen anything suspicious or different since you've been back at the shanty?"

Another gust blew in. She shivered. "There's a guy named Darcie who's been nosing around for a couple of weeks now. I think he believes there's more gold to be located. He's never bothered me – I mean, he's been friendly and helpful and acted the complete gentleman whenever he's around."

The wind hit her full force so hard that her hair flew straight back. The closer you got to the actual Atlantic, the more aggressive and daunting the wind, the more wild and menacing the sea.

She wrapped her arms around herself and tried to think warm thoughts. "Cavan doesn't think I should trust him."

Daisy shivered and watched as the detective jotted something down in his notebook. "Cavan gets this weird vibe from Darcie.

Cavan picks up on stuff like that. Me, I'm either more dense or trusting, or some combination of the above. Anyway, Cavan doesn't want me to see him or to be alone with him."

"Can you give me a description?"

She told the detective about Darcie's long black hair and sometimes man bun, and his dark eyes and long eyelashes. "I'm guessing he's almost 2 meters tall."

"Do you have any knowledge of the rocks he's been moving from the front of what looks to be a sea cave on your property?"

Her heart beat a little faster. So Cavan was right about Darcie. He was after the mythical gold that both he and Cavan seemed to believe was still hidden somewhere on Granny's land – hopefully where the last X on the quilt was planted.

"I was afraid something like this was going on, but I've been scared to go down to the cliffs and see what he's actually been up to."

The detective made a few more notes. "Until we know more about this fellow and what his intentions are, I would heed your friend's advice and stay away from Darcie and the area where he's made camp."

"He's camping on my property?"

"He's trying to stay hidden from view, and taking care to cover his tracks, but I'm convinced he's been sleeping under a tarp near the deep tide pool on the west edge of your land."

Yuk. Darcie was probably using it as his own, personal hot tub so he could bathe in the water the rocks held back, just like she had been before she moved into Cavan's loft, well, her loft. The loft she owned and was leasing to Cavan. Well, that the bank owned.

"I have to admit I'm more than a little freaked out to hear that news. I guess I'll have to stop coming out here by myself like Cavan says. Can't you do something? Arrest Darcie for trespassing or tampering with private property or something like that?

"Your land isn't fenced or posted to prevent trespassing, and the public roadway goes through your property so anyone who parks their car and wanders down to the sea has open access to your beaches. He's not doing anything more than millions of tourists do every summer without your permission."

She sighed. "That's how Granny wanted it. She was a firm believer that although the land officially belonged to her, it was really a gift from the Good Lord, who put it there to be enjoyed by whomever he led to our banks."

"That seems to be the sentiment held by most of the old-timers along the Wild Atlantic Way."

"You're exactly right." She reflected for a moment on the ways in which the world was changing and finally said, "For the most part, I believe my generation remembers how things have always been and tries to respect the wishes of their grandparents and great-grandparents. What the next generation and the one after them will do is a mystery to me, but somehow I doubt they much care what someone who died long before they were even born thought about anything."

"I suspect you're right. And just between you and me, it frightens me no end, but it seems to be the way things are headed."

She looked around and took note that the sun was high in the sky and shimmering over the waves.

"Feel free to ask away if you have any more questions, but if you don't mind, I'd like to start packing up my paints and the rocks I've been working on so I can hike out with you."

"I didn't mean to scare you off your own place."

"It's not you who's scaring me. It's Darcie."

"I do have one more question. Do you know an Aodhan Byrne?"

What? She dropped a tube of paint and swallowed hard. "Sure. I mean, he's my ex-boyfriend. We dated when I lived in Killarney."

"Okay." The detective wrote something in his notes. "That explains why his car has been sighted in the area."

Actually, as far as she knew, it didn't explain anything – unless Aodhan had realized what a jerk he'd been to her and tried to find her so he could apologize. She didn't share her thoughts with the officer because of the personal nature of the matter. Who knew what or why Aodhan did anything? All she knew was that the way he'd treated her was embarrassing.

She lowered her voice. "May I ask – I mean, I understand if you can't divulge anything about the investigation – but I would like to know if I'm being interviewed as a neighbor, or am I still a person of interest in the investigation? More important, is Darcie under suspicion for the murder of the priest?"

"I cannot tell you any of the details – but I would recommend that you stay away from Mr. Sneem and anyone else you see nosing around your property until we've completed our inquiries."

15

Cavan stepped outside the bicycle shop and flipped the sign from open to closed. For once, all his bikes had been returned early and he didn't have to wait for anyone to come straggling in. Eighth wonder, as the sky was fair and the winds were nay but a wisp.

Daisy was at her sea shanty, sitting outside at her picnic table painting mermaids and rainbows and fluffy, white sheep – and in her glory, if he knew her. He had not felt entirely comfortable about her being out there by herself, even in the bright daylight, but she was hardly some grunter he could keep cooped up in a gated pen during the hours he was working. He'd made her promise to skedaddle back to her bicycle and take off as fast as she could fly or flag down a passing motorist on the road and hitch a ride into town if she should but catch a glimpse of Darcie's head appearing over the edge of the cliffs.

She'd promised she would be back long before dark – a sacrifice on her part for sure since he knew how much she loved to watch the sun setting in the west over the Atlantic.

He thought about riding out to the shanty to act as her bodyguard now that he was closed for the day, but she'd mentioned needing some time alone to concentrate on her painting, and he had no desire to smother her.

He hoped she'd felt safe and gotten a lot done. He was somewhat torn, as he really did not want her underfoot every minute of every day, and most certainly did not want her to move all of her paints and the half ton of rocks she'd collected into his loft.

That left him with some free time – a rare thing in his life as of late. He didn't feel like cooking, which gave him the perfect excuse to head up to O'Flaherty's Pub for a wee bite of dinner and perchance a first meet up with the fair Mandy, who still came highly recommended by Rory and Lisette.

He took the stairs to the loft two at a time and took a quick shower to get rid of the smells of rubber tyres and stale air and to wash the grease out of the creases of his fingerprints. He fluffed up his hair with a towel and donned a clean rugby shirt with blue and red stripes – or, as Daisy would say, sea blue and cherry red stripes. She had a habit of calling colors the names on her paint tubes. But that was okay. It suited her. Daisy was a colorful person and very descriptive in both her words and her artistic expressions.

He pulled up his jeans and added a belt made from a recycled bicycle tyre. Socks next, and then tennis shoes, which were also blue and red. Coordinated colors. Daisy would approve.

When he was dry and dressed, he grabbed his baritone ukulele, dashed downstairs, and took off for O'Flaherty's on his bicycle. A few minutes of flat and one steep hill later, he was securing his bike in the stand and walking through the door.

He scanned the room for Rory, and didn't see his friend. Probably the better of the two scenarios. He didn't always appreciate Rory's running commentary on romance and thought it best if he made first contact with Mandy on his own.

He found an empty stool and bellied up to the bar. Good. The wait staff wore name badges. Mandy was not among the men and women manning the bar. Maybe she wasn't working today, or maybe her shift hadn't started yet – or had already ended. He wandered through the tiny, interconnected rooms that comprised the pub until he found a two-seater booth. It was near a small stage – if he nursed his drink long enough, he would most likely get to enjoy playing a wee bit of trad. There was no band advertised for a performance, but he felt sure some musicians would be by before the night was over.

What usually happened was that any musicians who favored the pub would wander in willy-nilly and start playing. Each new one who came through the door would get out their instrument and pull up a chair. The circle kept growing and stretching to accommodate whoever showed up until the room was filled with fiddles, accordions, flutes, recorders, guitars, and the occasional ukulele like his. He didn't know who usually jammed at O'Flaherty's, but he had no doubt he'd be welcomed if he wanted to join in.

He left his case in his booth and went to the bar to order a drink. A few minutes later, he took his Guinness back to the booth and waited.

He found himself thinking that Daisy would like O'Flaherty's. It was comfortable and down to earth, like Daisy, but it had a certain class about it, too. She would love the artistic renderings of the sea on the walls, and the more cutesy images of sheep grazing against the hills overlooking the Atlantic. There was a fair amount of history reflected in the décor, and an old doll house that he knew Daisy would love.

The walls were painted the leafy green of an Irish hedgerow. He smiled at himself when he realized he was starting to think of the green as leafy green. He was doing a Daisy.

The two women in the booth behind his ordered two glasses of white zinfandel, as if he hadn't already figured out they were Americans by their accent. In the booth on the other side of his, two men with grey hair were speaking Gaelic.

The whole place was humming with craic. Daisy would feel very at home here for a lot of reasons. He'd heard the two mainstays in the bar were rendered from a ship lost at sea – a detail Daisy would be particularly interested in since her sea shanty had also been built with wood washed ashore after a storm had wrecked a ship.

"Another Guinness?" A woman with dark brown hair retrieved his empty glass. So much for nursing his drink. "Sure. I guess so." It was after nine. The music should be starting soon. Hopefully by then he'd be playing instead of drinking.

The barmaid disappeared. The pub was definitely a testament to the history of Dingle Town - every inch of its walls was adorned with photographs and memorabilia. The signage was in both English and Gaelic, another idiosyncrasy that Daisy would appreciate.

"Here you go." His barmaid put his Guinness on a coaster and slid it across the table. He looked up to thank her. Mandy. Her nametag said Mandy. He'd been so busy thinking about playing with the musicians that he'd completely forgotten about her.

She had already turned and started to walk away when he found his tongue. "Mandy?"

She turned and said, "Yes?"

"I think we have a mutual friend. Rory O'Neill."

She hesitated. "Sure. He's dating my sister."

"Right. I met her the other day."

"She was telling me about your bike shop." Mandy smiled.

He stuck out his hand. "Cavan Donaghue."

"Mandy Moynahan."

"Nice to meet you. Maybe we can talk a little more when things calm down."

"I'd like that."

Mandy left and he settled back into his booth. She seemed nice enough. Daisy had a shirt just like the one she was wearing.

A man was opening a guitar case a few feet from where he was sitting. Another walked up and shook his hand, then opened a fiddle case. A woman with bright red hair appeared next with a concertina. The first man pulled a few chairs into a circle. Cavan stood and walked over to join the group.

A half hour later, he was having a gay old time playing The Rocky Road to Dublin, The Wild Rover, Fiddler's Green, The Boys of Killybegs, and one toe-tapping instrumental after another.

One musician after another filtered in as the night drew on until there were ten or twelve of them. He'd always found bike riding exhilarating, but tonight, his heart was tuned to the music. He caught a glance of Mandy every so often. It was free beers all around for the musicians, but he was having enough fun without it and didn't want to take a break to drink.

He'd left Daisy a note so she'd know where he was going, but he started to worry about her about half ten when he knew the sun was setting. He thought he should probably head home just to make sure she was okay. He could almost hear Rory taunting him about Daisy's and his shoestrings being tied together but he had good reason to be concerned for her wellbeing with Darcie sniffing around and a murderer on the loose. If they weren't one in the same.

The song came to an end and there was a lull while the leader debated which one to do next. Cavan started to strum and sing a tune that had been floating through his mind all evening.

In early morn out on the sea,
The fog gives way to sun.
You can hear the seabirds singing
As the waves come crashing in,
As the waves come crashing in.

Where my Seaside Daisy's shanty's
On the Wild Atlantic Way
There's a treasure at the rainbow's end
In the caves on Dingle Bay.
In the caves on Dingle Bay.

He slowed the tempo and mellowed his voice to a serious pitch.

For gold can be a blessing,
And gold can be a curse.
But true love is the greatest gift
Through better and through worse,
Through better and through worse.

"Sweet song. Is it yours?"

Cavan nodded.

"Love the trad vibe." The leader started to strum the chord progression. "You can take the lead if you want to teach us."

Cavan shook his head. "Maybe when it's finished."

Someone in the crowd called out "Whiskey in the Jar." The leader choose a key and strummed a few opening chords. One by one, the other instruments joined in and the patrons started to sing.

He pushed back his chair. It would be fun to play until the pub closed down, but he had to be up early in the morning, and if he waited much longer, Daisy might be asleep before he got home and he wouldn't get to hear how her day had gone. Assuming she was home. He hadn't tested the key he'd given her to make sure it worked. He felt foolish then. For all he knew, it was her old key. If anybody should know how to get into the place, it was her.

The music swirled on around him. If he stayed until closing, he could talk to Mandy for a bit, get to know her a little, offer to walk her home. It wasn't like Daisy needed a babysitter. They'd discussed all of this before they'd each gone their respective ways that morning. She was a big girl. They each had their lives. She was staying at his loft as an extra precaution – that didn't mean they had to be joined at the hip every hour of every day.

He saw Mandy approaching him out of the corner of his eye. She probably assumed he was going to take a break so he could get something to drink.

He stood, turned to face her and smiled.

"The band sounds great tonight! You should join in more often."

"Thanks. I enjoyed it. It's probably been two months since I've played."

She smiled and looked like she was debating whether or not to say more.

It was hard to talk with the music still loud in the background. "Just a lot going on right now."

She said, "No worries. I understand."

Had she thought he was going to ask her out? What had Rory told her? Had he thought he was going to ask her out?

Even he didn't know what he'd intended to do. "I guess... I guess I should get going."

"Sure. Maybe another time."

Again, he had the feeling that she'd been expecting more. He certainly hadn't led her on with the few limited words they'd shared, so if she had, her expectations were obviously based on something Rory had said.

"I'm glad I got to meet you." He didn't want her to think he wasn't interested.

She nodded and he turned to bundle up his ukulele.

When he had his instrument in its case, she was gone.

He sighed. Just as well. He didn't know what he wanted. Well, except for Daisy. Arg!

Sometimes he wanted to pound his head against the wall.

He raced down the hill to the harbor at breakneck speed. It felt good. When he got to the shop, he could see the light on in his flat. Daisy was home. The glow from the window filled him with warmth and anticipation. Of what, he didn't know. He felt happy. That was all that mattered, wasn't it?

He unlocked the door to the shop to store his bicycle in the back room.

It was then he heard the words, "Your feet will take you where your heart is." Well, it was more like he'd thought the words, except they didn't come from his thoughts. He'd never heard the expression before. It was as if they were spoken by someone else, but inside his head, not out. How could that be?

He stood quietly and listened to see if whoever was speaking to him had any more to say, but the only noise he heard was of Daisy pattering around overhead.

16

"Aye! He could hear me! I'm sure he could!" The sea captain pumped his fist and beamed at Granny. "The lad is so in tune with me that he could hear me clear as day!"

Granny rolled her eyes. "If he's so closely knit together with ye, then why don't ye tell him to quit dinging around and tell Daisy he loves her?"

"Wishful thinking on yer part. I know ye care about the girl, but ye can nay impose yer wishes for the girl on Cavan. Ye can only hope. Patiently."

"What? He went to that bar to meet a woman and barely glanced at her the whole time he was there. All he could think about was Daisy! I'm telling ye, he 'as it bad."

"Now listen here, Siobhan. Ye know I agreed to help you out, but I do nay want your granddaughter breaking my great-grandson's heart. And to be quite frank, she's a bit of a loose cannon. I do nay want him involved with the likes o' someone who does nay know their own heart."

"And ye can nay practice a little patience of yer own, eh? Daisy's been through a trauma. But once things settle down, she'll realize Cavan is the one she loves." Granny's voice softened. "She always has."

"And ye do nay think ye're a wee bit prejudiced?" The sea captain wanted none of it. Cavan was far more sensitive than this Daisy girl. He deserved someone better and he would have it, if the captain had anything to do with it.

Granny harrumphed. "At least she's off that spawn of the pirates, Darcie Sneem. I was about ready to strangle her over that lapse in judgment."

"Now ye're finally being honest. The girl has poor judgment. Cavan is better off taking his chances elsewhere."

"That ship has already sailed," Granny said a wee bit smugly.

"That ship has already sunk – and her chances along with it."

Granny snorted. "My whole life has been built on the premise that you salvage the wreckage of what's gone wrong and make something beautiful out of it."

The sea captain looked at her and did nay even bother to hide his distain. "Do ye nay realize how offensive those words are to me? Those boards you used to build yer house were very possibly floating around in the sea because my ship broke up on the rocks. Using them was akin to cannibalism if ye ask me! Ye took the shipwreck of my life and other precious souls and used it to profit yer own needs."

"I used those boards to survive. And nay without praying for every man who lost his life, and thanking the good Lord that what they lost turned out to be my gain. My very humble gain."

The sea captain sighed. "I guess if the sea was going to take them from me, I'd rather they do someone somewhere a wee bit o' good."

"Nowadays, they call it repurposing." Granny chuckled. "It's the trademark of the millennials. They steal an idea I and my generation thought of decades ago and give it some fancy new name so they can take credit for it themselves."

He chuckled in spite of himself. "Isn't that the truth."

They both quieted so they could listen in on Daisy and Cavan. They had to tread carefully now that both Cavan and Daisy believed there was more gold to be found. If they clued them in on too much, too soon, Darcie – or even that Aodhan fellow - could end up with the gold instead of them. And who knew what either of them might do to keep Daisy from getting back what they thought was rightfully theirs.

#

Daisy stood in the personal products section of the grocery looking for the things on Cavan's shopping list. He might have more money than she, but she had more time, and she wanted to be helpful. He deserved that for giving her a place to stay and paying for most of the food they ate.

Old Spice shaving cream. Check. She was tempted to tell Cavan they'd discontinued the scent and pop a tube of Jack Black Beard Lube in the trolley instead. Hmm. She picked up the tube and read the label - lather-less with hints of eucalyptus, peppermint, macadamia nut oil, jojoba oil as key ingredients. Lather-less. Designed to not only invigorate your whiskers, but deliver a rich splash of moisture and nourishment to your skin after you are done shaving. She was tempted to try it herself.

She put it in the cart but couldn't bring herself to put the Old Fogey Spice lather back on the shelf. She didn't like to lie, especially when she was skating on thin ice with Cavan already. He'd been defensive and in a wee bit of a bad mood ever since he'd returned from the bar and found her spreading out a small selection of her paints and few dozen rocks on the kitchen table. She'd kept it to one end, so she wasn't sure what the problem was. It wasn't like his table was wood or that she'd neglected to take off the tablecloth. She had. And the table was glass topped, which meant she could use a razor to scrape off any random spills.

She looked back down at the list. Razors that will cut a thick beard (in any color but pink.) Fine. Cavan obviously didn't appreciate the one she'd loaned him when he ran out earlier in the week. She perused only the manliest looking razors and made a selection. Check. Men's boxer shorts. What? How was she supposed to pick out boxer shorts? She found the aisle with underthings and then the men's section, which was much smaller than the women's. Oh good. The next line on the list included the exact brand, size, style and color Cavan preferred. As they were out of black, she chose a nice navy blue.

"Good grief, Daisy. Must you be so obvious about flaunting your indiscretions?" Auntie Ailene's voice cut through the Tesco background clatter and her own personal shopping haze like a razorback clam.

She froze with Cavan's boxer shorts held high in her hand.

"What are you talking about?" She turned and saw the dastardly duo were both present. "Hello, Auntie Ailene. Auntie Sheelagh."

She lowered her arm slowly and tucked the boxer shorts in the back corner of her trolley as Auntie Ailene peered at her purchases and Auntie Sheelagh pretended not to know her.

Auntie Ailene snorted. "No need to play coy at this stage of the game, Daisy. We've heard all about your ill-timed pregnancy – and that Cavan has taken you in even though the child is not his."

"What? I am not pregnant. Who told you that?"

"No need to deny it, dear." Auntie Ailene frowned. "Our source is very reliable. A dear friend of ours and your granny's, too, when she was living, bless her soul. Our friend's sister is from Killarney. She's probably heard it from both sides."

"I am not pregnant! And Cavan has not taken me in so he can be a father to my non-existent child! In fact, when I'm done picking up these things for Cavan – which does not mean what you think it does – I was just going to head over to the woman's aisle to buy some tampons."

"No need to be vulgar, dear," Auntie Sheelagh said. "And you must know those tampons can kill you. Toxic shock syndrome, I think it's called. Plus, any respectable woman would know that once you've started using them, no man is ever going to be fooled into thinking you're a virgin."

The ludicrousness of it all was amazing. But no matter how unfounded and unreasonable, it still struck her like a ton of rocks, "No man is ever going to think I'm a virgin if the two of you keep spreading gossip about me being pregnant!"

Auntie Ailene turned to address Auntie Sheelagh. "The boys her age probably don't even care if a woman is a virgin anymore. They probably prefer someone who's experienced." She huffed and turned back to Daisy. "We know all about yer promiscuous ways, Daisy. I don't know what Granny was thinking when she left you the sea shanty."

Okay. Daisy had had enough. "Right. Because if Granny had known I was going to be running a house of ill-repute out of her home and entertaining a different man every hour of the night, she'd have left it to one of her homely, unappealing nieces so none of that kind of hanky-panky would be going on."

"Daisy Fitzpatrick! For shame." Auntie Sheelagh said.

She could almost see Auntie Ailene bristling and shifting into hyper-judgmental mode.

"I was just reading Psalm 62:10 in my daily devotional. It says, *'If riches increase, set not your heart on them.'* If that doesn't sum up the crux of what you did wrong, I don't know what does. You can't let a sudden jump in your income dictate your lifestyle. If you hadn't bought that big house in Killarney and that luxury automobile of yours when you found the gold, you wouldn't be in the trouble you're in now."

Daisy swallowed. She hated having to admit that Auntie Ailene was right – about anything. But even she could see – in hindsight – that she could have tempered her reaction to finding the gold and taken things a little slower. It had just all been so exciting when it happened.

Auntie Sheelagh chimed in. She looked at her sister. "We must have the same devotional book – James MacDonald?" She turned to Daisy. "The article recommended choosing a comfortable level of living that meets your needs, and not compromising that with more spending when more income arrives. Instead of living beyond your means like most young people do, be counter-cultural. Choose a lifestyle that's biblically based, eternally focused, and others-oriented."

Again, Daisy had to admit they were right. But she sure wasn't going to tell them that. And she definitely wasn't going to mention the fact that she had the same devotional or that she'd also read Psalm 62 that very morning.

Whether she said it aloud or not, there was no denying it was sound advice. She'd had a good, happy life before she'd found the gold. She'd had everything she needed and even wanted in the pre-gold days. If she had let enough be enough – been content instead of covetous – she could have saved herself a world of hurt.

"Listen, Aunties. I've got a lot of things on my list and I want to get home in time to fix Cavan a little lunch since there's basically nothing to eat in his icebox. Please know that I do take your advice to heart even though you may not believe it. And as to the question of why Granny left me her house and everything in it, I believe it was because she knew I would never sell it, or have it bulldozed. She knew I loved the land, and her, and the sea shanty, with all of my heart. I still do."

"Then why in God's name are you living with Cavan?"

"The answer is complicated, and I don't have time to go into it now. Just know that I'm trying my best to figure it all out, and when I do, you'll be the first to know." Well, there went her truthfulness streak after all – because if and when something good finally came of all of this mess – if and when they finally found more gold – the very last thing she intended to do was to call either of her aunts.

She'd just turned away from her aunties when her mobile rang. She glanced at the number. Maybe Cavan had forgotten something else he needed from the grocery.

Not. It was a Killarney number, one she unfortunately recognized as the collection agent who'd been hounding her about the bills she'd accrued when she had money. Not only did she not want to talk to him – what was the point when she currently had no money and no way of earning any – but she could hardly pick up when the aunties were still within earshot.

She looked around and silenced the ringer. What was she going to do? If Granny really had more gold buried somewhere on her property, she needed to find it fast or admit defeat and sell the shanty and get a job waiting tables in Dingle Town.

#

Granny wiped a tear from her eye. She loved her sisters, but she hated the fact that they couldn't find it in their hearts to be kinder to Daisy.

"I think I'm starting to change my mind about Daisy," Captain Donaghue said abruptly.

What was he doing here? She'd only ever encountered him down by the shore. Were their auras now so linked that they could be together anywhere? Granny didn't know how she felt about that. If the man was finally coming around to recognize that Daisy was a rare gem, it would help. If he was nay, then he'd better watch out because she'd had it up to here!

Captain Donaghue tipped his half-materialized hat. "Daisy obviously loves ye a great deal."

"Aye. And she cares for my sea shanty like it was her own."

"It is, now ye're dead."

"Well, of course it is." She felt blustery and prickly today. Mostly, she was sick of having to defend Daisy when the truth was, the girl was as fine a lass as she'd e'er known. If Cavan Donaghue and his bloody great-grandfather could nay see it, they were the ones who needed to get a better grip on reality. And she was adding her sisters Sheelagh and Ailene to the list.

"The more I think on it, the more I'm inclined to think my Cavan could nay do any better than your Daisy girl. All they can think about is the other."

"If they do nay realize it soon, we may have to clunk their heads together to get them to wake up to the idea."

The Captain repositioned his hat on his head. "It's complicated. Is that nay what the young people say nowadays?"

Granny smiled in spite of herself. "It would help if they could catch whoever killed the priest and put that much behind them."

"And recover the gold so they can do as they would with it."

Granny coughed. "Thank ye for that."

"Aye." The sea captain vanished and Granny found herself back at her shanty by the sea. The title on the deed might say Daisy Fitzpatrick, but it would be hers as long as she was granted the privilege of watching over it.

#

Daisy filled the basket on her bicycle with everything she'd purchased at the grocery, lopped the last shopping bag over the handlebar, and swung her leg in front of the seat. She was just ready to start pedaling when she heard a familiar voice.

She turned and saw Rory walking beside a tall, slender woman with gorgeous hair. Not feeling like another encounter, she turned her back to them. It wasn't her intent to eavesdrop but they were only a few feet away.

She could hear Rory's voice. "I'm not saying I'm glad Father O'Leary was murdered. I just think that if he hadn't been so hardnosed about how much people gave to the church, he might still be alive."

"OMG," the woman he was with responded. "Do you really think someone would kill a priest just because he told them they were greedy?"

"He told me I should sell my Colnago and be content with a second hand bicycle, and that I ought to donate the difference to a charity."

The woman said, "Well, not everyone treats their bicycle like a member of the family. They're a mode of transportation. A lot of people get by with normal bikes."

"It's titanium." Rory laughed, but there was a serious tone to his voice that made Daisy think he wasn't kidding. "All I'm saying is that an opinionated priest like Father O'Leary is going to ruffle some feathers and make a few enemies along the way."

"So, do you still think Cavan's friend, Daisy, had something to do with the murder?"

"She might have. I guess..."

Rory's voice trailed off to nothing. They were out of range, and she could hardly follow after them.

She stood frozen to the ground for a minute. Rory didn't know her, not really. In that sense, his words didn't hurt as much as dear Aunties Sheelagh and Ailene's. But it bothered her that a man she might have liked to impress because he was a good friend of Cavan's could honestly believe she might be a murderer. She wanted to cry. Could this day get any worse?

17

The next day, Cavan decided to do a 'take two.' For better or worse, Daisy was out at the cottage again, having insisted on hauling her paints back to the picnic table on the back of her bicycle. He'd let her leave her rocks at the loft for the time being, but only because they were too heavy to transport back and forth willy nilly. And she had plenty more to work with down by the sea, where the tide brought in a fresh crop every day.

If his rental bikes were all returned by a decent hour, he'd head to O'Flaherty's again and hope that Mandy was working so he could have a do over. He debated on whether or not to take his instrument along, and in the end, decided it would be nice to have it. Sort of a security blanket in case Mandy didn't want to talk to him, or was too busy, and a convenient excuse for why he'd returned to the bar a second night in a row.

He tried to sort out his motives for giving things with Mandy another go while he caught up on some paperwork. He'd not felt any great fireworks when they'd met, but she was attractive enough. He wasn't even sure he wanted to be in a relationship right now say nothing about not having the time.

Maybe he was trying to prove something to Rory, which he knew was not a good reason. Or maybe he just wanted to enjoy the attentions of a girlfriend instead of a girl who was just-a-friend. Was that so wrong of him?

His feelings for Daisy were the biggest stumbling block. He

didn't have a clue what to do about her.

A few hours later, he'd taken in his last two rental bikes and locked up the shop so he could shower, don clean clothes and head up the hill to O'Flaherty's. Daisy still wasn't home from the shore, which left him mystified as to why he felt he was sneaking around on her.

This time, Mandy was behind the counter when he arrived. She smiled at him right off, but then, she seemed to do that to everyone who walked in the door. He didn't know if she was particularly glad to see him or not.

He ordered a Guinness and stayed seated at the bar so he could pay her a little more attention than he had the previous night. For over an hour, a steady stream of customers kept her occupied. His mind wouldn't calm, and soon, the melody of another song started to weave its way through his head.

> Is it love or just a friendship?
> Fleeting feelings or forever?
> Might she love me – feel the same way?
> Would she try to understand?

The words flowed from his heart without any particular shape. He could hear notes gathering into a melody like a sky full of color just before a rainbow forms.

> Should I risk it? Take my chances?
> Or accept the status quo?
> If I don't, I'll never know
> If our love can somehow grow.

He looked around, embarrassed, afraid that the others could read his mind. The band hadn't started up, but he'd seen a handful of the musicians he'd played with the night before wander in and head to the back room.

The song wouldn't leave him alone.

> The best loves are born of friendship
> Sharing conversation, pleasure.
> Love and passion, merged together
> Bring to life the greatest treasures.

Mandy finally came to see if he needed a refill.

"Thanks."

She smiled, although rather half-heartedly. "It's what I do."

"Well, you're really good at it," he said, sincerely appreciating Mandy's people skills and deftness at multi-tasking.

"Thank you," she said, looking past him and a little to the left.

When she finally looked back at him, Cavan said, "Rory seems to think we'd hit it off, but with me working days and you working nights, it might be hard to find a time to get to know one another." He didn't know why he had blurted out something so negative sounding right off the bat. It made it sound like he was giving up on a relationship with her before they'd even tried.

"Listen," she said. "I know you told Rory that this Daisy is just a friend, but now that she's pregnant and living with you, I think it would be a very bad idea for us to get involved. I mean, you've obviously already got a lot on your plate if you've got her and her baby to worry about plus your business and whatever else you've got going on in your life. Don't get me wrong. You must be a pretty special guy to agree to help Daisy raise her baby even though it's not yours. I admire that, but I just don't think I want to get involved. I hope you understand."

His jaw dropped open and stayed open. He couldn't find the words to reply. How could he? And what would he say even if he could find his tongue? He was in complete and total shock. Daisy was pregnant? Why hadn't she told him? No wonder she was eager to find a way to get some income coming in and secure an alternate place to live. The sea shanty was cute and comfortable in the summertime – a dream home in its own unique right when the weather was fair, but come winter, it would be no place to be with a newborn babe.

He heard a moan escape his lips and felt a dead weight settle over his body from his face to his feet. He couldn't move.

"OMG," Mandy was saying. Maybe she'd said more. He didn't know. "You didn't know about the baby, did you?"

Cavan tried to shake his head no, but he felt so frozen that he couldn't tell if he'd been successful.

"OMG. I'm so sorry," Mandy said. "I'm not one to gossip and the last thing I want to do is to meddle in your affairs..."

It wasn't his affairs they evidently had to worry about. He felt his eyelids drooping and his shoulders falling as an overwhelming tiredness settled over him. The music started up with a jolt, but what had been so rejuvenating the evening before did nothing to revive him tonight.

Mandy looked as distressed as he felt. "I have nothing against you personally, Cavan. If you knew me better, you'd be aware that I believe it's always best to be very direct, which of course you wouldn't, since we're relative strangers. I would have liked to get to know you better, but... And the person who told me Daisy was pregnant heard it directly from her great-aunt, so..."

"I should go," he said. At least he would if he could. He forced himself off the stool and managed to stand upright. "No. I hadn't heard. Daisy never said a word."

Another customer held up an empty glass and motioned to Mandy to come. She shrugged and gave him a pitying glance.

What had he been thinking? Of course Daisy had had sex with her rich boyfriend. That's what couples did. It was the twenty-first century. Casual sex was not only accepted – it was commonplace. He hadn't wanted to think about Daisy having sex with another man. He certainly hadn't wanted to learn that she was pregnant with another man's baby – least of all from a woman he was interested in seeing. Well, a woman he'd been told he should be interested in. He really hadn't seen enough of Mandy to know if he was into her or not.

He slinked out of the bar like he was afflicted with chronic wasting disease. He felt dead. Shell-shocked. This certainly explained why Daisy had been given no help from her great-aunts, both of whom, although not considered rich, had plenty of money and more than enough space in their homes to take in a relative who was in need of assistance. He knew Daisy had had words with them over the quilt, but if the deeper problem was that she'd gotten herself pregnant out of wedlock, it made sense that they would turn their backs on her entirely. The older generation did not share the loose attitudes of the young.

He took a deep breath once he was out under the stars again. The music faded with every step he took until he reached the relative quiet of a cobblestone side street. He felt so unsteady on his feet that he walked his bike down the hill to the flatscape of the harbor.

When he first heard the voice, he thought he was dreaming. It made sense. He felt half asleep, and wholly numb.

"Believe what she tells ye or nay, lad. Just follow yer instincts and all will be well."

"What?" He jerked his head around to see if someone was following him. He saw no one. He focused his eyes away from the light and let them adjust to the darkness. Was someone clinging to the side of an alleyway, out of sight? When he saw no one, he returned to the message, still echoing in his mind. Believe who? Mandy? Daisy?

And his instincts? Hadn't they gotten him in enough trouble already? He resumed walking and reached the shop a little before ten. Every light in the place was on except for the one in his bedroom. The warm glow that had greeted him the night before was gone and a deep sense of dread filled his heart.

#

Daisy looked at the dining room table just past her rocks and hoped Darcie couldn't see past them to the spot at the other end of the table where the photos they'd taken of the quilt were spread out in full view. Of course, Darcie might already have some of the photos. But he might not. And she could only hope he hadn't cracked the code that had enabled her to link the photos together in the correct order.

"Daisy?" Cavan's voice echoed up the stairs. He sounded tense, out of sorts. Why, she couldn't imagine – unless it was still the ridiculous spat about her rocks. Cavan had no way of knowing what awaited him when he reached the living room, so it couldn't be that.

She glanced over at Darcie, who didn't flinch. He was quite obviously not afraid of Cavan.

"I'm up here, Cavan."

She heard his footsteps coming louder and louder. Cavan rounded the corner, saw Darcie, and instantly turned a deep shade of red.

"You'll never guess who dropped by, Cavan." Daisy tried to calm her voice, which had started to shake ever so slightly. She was simply not that good of an actress, especially at the end of a long day when she was exhausted.

She gulped and tried to sound cheery, as if she had no worries.

"Darcie came by to see if I was okay after not seeing me at the shanty for the last couple of nights. He seemed to think I might be staying in town and came round to check on me."

"How very nice of you," Cavan said to Darcie, looking like he was about to burst. "But it is getting quite late and I have to be up first thing tomorrow for a couple from Scotland who'll be picking up bikes." He took the door knob and stood to the side to wave Darcie through. "I'm sure your concern is much appreciated."

"Daisy was just fixing me a cuppa," Darcie said.

"Oh. That I was, as Darcie seemed in no hurry to go and I had no idea when you would be home." She gave Cavan a disapproving look. If he'd been home, Darcie would not have had the opportunity to force his way into the loft in the first place.

The two men stared each other down.

She could understand Cavan being irritated, although in a way, it was his own fault for not being around when she needed him. The important thing was that Darcie hadn't yet noticed the photos. She stood and started toward the kitchen. "It sounds like the pot is boiling." She smiled and tried to look happy. "The sooner we have that tea, the sooner we can all get to bed."

Darcie smiled drolly. "I was out to check on you last evening when a policeman approached me. Treated me like I was up to no good until I told him I was a friend of yours."

Daisy's hand shook as she picked up the pot and proceeded to pour the tea.

Cavan cleared his throat. "Well, with Daisy's neighbor just murdered a few weeks ago, I for one am glad they're keeping a close eye on things."

Darcie spoke again. "None of the land is posted against trespassing, which nowadays is an open invitation for trekkers and bicyclists."

"If you're implying that a trekker or a bicyclist murdered the priest, I can tell you you're dead wrong about that." Cavan's voice came out in a snarl, which in Daisy's opinion, did nothing to confirm his ascertainment that bicyclers and trekkers were a gentle lot not prone to violence.

She jumped in to try to diffuse the tension. "Granny believed that the whole Wild Atlantic Way should be open to local goers by and touristy sightseers alike just the way God intended when he made it. But that doesn't mean she would have tolerated anyone setting up camp or poaching off the land or squatting on her property. She was very territorial that way." She didn't look at Darcie. She'd made her point.

She took two tea cups in her hands and started toward the living room.

Darcie jumped up from his seat. "Let me help you with those."

"No! I've got it." Her mind flew to the photos of the only part of the treasure map that Darcie didn't already have that lay in clear sight between her and the living room.

But Darcie kept coming. She saw his eyes scan the tabletop and land on the photos. She took one big step, pretended to trip, and dumped a cup of tea on top of the pictures.

Cavan came beside her a split second later and whisked the photos out of sight, but she could tell by the look on Darcie's face that the damage was already done.

"Oh, I'm so sorry, Cavan! Let me get a towel to blot up the rug." Tea was full of dyes, albeit natural ones. They'd probably have to tea stain the entire rug to avoid having a noticeable spot of a darker color front and center. She tried to catch Cavan's eyes. He did not look happy, but she could tell he understood full well why she'd *spilled* the tea.

"I'll get it," Cavan said sternly, glaring at Darcie, which was better than him glaring at her.

Darcie looked like he wanted to duck down a hole except that there was none to be found.

"I'm very tired, Darcie," she said after they'd made a cursory sweep of the rug with a microfiber cloth.

Darcie glanced furtively at the spot on the kitchen countertop where Cavan had stashed the photos but Daisy felt sure he couldn't see them from where he was.

"Cavan is tired, too, as you can probably imagine" she said, when Darcie still hadn't offered to leave. "We'll have to do tea another time."

"I'll be back," Darcie said. "Soon."

She wanted to point out that it wasn't an invitation and that she'd only been being polite.

"Please call first next time." At least she got that out. "I'm very unsettled now, and I don't ever know where I might be. So I'd really rather you didn't bother me and Cavan."

Well, if looks really could kill, Cavan would be dead, and so might she.

Cavan was fingering his mobile as if to remind all of them that the harbor police were just across the street.

Darcie got his meaning and began to inch toward the door. "Until next time." He grinned, exposing a patchwork of different colors of teeth.

Cavan bolted the door as soon as Darcie was over the threshold and then watched out the window where the quilt was flapping in the breeze until they heard Darcie's Harley snarl to life and drive off.

Neither of them said a word. The roar of the engine finally faded.

18

Daisy went to Cavan and reached out her arms to hug him. She'd been terrified until Cavan had come home. Darcie was gone, but her muscles still felt like jelly and her legs, like they could collapse.

Cavan stiffened and stepped back.

Her arms fell to her sides. How could he not share her emotions?

Cavan didn't say a word.

She forced a smile. "I'm sure finding Darcie here wasn't what you'd hoped to see when you walked in. All I can say is that I heard a knock on the door, assumed it was you and said, 'c'mon in.' I tried to block him from coming in any further, but he was very aggressive and forced his way past me. I was terrified."

Cavan still didn't speak.

"Is it the rocks? I left my paints out at the shanty because I thought I'd be going back tomorrow."

Still not a word.

"Cavan, I hate it when you're unhappy. Please tell me what's wrong."

For a second, he looked as though he might speak and then his jaw clamped shut again.

She tried another tack. "I want you to know how much I appreciate everything you've done to try to help me. I've been so happy since we renewed our friendship that I-"

"I don't want you to be happy!" The words burst out of him like a dam had broken somewhere deep inside of him. "And I don't want you to get comfortable around here, or to settle in, or to feel at home here, because it's only temporary. Crisis management. And that is it."

Not only did her bubble burst, but her heart cracked wide open. She'd thought Cavan was – was the one person in the world she could count on.

She thought she'd felt shaky before, but now, it felt like the earth was quaking under her feet, and the bedrock of her entire world was caving in around her. And it was in that moment that she realized how truly unfair this had all been to Cavan. He'd given her a simple offer of help, and she'd built a completely new life based on the comfort and security she'd felt when he was around.

Cavan loved her – maybe tolerated her would be more apt – like a sister. Who wanted to spend their life catering to a pesky, sometimes demanding, always needy, sister?

"Well, I can see you're tired," she said meekly. "So I'll be off to bed. Should I use the bathroom first, or would you like to?"

"Go ahead," Cavan said.

"Thanks." She turned to go to the porch to put on her nightclothes and get her toothbrush.

"Daisy?"

She turned. "Yes?"

"We need to talk in the morning. Now that Darcie has seen the photos of the four corners of the quilt and knows that you're here and the quilt is, too, we're going to need to follow a whole new protocol to make sure you stay safe."

"I understand."

He coughed, almost choked, like he was on the verge of being ill. "Are you sure this gold is worth the price we might pay? And that's assuming we even find it. Is being rich worth that much to you?"

"Is that what you think? That it's about being rich?"

Cavan looked completely and totally disgusted. "When I look at how you spent the money last time around, I would say yes."

The room started to spin. She finally found the cheek to say, "Well, maybe I've learned some things since then."

Cavan said nothing. His face was closed. His eyes were glassy.

He looked almost as judgmental as Aunties Ailene and Sheelagh - the complete opposite of the vibe she'd been getting from him until now.

He spoke first. "We can talk about it in the morning. I have an early appointment scheduled for two hours before the shop opens. Once the customers have picked up their bikes, I'll be back up to have a bite to eat. We can talk then." His voice still sounded somewhat hostile and even bitter.

She knew when she was being dismissed. "Fine. I'll hurry up and use the bathroom so you can have your turn."

#

Cavan tried his best to be quiet the next morning when he got up to meet the Scottish couple who had reserved bicycles. Or maybe they weren't Scottish. They had a Scottish phone number, but he'd spoken to the guy on his mobile and it had sounded to him like he had an American accent.

He hadn't seen or heard anything from Daisy when he left to go downstairs and let them in – which was fine by him. He'd speak to her later – if he figured out what to say to her by the time he was done leasing the bicycles. He took a second to take the trash out and deposit the bags in the dumpster round back and then unlocked the bicycle shop.

The couple was right on time. Good thing - he'd have been pissed if he'd opened up early only to have them not show up.

The man extended his hand. "I'm Michael St. Dawndalyn and this is my wife, Isabelle." American for sure.

"Nice to meet you." He handed the man a registration form and watched as he entered the address – Tobermory, Isle of Mull, Scotland. So. Americans living in Scotland. He wondered why they'd chosen to settle in Scotland instead of Ireland. Everyone knew the Irish were more friendly when it came down to it. Not that the Isle of Mull wasn't beautiful enough, or so he'd heard. But very few places on God's green earth could compete with the Wild Atlantic Way.

"Thanks for meeting us early," Isabelle said in what sounded to his ears like a Southern drawl. Not that he was an expert on Americanisms. Anyway, she seemed like a nice woman. Her eyes were merry and quite blue.

Michael continued where she left off. "We want to ride the entire loop, and not knowing how often we'll need to stop to rest-"

"And take pictures," his wife added with a wee smile.

"-along the way, we thought we'd better get an early start."

"Wise choice," Cavan said. "You'll find the traffic a lot lighter in the wee hours of the morning than at midday. For the most part, you'll find the cars going as slow as you are, taking in the sights, but you should watch out for the occasional maniac who thinks the single track curves are made for high speeds. It's not supposed to rain, which is a miracle in and of itself, but they're saying the wind could get quite gusty this afternoon, so you may need to factor in some time to take shelter down in the sea caves to wait out the weather." Cavan checked the tide table taped to the counter and informed them when the high and low tides would be. "I only mention it because you don't want to get caught down by the sea caves should you decide to go exploring."

"I understand," Michael said.

Cavan didn't know what it was about the man, but he somehow got the feeling that Michael St. Dawndalyn really did understand his words of caution, and a lot, lot more than that. Maybe the 'ghost' whose voice he'd been hearing had sent this couple to shed a little light on what was going on with Daisy and the hidden treasure.

"So what brought the two of you to Scotland?" Cavan said, both in a cursory and curious way. He thought about what Daisy said, about never seeing her customers more than once except in extremely rare cases. That's exactly how it was with the bikes he rented to tourists. But this couple... He felt a strange connection to them.

Michael and Isabelle looked at each other and laughed.

"Long story. The funny thing is, we didn't meet until we got here."

It was her that spoke, but Michael who started to sing. "Two drifters, off to see the world. There's such a lot of world to see." And then she joined in, singing, "We're after the same rainbow's end, waiting, round the bend, My Huckleberry Friend, Moon River, and me."

It was a little weird, but very touching. The two of them were obviously very deeply in love.

"Don't mind us," she said.

"I don't." He smiled and continued to get the rental agreement ready to sign.

Isabelle asked, "Do you have someone special? A Mrs. Recycled Cyclery?"

He picked up the papers to hand to them and felt a flash of pain slice through the soft spot between his thumb and pointer finger. Ouch! He clenched and unclenched his fist in hopes of offsetting the pain.

"Ouch," Isabelle said. "Nothing hurts as bad as a paper cut."

"Not really," Michael said.

Isabelle handed him a tissue. "Don't mind my husband, he's a psychologist. Pain is all relative to him."

Michael bristled noticeably. "Emotional pain is very real, and can hurt much worse than actual pain."

Isabelle laughed again, "Says a man who has never had a baby and never will."

Michael rolled his eyes. "But as I'm very empathetic, I can well imagine..."

"My friend, Daisy, is going to have a baby," he blurted out of the blue. "At least that's what I'm told."

Michael looked at him in a careful, calculated way. "So I take it you two are pretty close."

"I thought we were. But when you have to hear stuff like this from a stranger on the street, a guy has to wonder."

"Is she married?" Isabelle asked. "Happy about the pregnancy?"

"No, and I don't have a clue. I'm assuming not since she barely has a cent to her name. Her old boyfriend dumped her, so she's going to be a single parent. And I don't think she ever really wanted kids in the first place."

Isabelle said, "That sounds pretty rough."

"It sounds painful," Michael said. "And your reaction would signify that you're acknowledging the pain she must be feeling."

Isabelle opened her mouth to respond, but first Cavan said, "Do you think that's why she hasn't told me?"

"Maybe she just hasn't found the right moment," Michael said. "How often do you see her?"

"She's upstairs in my loft," Cavan said, feeling sheepish. "Sleeping on the back porch. I mean – we're not – I mean – the baby isn't mine. Because we haven't, um..."

"But she should have told you," Isabelle said. "Even if she's in a lot of pain." She looked at Michael. "But then, you and I had a lot to learn about being honest and truthful when we first started to get to know each other."

Michael frowned. "It takes time to build up trust in a relationship."

Cavan handed Michael a pen. "We've known each other since we were kids."

Isabelle said, "Sometimes it's easier to talk to a stranger about sensitive issues than it is someone who's very close to you."

"Yes," Michael added. "It can be very embarrassing to admit something to someone who knows you well. And then there's the risk involved – the possibility that you might reject her or criticize her. She may not be willing to take the chance of losing your friendship."

"Maybe she'd talk to the two of you about it." Cavan thought it made sense. "If it wouldn't be too much of an imposition. I don't know what a counseling session goes for these days, but I could let you use my bikes for free if that would help. She's really had a rough go of it lately and everybody in the whole town knows her and already has their nose in her business. I think it would mean a lot to her."

Michael and Isabelle gave each other a look. "Sure. Is she up and about or would you like us to try to meet up with her when we return the bicycles?"

"I'm not sure." Cavan didn't think he'd heard any noise from upstairs, but then, he'd been distracted between talking and working. "Why don't I run upstairs and see if she's dressed."

"Sure." Michael nodded.

He dashed up the stairs two at a time so as not to keep them waiting.

"Daisy?"

No answer. He called out to her again, a little louder. "Daisy?"

No reply. Either she was still sound asleep, or in the bathroom. The bathroom door was wide open. There was no sign of her.

"Daisy?" He turned to go to the porch where she was sleeping and looked out the window. The sun was streaming through the small panes of glass and the beveled bit at the top was casting rainbows around the room. Daisy used to tell him how much she loved it when the morning sun shone through her beveled glass windows. Come to think of it, he hadn't seen the room slathered in rainbows once since Daisy moved in.

Because the quilt had been blocking its rays. The quilt! Daisy's granny's quilt was gone. At least, it wasn't hanging on the line outside the building. He looked closer. It looked like the whole clothesline was missing!

He quickly stepped to the room where Daisy's bed was, rapped on the door, waited a second, and opened it wide. Daisy's quilt was gone all right. And so was Daisy.

19

Cavan's eyes scoured every detail of the apartment. Daisy's purse was still there. Her mobile was in the kitchen charging. She'd left in a hurry, or without thinking about leaving. That much was obvious.

He dashed back down the stairs. "Now isn't a good time," he called out to Michael and Isabelle. "Hopefully Daisy will be around when you return the bikes."

He grabbed one of the bikes they'd rented from the back room and wheeled it out to them, then returned for the other. He wished them well one more time, opened the front door and held it so they could exit with their bikes, then went back to lock up.

Wait! Was that Daisy? And Darcie? And Granny's quilt? What? The quilt was airborne. Daisy was running, trying to catch up to Darcie by the looks of it.

Cavan stepped outside and started to run after them, watching the sky for more signs of the quilt, which looked like some sort of magic carpet ride soaring where it would. The whole scene was surreal. He heard the beep beep beep of a garbage truck backing through the alleyway, saw the baker opening the door to his café next door, got a whiff of cinnamon and fresh baked bread that mingled with the smell of yesterday's catch from the harbor.

He had just run round the corner by the harbor when a huge gust of wind puffed the quilt up like a ship's sail. It sailed over the roof of the police station, heading out to sea. He could only hope it would catch on one of the sailboat masts punctuating the harbor, but the wind pushed it higher aloft until it cleared the boats, then let it plummet until it was skimming the water, lifting and falling over the surface.

Darcie had reached the end of the pier. Daisy was close behind, now lagging back. Either she was out of breath or didn't want another encounter with Darcie.

Cavan kept running. He had no clue what had happened between them, or how they ended up here or how the quilt had ended up on the loose but he had to try to help Daisy. That much he knew for sure.

He looked up again and saw the quilt well past the pier where the sailboats were docked. And now, there was Fungie the Dolphin following along with a leap, bounding out of the water here and there like he did when he followed boats into the harbor.

What a freak show! He looked for Daisy and didn't see her. Probably watching from behind a boat to keep out of Darcie's sight. If Darcie couldn't have the quilt, he'd want Daisy and her photographs all the more. Nothing anyone could do about the quilt now unless they were already out in a boat, unless the wind changed directions before the fabric hit the waves.

Darcie dove into the bay with a splash. What? He was that desperate to get the quilt? Greedy bugger. Of course he was! There was gold at stake, wasn't there? And everybody but Cavan seemed to think it was the end all, that the best thing that could possibly happen to someone was to strike gold. Arg!

He looked at the sea. He looked for Daisy. He looked at Darcie, who was almost dead center under the quilt, which was hovering over him like a banner, teasing, dipping, lifting, soaring like a flirtatious woman.

"Please! Somebody do something!" Daisy screamed from wherever she was hiding. "That's my Granny's quilt and it's all I have left of her. It was made by her own hands. I can't lose it!"

Cavan jumped. Into the water. Darcie was bigger than he was by a fair amount. He also looked stronger, but it was probably just the dreadlocks and the man bun and the pirate gear.

Cavan hit the water stroking and found his groove in seconds. The water was freezing, but he was in the zone, doing the breast stroke. Pumping each arm as hard as he could. He was strong, too, and he was motivated not only by gold, but the love of a woman.

"Cavan!" He heard Daisy's frantic cries, fear, cheers, the whole gamut of emotions mixed with water, and the occasional wail of the wind and Darcie's splashing. He must be getting close. He looked up, expecting to see the quilt, but it had disappeared. Did Darcie have it?

His competitor was still swimming frantically; probably in the direction he'd last seen the quilt. Cavan stopped and tread water, surveying the landscape.

"Over there!" Daisy shouted from the shore. He heard a motorboat springing to life. He swam in Darcie's direction, trusting that he'd seen the quilt go down. Darcie was diving, over and over again, looking underwater. Cavan did the same until Darcie grabbed him, got him in a headlock and tried to drown him.

"Dai-" he went under. His mouth filled with salt water. He wrestled free of Darcie's grip and bobbed to the surface.

"Daisy!" He sputtered and tried to say more until he was pulled back underwater. He kneed Darcie and fought his way back to air.

"Be careful," Daisy screamed. "He won't give up until you're dead. I know it!"

Well thank you for the positive word of encouragement, he thought, gulping for air.

She was frantic. He could hear it in her voice. He wanted to reassure her, but every time he opened his mouth to tell her not to worry, Darcie dragged him under again. Damn. If she didn't calm down, she could harm her baby.

His instinct was to open his mouth and take a deep breath. But he was still under water. He'd held his breath as long as he could. His lungs felt like they were going to burst. He tried to hit Darcie hard, or knee him again, but Darcie had the upper hand. He twisted his torso and tried to come at Darcie a different way, catch him off guard.

"Cavan!" Daisy's voice sounded far, far away, weak and off key – like a mobile with bad reception. How long had he been underwater? He had to tell Daisy how much he loved her before he died. He didn't want to die. He did not want to die! He clawed his way to the surface and got one chance to suck in air before he was underwater again.

Cavan swung his elbow back and smashed his arm into Darcie's nose. He heard a pop when his elbow connected with bone and sinew.

Darcie yelped and reacted like a bull who'd been stabbed.

Cavan took a deep breath and got ready for the next assault. This time, he had to be preemptive. He groped for Darcie. A vulnerable spot. He'd take anything – any chance to disable him. Darcie's body seemed to be floating away from his. Cavan's legs were strong, but the current was against him and he couldn't kick what he couldn't reach. The water around them was tinged with red, he hoped from Darcie's nose. Darcie's arms were like a vice around his neck and pressing down on the top of his head.

Lord, help me, he prayed.

He kicked one more time in a frantic attempt to do damage to Darcie. He strained and twisted and stretched his legs as far as he could. And then, he felt the brush of a fish. The fish buoyed him up so he could get a breath. At least, it seemed intentional.

And then, he was underwater again. But the fish was with him now. He felt less panicked, less frantic. The dolphin was there to protect him. It had to be Fungie. The Dingle Dolphin was a male bottlenose that weighed something like 500 pounds. He was long, Cavan guessed twice his length. He'd seen him rolling ahead of the bow wave as he escorted fishing ships and tour boats into the harbor. He felt a sudden peace.

Fungie flipped, and his massive body thrust its way between him and Darcie. Propelled upward by the dolphin's momentum, Cavan burst above the surf.

He breathed. Sweet, pure air. Once, when he was a wee lad, he'd seen Fungie jump high enough to clear the water to the height of a vessel's bridge.

His brain still felt like he was asleep – he struggled to leave behind his thoughts of the past and reconnect with the present. Daisy needed him. She was pregnant and she shouldn't be upset. And he needed to save the quilt. Where was it?

He felt the vibration of a motorboat. The giant fish disappeared. Fungie had saved his life.

The police sidled up to him and a plain-clothed officer he knew from the pub reached out his hand to pull him from the water. "Time to come aboard."

He shook his head. "Darcie's your man. I'll keep looking."

"We know all about Darcie."

"He was trying to kill me. Over a quilt."

"The quilt?" The officer looked befuddled. "I thought this was about a girl."

"No. I mean-" He dove back down into the water, trying to see the quilt. Daisy would be frantic if the quilt was gone. She'd slept in the same room with the thing even though it smelled like fox urine because it meant so much to her. There was no way he was going to get in the police boat until he found Daisy's quilt.

He bobbed his head up for air, shut his eyes, and went down again as fast as he could blink the water out of his eyes.

"Come here. Now!" The police yelled. "It's time to come in out of the water. I'm under orders-"

Cavan dove as deep as he could until he couldn't hear anything except the pressure of the ocean. His eyes stung from the salt water but he kept on peering into the depths, trying to see the quilt.

He came up for another breath.

"It's gone, lad. I can see everything from up top and your precious quilt is nowhere to be found."

"But if Darcie-"

"I'm under orders to bring you in before you drown. Seems you're a wee bit more important to the pretty lady than her quilt."

"But I have to find it." He gulped. "I have to find it before Darcie does."

The officer gave him a look and the boat eased away from him, carried by the current. He pointed to a second boat. Darcie was on board. They were handcuffing him. His nose was dripping blood.

The officer eased his boat closer and Cavan grabbed the gunnels.

Cavan let his legs rest against the side of the boat. "But has anyone found the quilt? Daisy needs it. It's her Granny's." He didn't want to bring up the whole subject of the gold. It should be up to Daisy if she wanted to involve the police in that. "I just want to try diving a few more times."

"You should probably go to hospital to be checked over. You look liked a half-drowned gutter snipe."

"Thanks, but I'm fine. Maybe you could just hover near by while I try to dive a few more times."

"We've got trained divers with wetsuits who can do that if it's deemed necessary, lad. And, as I mentioned, you are looking a wee bit peaked."

"But that's the whole thing. I'm the only one who understands how important the quilt is to Daisy. So I should be the one to keep looking for it."

The officer cleared his throat. "The lass told me you would say that, and she said to tell you that you mean more to her than the quilt. More to her than anything."

He felt a little zing of warmth in his otherwise freezing body. "She said that?"

"Come aboard," the officer said. "You're starting to look a wee bit blue from being in the bay and I've an inkling that what the lady has to say will warm you up faster than a hot water bottle tucked under your blanket."

#

Daisy paced back and forth at the end of the pier. Half of Dingle was down at the harbor watching by now. And she didn't give a hoot. They all thought they knew her business anyway, so they might as well get a show.

One of the boats hooked up to a mooring several yards away but they didn't have Cavan. Darcie. The creep. She'd already given a short statement. Trouble was, the police didn't put much stock in gut feelings or instincts and they probably didn't have much on Darcie in the way of proof positive. The fact that he'd tried to steal her quilt and drown Cavan should be good for something, but who knew what the police would believe.

At least she hoped it had been Darcie who was trying to drown Cavan and not the other way around. Cavan had a definite dislike for Darcie and it had been hard to tell at such a distance. And of course, there'd been a lot of splashing going on. She wasn't going to say anything to the police about that either.

She watched out of the corner of her eye as the police dragged a very annoyed, highly agitated, bleeding Darcie off the docks to the harbor police station. The other ship – the one that hopefully had Cavan aboard - was finally drawing near.

All she knew for sure was that she'd almost lost Cavan and it had nearly killed her. When she'd started to fall for him, she wasn't sure, but she did know that her heart was as entwined with his as a Celtic knot.

What was taking so long? She could only hope the extra time they'd spent rescuing Cavan had been arguing and not resuscitating. The man was stubborn and determined, that was for sure. Worry niggled at her brain as the ship grew closer. Lord, she hoped they were bringing in a kicking, screaming Cavan and not a half – or wholly - dead one.

Lord, she hoped he was okay. And that he'd forgive her.

.

20

The policeman gave Cavan a towel, but he was still soaked to the bone and the wind was not his friend. The same gusts that had carried Daisy's quilt off to sea were still whooshing over the relatively calm sea every few minutes and couldn't have been colder if they'd been straight off an iceberg. He'd learned at a very young age never to underestimate the Atlantic, even in the partial shelter of Dingle Bay. The sea was a fickle mistress who could lure you in with sweetness one minute and come crashing in on you the next.

They were near enough to the harbor that he was going to have to get out of the boat in a few seconds anyway, so he wrapped the towel more tightly around himself and came up from below decks.

Daisy was standing on the pier, looking freezing cold herself. The second she saw him, she started to wave her arms in the air and jump up and down. Were women who were preggers supposed to jump up and down so vigorously? He certainly didn't think it looked to be a good idea. What if the wee one got dislodged? Could embryos get seasick? Be beset by vertigo?

"Stop it!" He called out to Daisy. "No need to jump about like a mad woman, Daisy. I'm fine!"

"But I'm happy to see you!"

They were close enough to the pier that he could see Daisy's face. She'd stopped jumping, but now, she looked more than a wee bit offended. Emotional distress was hard on babies, too, wasn't it? He thought he'd heard somewhere that they could pick up on things like that through the umbilical cord.

"Is he okay?" Daisy yelled over the ruckus of the motorboat.

The policeman nodded and said, "He might do well with a dry set of clothes."

Cavan nodded his agreement. "Do I need to give a statement?"

"Yes, but you're free to go home and have a hot shower first since you're close by. You can come back to the station once you've warmed up a bit." The policeman winked.

Daisy missed it entirely, or at least, she acted like she had.

"But you're not going to let Darcie go, are you?" Daisy looked as scared of Darcie as she did happy to see Cavan. In fact, her face was a very strange mixture of emotions.

"No. We'll hold him at least until we have what we need. My supervisor messaged me while we were heading into the bay and said that the hardware store was robbed last night. Among the things that went missing were some picks and shovels and random digging paraphernalia and a branch clipper with a seven-meter extension."

"That's probably what Darcie used to cut the clothesline that my quilt was hanging on!" Daisy said.

"And he's probably using the picks and shovels to carve up your sea caves." Cavan added.

The officer raised an eyebrow. "I'm sure we'll find plenty to talk to Mr. Sneem about. I can't guarantee that it will stick, but we'll do our best."

Daisy's face paled. "But if he stole the tree trimming equipment and tried to steal my quilt, and tried to kill Cavan, isn't that enough to lock him up for at least a few years?"

Cavan took that one. "He could say that someone else stole the tree trimmer and cut down the quilt, and that when he saw the wind take it, he jumped in the water to try and save it just like I did."

The officer nodded his head. "Aye, and that Cavan was trying to kill him and he was only defending himself. T'would nay be the first time two drunken suitors ended up in the bay, fighting for the love of a woman."

Daisy blushed at that one. Or maybe the blood was rushing to her head because she was spitting mad. It was hard to tell with Daisy.

"Well, you can just tell them that Cavan Donaghue is one of the most honest, upright men I know, and that Darcie Sneem is a conniving thief who would lie even if telling the truth would save his soul," Daisy said.

"I promise you we'll take very good care of Darcie Sneem," the officer said with another wink. "Why don't the two of you run off and spend some time getting, um, warmed back up?"

Cavan looked down at his watch, which was stopped. He was a cyclist, not a surfer after all. Who would have thought he'd have need for a waterproof watch?

"I don't know what time it is, but I'm guessing it's time or past time I opened the shop."

"I can mind the till while you take a hot shower and get changed," Daisy offered.

The officer was starting to look frustrated. "I'm sure your customers will understand if you need a little – um – personal time to recover from your ordeal."

Daisy looked nervous.

The officer shooed them off. "We'll see you later today."

#

Daisy ran across the street as soon as there was a break in traffic. Cavan had hold of her hand as they went through the shop and up the inside stairs to the loft.

"We need to talk," he said.

"You need to warm up," she said.

Cavan shrugged. "I'll take a hot shower."

"You should put some lotion on. Two showers in the same morning and the salt water on top of it."

"I will."

She almost offered to help him with those hard to reach places but thought better of it.

He was still standing in the doorway, dripping.

"You should lie down," he said. "All this excitement. It's not good for-" He paused. "-you."

"I am pretty exhausted. Probably coming down after the adrenalin rush."

"Rest while I'm in the shower. When I get out, I'm going to call Rory and see if he'll mind the shop today. We can talk to the police first, and then we're going to take the pictures out to the shanty and find the sea cave that has the gold. With Darcie in jail, we don't have to risk leading him to the spot. It's the perfect time to do this."

Her mind flew in one direction and another. "Good idea!" She tried to sound bright and upbeat. "But there might be one little problem."

"If you're not feeling well enough, I understand-"

Why was Cavan so worried about her physical condition and stress levels all of the sudden? He hadn't seemed to care about her all that much last night when Darcie had been snooping around. And it wasn't Cavan who had almost lost her in Dingle Bay. If anybody should be worried about anyone, it should be her fretting about his well-being, not the other way around.

She peered at him curiously. Unless he'd thought he was going to die, and had a life changing realization when he was on the verge of drowning...

Cavan said, "If you're worried that they'll release Darcie before we have a chance to look for the gold, I think the officer who picked me up will be honest with us about what their plans are."

"It's not that." She looked down. "It's just that I ripped up the pictures and threw them away last night after Darcie was here. They were half ruined from the hot water spilling on them anyway and I didn't want to risk him stealing them and finding out where the gold was before we did."

Cavan looked a little confused but she'd expected as much. It wasn't like a man was likely to understand her reasoning – about anything.

"So I just need to get the pieces out of the trash and tape them back together. It shouldn't take long."

Cavan said, "Why don't I print up another copy from your phone to save time? I took out the trash first thing this morning so we wouldn't miss the truck. If they're on their usual schedule, they probably came while we were chasing down your quilt at the harbor."

Her stomach crashed and bounced up and down when it hit bottom. "The trash is gone? You're sure?"

"Why? You didn't lose your phone again, did you?"

"No. Worse. I deleted the photos."

Cavan dropped his towel. "You what? Why?"

"I was worried Darcie would steal it, or hack into my mobile account. I figured we could take more if we needed them. How was I supposed to know that the quilt was going to end up in the

Atlantic?"

"No worries. Let me think." Cavan hit his head with the heel of his hand. "They should still be in your trash file. The camera holds them for 60 days before it really deletes them. You should be able to restore them just fine."

"I thought of that, too. That's why I emptied my trash."

"You didn't."

"I was trying to be thorough." She sank into the nearest chair.

"I'm sorry," Cavan looked at her like he was more concerned than angry. "I didn't mean to upset you."

What was wrong with the man now? She'd have been angry with him if he'd thrown away the photos. He ought to be at least a little angry with her. Although it really wasn't her fault! It was him who had said they needed to come up with an entirely new protocol now that Darcie had gotten a glimpse of the photos and knew that there was more to the quilt than the center piece. But she would have thought Cavan would be upset. This was their chance to find the gold, and she'd blown it.

Cavan looked at her like he was trying to gauge if she was strong enough to go on. "Can you remember some of it? Because I think I could draw a sketch that might be halfway accurate."

"Assuming we had the blocks lined up in the right order, I think I kind of have a general idea of where the map led to. Maybe."

"Then we still need to go, and soon, while the map is still halfway fresh in your mind and Darcie's in jail."

Cavan's look boosted her confidence a wee bit. She did feel like she had a general idea of where the gold might be – if she was recalling things correctly.

Cavan closed the door to the bathroom. A few seconds later, she heard the shower start up.

She sighed and settled back into the chair. She'd been going to tell him the things that had gone through her mind when she'd realized she might lose him. She'd been going to tell him she loved him more than Granny's stupid old quilt. More than all the gold in the world. More than money and wealth or fortune or fame. More than anything.

She could hear the water pinging against Cavan's body and feel the warmth of the steam leaking out from under the door. That was another nice thing about the loft. There was always plenty of hot water and excellent water pressure.

21

Cavan let the hot stream of water run down his chest and pound against his freezing cold legs. The water in the harbor had been so cold it had almost paralyzed him. It hadn't seemed to faze Darcie all that much – the bastard probably had such a cold pirate's heart that he felt right at home in the icy water.

Speaking of cold hearts, or maybe he should say thinking of the cold harbor – what was it with Daisy anyway? How could she not be more excited about expecting a baby? And if she was even a smidgen happy about it, wouldn't she want to share the news with him? Did she trust him so little? Had he made her feel so awkward or stupid or unwelcome in his life that she didn't want him to know? He sure hoped not.

He was walking a fine line. If he let on to Daisy how much he cared for her, he could make her feel so uncomfortable that she might run, disappear from his life altogether. That was the last thing he wanted. When he'd found her gone that morning, that's exactly what he'd thought had happened and it had almost killed him.

Somehow, he needed to convey his feelings to Daisy without ruining their friendship.

He washed his hair to get rid of the smell of the harbor even though it had only been an hour since he'd shampooed. He inhaled the scents of coconut and vanilla in his hair products and tried to forget how it had felt when his lungs had been ready to burst.

Darn Daisy. She was driving him crazy.

That's when he remembered the couple who'd picked up their bicycle hires right before things got insane down at the pier. He honestly hoped they could talk to Daisy when they returned their bicycles. Under normal circumstances, he didn't see the need for a counselor, but at this point, he was ready to admit he was in over his head with Daisy – no pun intended.

Five minutes later he was blissfully warm and dry.

"Ready to head out to the sea, Daisy?" He looked around. "Daisy?" She was nowhere in sight. "Daisy!" His heart started to beat a little faster. "Daisy?!?!" Not this again.

"We're down here." Her voice was muffled. The bike shop. But *we're?* He started down the steps two by two. Just his luck that he'd escaped the icy grips of the Atlantic only to break his neck falling down the stairs. All he could think about was what Darcie would do to Daisy if he wasn't there to protect her. Surely they hadn't released him already.

He was almost to the back room when he heard Rory's voice. Of course. *We* was Daisy and Rory.

He slowed down and tried to look nonchalant and unflustered, as though he hadn't almost lost the woman he loved – but wasn't supposed to – twice in one day.

"Hey, Rory. Thanks for giving me a hand. Did Daisy tell you what happened?"

"Yeah. I'm sure glad Fungie showed up when he did. You know you're going in the history books, right? Fungie escorting boats in and out of the bay is pretty old hat, but saving the good guy in a fight to the death. Pretty legendary if you ask me."

"Well, no one did ask you," Cavan said. He did smile. But really, it was pretty embarrassing to have to admit that he couldn't take down a loser like Darcie without help from a dolphin and the police. And that he hadn't been able to save Daisy's quilt to boot.

Daisy made it worse by beaming at him like he was some sort of hero and going on and on about how brave he was.

The phone interrupted their conversation. He answered, "Hello. Recycled Cyclery."

"I'm looking for Daisy Fitzpatrick. Is she available?"

He eyed Daisy. The man on the other end of the phone didn't exactly sound friendly. "Can I ask what this is in regard to?"

The man hesitated. "I'm told this is where she lives now, and since she refuses to pick up her mobile, I had no other choice but to try and track her down this way. My name is Maurice Jones, and I'm a debt collector from Killarney. I've been retained by the company who sold her the Mercedes that was repossessed and the furniture company she used to furnish the home she owned in Killarney, which by the way, remains her responsibility since it has not yet sold to another buyer. If I could please speak to her, or if you can tell me when she might be available, I would certainly appreciate it."

He looked at Daisy and Rory. The last thing he wanted was for Rory to know about Daisy's legal problems. "Um, I'll make sure to pass the message along. Can I get your number?"

He wrote down the information and set the phone back on its base.

Daisy was still going on about the episode with the quilt. "Cavan really did save the day. I mean, when I woke up, I saw the quilt slipping and falling from the clothesline, and I couldn't imagine what was happening. So I jumped out of bed and caught a glimpse of Darcie with a tree trimmer on an extender pole, snipping the clothesline from below. And then a gust of wind puffed up and the quilt got all buoyant and went airborne, flying one way and then another. Darcie went running after it like a chicken with his head cut off and all I knew was that I had to catch it before he did. And you know the rest of the story. Thank God Cavan showed up when he did!"

Except his showing up hadn't changed anything, Cavan thought. The quilt was still gone and they had no way to find the gold, and Daisy's debts were obviously still mounting.

"It was really odd," Daisy said. It was like someone was waving a cape in front of an angry bull, and every time Darcie got almost close enough to grab it, whomever was orchestrating the wind gusts would blow and whip one end of the quilt into the air just high enough that he couldn't reach it."

Cavan hadn't thought of it that way. He thought about the sense he'd had that someone was watching over them, trying to help them find the gold. At times, he'd almost felt like the presence was a ghost, someone he should know, but didn't quite recognize, and that the mysterious whatever-it-was that was following Daisy and him around, was trying to help. Maybe he, or it, or they had been trying to keep the quilt out of Darcie's hands. Or maybe the wild winds of the Atlantic Way were finally doing some good. Whatever the case, he was not going to bring up the possibility of some sort of benevolent ghost hovering 'round to assist them.

Rory gave him a look. "So I was just telling Daisy how good she's been looking lately. Whatever's going on in her life must really agree with her. She's really got the glow, wouldn't you say?"

Could Rory be any more obvious? Of course, he would know about the baby if Mandy and Lisette knew. But glowing? Rory might as well scream out the news that Daisy was expecting.

Daisy blushed. "I told him it was too much sun and windburn from being down on the pier this morning."

"Right," Cavan said. At least Daisy wasn't buying into Rory's not so subtle taunting. "So let me show you how to use the Mastercard Visa machine and where I keep the change in case someone wants to pay cash."

"Sure," Rory said.

He pulled out a bike hire contract. "These are pretty standard and I've got everything marked in the back room so you know which bikes go to whom. Not to cut you short, but Daisy and I need to get over to the police station and then we have some business down at Daisy's granny's sea shanty. It shouldn't take too long. Will it be okay if we're back by three o'clock? That way, I'll be here by the time most people return their bikes."

"Yeah," Rory said. "I have plans tonight, so if you can be back by mid to late afternoon, that would be great."

"Thanks again, man." He turned and looked at Daisy. She did appear to be glowing. "Daisy? You ready?"

#

Two hours later, they were out on Granny's beach along the Wild Atlantic Way looking for the sea cave that - based on Granny's stitched treasure map – was where the gold should be. Daisy tried to mentally warm up her brain by visualizing the photos of the quilt. Everything hinged on the quilt, and since they'd lost it and inadvertently deleted the photos she'd taken of the pertinent parts, all they had to work with now was a vague notion she'd formed in her head when she'd first glanced at the pictures they'd taken of its four corners.

Daisy was just about starving to death. Too late, she'd realized she'd never had breakfast or lunch because of all the commotion. She swept her eyes across the completely undeveloped waterfront and wished for once that there was a crab shack or a food truck or something along this part of the ocean. Because, unfortunately, food just didn't magically appear from rocks or sand, or sheep grazing amid sea grass and seaside daisies or foxglove. And neither, it appeared, did gold.

Cavan circled around her. "Okay, let's talk it through one more time. We started at the shanty and then worked our way over to the sea cave which was at the X in the center of the quilt."

"Which Darcie has completely ruined with his pick axes and dynamite."

"He's been a busy boy all right. If the police didn't already have enough to hold him, I'd be snapping some photos of the mess he made and taking them in right now."

Daisy felt both relieved and nervous about that. "I'm glad the video surveillance camera at the hardware store caught him in the act of stealing the tree trimmer, or he'd already be out of jail."

"Yeah, like – what did he say again?" Cavan mimicked Darcie's voice. "I wasn't trying to drown Cavan, I had a cramp in my leg. I was trying to hang onto him. I was nearly drowning myself. I know when in trouble in the water, you're supposed to relax and lay on your back so the person who's trying to rescue you can do their job, but I was so frantic that I made the classic mistake of flailing my arms around and fighting the very person who was trying to help me."

Daisy snorted. "Likely story."

"I can't believe they bought it."

"Oh, I don't think they did. But he has his rights I suppose. I'm sure they gave more credence to what you said than that line of bull Darcie was feeding them."

Cavan knelt down and peered into the cave. "All the more reason that we need to find the gold now, before they release Darcie and he has another chance to get his hands on it."

"This is impossible." At that exact moment in time, she not only cared about Cavan more than she cared about the gold, she cared about food more than she cared about the gold. Of course, if she didn't find some gold or figure out a way to make money pretty soon, she'd have neither gold nor food.

Cavan moved a few rocks and used the flashlight on his mobile to shine a light into the cave. "You're sure this is where the last X on the last corner of the quilt led?"

"I'm not sure about anything! I looked at the photos one last time before I deleted them, but I realized that until we could actually get out here and look with our own eyes and trace the maps on real ground, there was no way to know if we had the squares put together in the right order. So I didn't look at them as closely as I might have."

Cavan sighed, moved some more rocks, and dug around at the entrance to the cave a little more.

"You have to remember that the treasure may be buried under so much silt and sand that we might never find it even if we know exactly where to look."

Cavan said, "Yeah. The sand and silt that the sea took from the cave where you found your neighbor's gold in that last big storm of the winter could have been washed into the sea cave where your Granny's gold is."

"Or was. A storm like that could have washed the coins back out to sea and buried them at the bottom of the ocean."

Her stomach growled and Cavan said, "You did eat something before we left Dingle, didn't you?"

"No, I'm sorry to say. I was too distracted to think about food. Did you?"

"No," Cavan said. "But I'm not-"

What? She eyed him suspiciously. "What are you not?"

He gulped. "I'm not always half-starved like you are."

It might have been a veiled insult, but it wasn't an outright slur, so she let it slide. Besides, she was too hungry to care. She did have a big appetite. Always had. And it made no sense. Cavan had twice her bulk and was far more active than she was. Yet she could down twice again as much as he could in half the time. Thank goodness she had a high metabolism or she'd probably weigh 400 pounds.

Sadly, her need for a lot of food only made her financial woes worse. Cavan might be able to get by on a little bit of nothing, but she sure couldn't. Food wasn't free.

She swatted at her neck. It felt pinched again, like midges were taking a bite out of her – which made no sense on a day like today when the wind gusts should have been keeping them away. It was the one thing the wind was good for.

"Ouch!"

Cavan was at her side in less than a second. "What's wrong?" He hovered over her like she was an Irish crystal goblet in danger of breaking. She'd never seen anyone move so fast.

"Are you okay?"

"I'm fine. It felt like something bit me."

"Are you sure? You're not feeling lightheaded or nauseous or dizzy, are you?"

"From a bug bite? No. I'm fine. Probably just a sand flea or something. It's too windy for midges."

He touched her waist. "No stomach pains or cramping or anything like that?"

"No! Why would I?"

Cavan looked odd – like he was mildly irritated. What was wrong with the man?

"I just thought..." Cavan stopped and appeared to be scrambling for an answer. "Well, someone told me there's a bug going around. I hope you're not getting it."

"I'm fine," she insisted. "Just a little hungry."

But a few seconds later, she really did start to feel dizzy. Her ear was still hurting from whatever had bitten her and she felt like her legs were trying to go in an entirely different direction than she was attempting to head. She'd had sea legs once upon a time when she'd been out on a boat for hours and then come ashore. That's what it felt like – like she was unbalanced. She tried to walk toward the water, but her legs felt like someone or something was trying to push her back toward the sea caves. She really hadn't slept well the night before and the stress of the morning had certainly taken a toll. Probably the change in the weather.

She was so discombobulated that she felt like launching into a rousing chorus of 'That's what we do with a drunken sailor.'

Cavan pulled a Cadbury Flake bar out of his pocket. "Hey! Nourishment! If we share it, we should have enough energy to circle around to Darcie's Folly one more time to try to step off the continuation of the path. Maybe we'll see something different now that the sun is starting to sink in the west."

"Sure," Daisy said, reaching for her half of the chocolate bar. "I'm game."

"Only if you feel up to it." Cavan was acting like an old mother hen who couldn't stop hovering round her chicks.

"I'm fine." She stifled a scream. "But only one more time, and then, we need to walk home via a different route. If Darcie is released and sees our footprints circling round and round the mulberry patch, he'll figure out soon enough that he needs to start digging here."

"The tide will wash it away in another couple of hours."

Daisy looked up to the top of the bluff before she started to ascend. "All the more reason for us to get back to Dingle sooner rather than later. You've already had one run in with the icy waters of the Atlantic today. We don't need another."

22

"No!" Granny screamed as loudly as she could. Ye're so close! If you get any closer ye're going to get burned!"

"She can nay hear ye," the sea captain said sadly.

"She senses something. We used to play this game all the time when she was a wee one. C'mon, Daisy girl! Listen to your Granny. Ye're getting colder now. Freezing cold. That's right! Now ye're getting a little warmer. Aye! Ye're starting to get hot again. Stop! Do nay move an inch! Ye're so hot ye're burning up!"

They both watched – held their breaths, except that ghosts did nay really have any – and watched some more as Cavan and Daisy circled the perimeter of the sea cave, dipped their toes and then their fingers in the nearby water, and started to leave the area.

"Nay!" Granny bellowed. "Can ye nay see it? The cave is the same exact shape as the cave I stitched on the last corner of the quilt. Nay. Nay. Nay. Now ye're cold. Ye're icy cold. Ye're freezing to death. Ye're..." Granny started to sob. "Have some confidence in yerself, Daisy girl! Ye were right there! It's the X marking the spot where the gold is hidden! Ye're remembering correctly – ye just have to dig a little!"

Captain Donaghue looked on sadly. She turned away so he could nay see her cry, embarrassed because she had nay the ability to get through to Daisy.

"Ye did yer best, Granny. The lass has had a hard day, what with almost losing my great-grandson. I would nay expect her to be receptive or even especially keen with all that's on her mind today."

"She does nay believe in me. If she did, she would hear me loud and clear. And the thing with the midges! What does she think? That they follow her night and day, where e'er she may be, always biting her in the same spot? Does she really think that midges only bite her in the ear lobe? Does she nay think it's a wee bit suspicious that she's nay had a bite on her ankle or her knee or her arm?"

Granny collapsed onto a rock that was large enough to use as a seat. In fact, she remembered sitting on it many a night while she watched the sun set over the Atlantic.

"I can nay take the stress of it," she moaned, her head in her hands.

The sea captain chuckled. "Too bad yer granddaughter is nay really with child. If she were, you could give up on Daisy and try again with her wee one in a few years."

"But Daisy is in trouble. She needs the gold to pay off her bills and get a start on whatever life holds for her. She's like a wee lost lamb."

"Aye, but she is very determined, and she has the love of one of my kin to help guide her. If Daisy and Cavan do nay find the gold, they may be more likely to find each other. If ye had to choose one or the other for Daisy – the gold or true love, wouldn't ye rather she find true love?"

"Well, when ye put if that way, I get yer point."

Captain Donaghue sat down beside her. "Let's stay here to guard the gold and see if they circle back to the same spot one more time. If they can verify what they thought was right the first time around, they'll be more likely to listen the second time they come round."

Granny felt a wee bit warmer as she sat on the cold, hard surface of the rock. The sun ne'er reached this one, as it sat in the shadow of the sea cave. She'd chosen it especially for this time of night as the ones that got the full sun were so hot by the afternoon that you could fry an egg on them.

Captain Donaghue tried to pat her on the knee. The man had good instincts, but of course, he could nay do it. "I'll try to talk to Cavan when he's alone. These days, when he's with Daisy, she's all he can think about."

"Aye. When a man is in love, it's hard to hear anything but the one ye've set yer eyes upon." She thought for a moment. "Tis probably the reason I was able to work so hard and get so much accomplished in my lifetime. I did nay have the distraction of being in love for much o' my time here on earth." She sighed. "Not that I e'er stopped loving my man, but it was different once he was gone."

"Aye. 'Tis a sadness I know from the other side. My biggest regret is that I had to leave my lovely wife alone to raise our children on her own. She wept into her pillow many a night and I could do nothing to comfort her except to sit by her side and hope she could feel my presence from afar."

Granny sniffled. "Ye're right, ye know. Even if Daisy ne'er finds the gold, but discovers true love with Cavan, she'll have the richest of the two treasures."

"Amen to that," the Captain said.

\#

Cavan didn't really care if they ever found the gold. It had already caused far more trouble than it was worth – to him anyway. But he trudged along in the sand beside Daisy without voicing what he thought because he wanted Daisy to be happy, and finding the gold would make her very, very happy. At least he hoped it would. No matter what her frame of mind, she was going to need the gold to support her baby. Raising a kid wasn't cheap and without the gold, Daisy had no way to support herself.

He rested his hand on her shoulder for a few seconds to steady her while she climbed over an area that was knit together with rocks so dense that there was no way around them. If he ever got up the courage to suggest to Daisy that they try to transition from friends to – more than friends – then he wanted to build their future on things like common goals and shared dreams. He loved Daisy – he really did. But desperation and having no other alternatives were not a good basis on which to begin a new relationship.

"I appreciate the taste of Flake," Daisy said a few minutes later, "but if I'm going to keep going, I need something a wee bit more substantial in my stomach. I hate to say it, but I think we need to give up for now and head back into Dingle."

"I agree. Hopefully the police will keep Darcie in custody for at least a few more days or deny him bail altogether so we can keep searching without having to dodge him."

Daisy started to giggle. "It is kind of funny, having to lose a pirate to find the buried treasure."

"Aye," Cavan said. "It's like we're in a time warp and we landed back in the days of my Great Grandpa Donaghue, the brave sea captain who fought the pirates to get the gold in the first place."

Daisy stopped, turned and looked him square in the eyes. "Just so we don't end up dead like he did."

"No amount of gold is worth the cost of a life."

"Right," she said. "Earlier today, when you were out there in the bay and Darcie was trying to drown you and the wind was gusting and the waves were crashing around you, I realized just how much you mean to me. I felt like I was going to lose my mind until I could see that you were safe."

His heart quickened and he started to warm up even though the wind was as cold and sharp as icicles.

"I feel the same way about you, Daisy." She hadn't used the word love, so he didn't either, but at least it was a start.

She gulped. "Sorry to get all emotional on you. I just feel like I'm about to crash after that huge adrenalin rush this morning."

He put his arms around her and pulled her close. "Your blood sugar is probably all whacko from not having a decent breakfast or lunch."

He turned her in the direction of his car and they started the uphill climb to get off the beach and back on high ground.

Maybe he should have left well-enough alone, knowing how exhausted Daisy was, but he really needed to know one thing. "Daisy?"

"Yes?" Her voice was soft and tender.

"Why is the gold so important to you? Besides the fact that it's gold. Were you that much happier living in your big house in Killarney after you found gold the first time?"

"Oh, Cavan." She started to cry, quietly at first, and then with wild abandon, sobbing like he'd never heard anyone cry. It was a few minutes before she could speak – or walk.

"Don't say I didn't warn you, okay?" She smiled faintly.

"I'm listening," he said. And he was. Whatever Daisy was about to say might not be what he wanted to hear, but he had to know her answer to be able to gauge what he was getting into.

Daisy took his hand and squeezed it as they started scrambling up a set of rocks just up from another sea cave. "I've been thinking about this a lot, and the one thing I have to say first is that the main reason I want to find Granny's gold, if it's even out there, is because she wanted me to have it. She went to all the work of stitching the treasure map and leaving me the shanty and everything else because she knew I would treasure it – and never part with it.

"When I found the first stash, it was by accident. I didn't know that Granny had anything to do with it. But even then, it was never about the gold as such. Sure, I liked having enough money to go wherever and do whatever I wanted without having to worry about it. I liked not having to work all the time. Who wouldn't?"

Cavan shrugged. "I wouldn't. I like my work. Did you really mind the long hours at your shop all that much?"

"Well, I kind of did, but not because I didn't enjoy what I do. It's just that I was creating my own inventory, so when I wasn't at the shop, I was always painting and making things and gathering materials and trying to bulk up my product reserves so I wouldn't run out in the busy season. It just got to be too much. I didn't have time for anything else. I lost touch with everyone I knew. My whole life was about the shop."

"I never thought of the fact that every time you had a good day and sold a lot of things, you had to start over and make that many things all over again to restock your shelves."

"Yeah. I loved it when sales surged, but it was traumatic at the same time because – and this will sound weird - but it's true. Each of the little things I make is unique. They're like my babies."

He froze for a second, thinking she was finally going to tell him about the baby growing inside her. But she kept going on about her artwork. He was half disappointed and half relieved.

"Like the little Fuchsia Flower Fairies I make. Each of their faces is a little different than the last, and I make them in different colors, so in a way, they each have a personality of their own. I make the Irish Wool Fairies from random scraps and salvage bolt ends I would get from the Kerry Woolen Mill so no two of them were ever alike. I was attached to each and every one of them. I never wanted to let a single one go."

"But didn't you find it fulfilling, knowing how happy your art was making the people who bought it?"

She sighed and stepped around a large rock protruding out of a stand of sea grass. "I guess so. In a way. I would have kept them all if I could."

"Really?" He squeezed her hand. "I love the feeling I get when I sell someone a bike that's well matched to their needs."

"But you don't make – create – your bicycles. And when one is gone, you can call your supplier and order another just like it. And, you deal with locals. My entire business catered to tourists. I rarely saw a customer more than once. I loved it when people left happy with a bag full of treasures, but I didn't get to build relationships with any of them because I never saw them again – with rare exceptions. There were a few who came every summer. But once a year contact doesn't make a friendship."

Cavan helped her up a seriously steep incline paved with nothing but loose dirt and a few strands of grass striving to keep their grip on the land. "Sounds like you were lonely."

"I was. Especially after Granny died."

"I'm sorry." He tried to look at her kindly, but not to let her detect the pity he felt now that he'd realized her plight. "I wish I had known."

"See, that's what the gold was really about. It was me wanting to belong, to have a crowd of friends with whom I could relax and laugh and go places and do things."

He knew her family was small, now almost non-existent, and he hated himself for not thinking of occasionally including her in a Donaghue celebration or holiday gathering. "Are you in touch with any of our old classmates?"

"I never fit in even back then. How old were you when you moved into Dingle? With me living out by the sea instead of in town, I never got to play with the other kids or get close to them. Besides, Granny had rules, you know? I suppose she had to, to survive and provide for me. She always had a homemade snack waiting for me when I got home from school – and a long list of chores. When I look back, I'm thankful she taught me how to work and work hard, but Granny's lifestyle didn't leave much room for playtime when I was a wee one, or for socializing when I got older."

"I actually remember that about you," Cavan admitted. "And that you could only come out to play if you were done with your chores." He kicked at a loose rock and it skittered down the trail behind them. "So you never rebelled or tried to negotiate better terms?"

Daisy smiled but there were tears in her eyes. "I respected her too much to break the rules, especially when I thought about all the sacrifices she'd made to care for me, to feed and clothe me. Most of all, I loved her too much to want to break her heart. That's why I tried never to do anything to upset her."

Cavan squeezed her hand and they walked in silence for a few minutes.

"So once your Granny was gone, why did you go into – stay in – a business that would require you to keep such long hours and work so hard?"

She laughed, but her voice sounded a little brittle. "When Granny started getting on in years and started to slow down a little, she asked me once why I worked so hard all the time and suggested I should relax a little."

Cavan laughed. He could see where this was going. "She taught you too well."

"Yes." Daisy's voice was gruff and heavy with emotion. "And then she said that the reason she worked so hard her whole life was so I wouldn't have to."

Thank goodness they were back on flat ground because he had to hug her. Daisy rested her head on his shoulder and snuggled her face in the crook of his neck.

He was almost afraid to ask the next question that was on his mind. They were almost back to the car. Maybe that was a good thing.

"So did you find what you were looking for in Killarney then? Good friends, good times, good cheer? Happiness? Contentment?"

"I-" They rounded a corner and Daisy's sea shanty blossomed in front of them like a shy wildflower rising up out of the grass. Parked beside his modest, economy class Honda Jazz was a brand new Jaguar E-PACE.

"What?" Daisy unlatched her hand from his. "It's Aodhan. Aodhan Byrne. My boy – um, my friend from Killarney." She took off running across the field to greet her – um – friend.

His throat constricted and he felt an intense dislike for the man. And all that before he even got his eyes focused on the perfect specimen of a man who was most likely the father of Daisy's baby.

23

Daisy tried to hide the fact that she felt more than a little lightheaded as she ran toward Aodhan. She felt like she had an anchor tethering her to the ground, like someone's arms were wrapped around her middle, trying to hold her back.

She finally made it to Aodhan's side. "Hey!" She said it cheerily because she was still happy to see him in spite of the way he'd treated her, but hopefully not too cheerily, as she didn't want him thinking she'd been sitting around pining for him the whole time she'd been back in Dingle. "What brings you here?"

"Are you kidding?" Aodhan leaned back against his Jaguar and smiled in that slow, nonchalant way of his. "The whole escapade with you and those men who were fighting over some quilt that flew into the water made the midday news. I had to make sure you were okay. Hopefully the two gay guys who were squabbling over the quilt found their blankey and won't bother you anymore."

"Gay?" Cavan said, his voice bristly and all offended.

"Um, this is my friend – the guy who rents my building in Dingle - Cavan Donaghue. And he's not gay – not that there's anything wrong with that – and he was trying to help me rescue Granny's quilt before the other guy, Darcie, who's related to these pirates who used to roam the waters off the Wild Atlantic Way, stealing gold and pillaging and raping, found it and took it from me."

"Whoa, Daisy."

He was doing it again. Brushing her off. At least, that's what it felt like. But he must have cared about her enough to come all the way from Killarney to make sure she was okay, hadn't he?

"You always were a little overly dramatic." Aodhan added.

She narrowed her eyes and frowned. "It's a very serious matter." Cavan was standing so close to her that she could hear his breathing. She could feel the tension building up from inside him like a cloud going cumulonimbus and getting ready to silently explode into the atmosphere.

She shot a worried glance at Cavan and glared at Aodhan. "There's a lot at stake."

Aodhan looked like his typically smug self when he shot back with. "Yeah. I gathered that when your name was mentioned alongside the murdered priest's with the chilling supposition that there may be more gold buried somewhere along the Wild Atlantic Way, and that the gold might have been a possible motive for his murder."

Daisy closed her eyes and tried to gather her thoughts, which were swinging and clanging like a chime in the wind off the Atlantic. "They said all that on the news?" This was awful. Just awful. The last thing they needed was every looky-loo and fortune hunter coming out to try their luck at finding the pot o' gold at the end of the rainbow – a thing the Irish were notoriously famous for.

"I hope you didn't give heed to everything they said. The interview was obviously given without Daisy's permission." Cavan wasn't just quietly exploding now. He looked and sounded angry.

She huffed. The whole situation was already so out of control that she didn't know what she was going to do. She couldn't let it escalate any further.

"So once again, Aodhan, can I ask what brings you here? As you can see, I'm fine, although a little exhausted from all the excitement and missing a good night's sleep and my midday meal."

Aodhan looked at her from some distant spot far deeper than the surface of his lazy blue eyes and said. "Seeing the conditions in which you grew up certainly explains a lot." He gestured toward the shanty and the harsh, desolate landscape.

She held her head high. "I couldn't have been raised in a more beautiful place or by a more loving person." She reached back and touched Cavan's clenched fist whilst she said, "Did you come to lend a hand, Aodhan? If not, then Cavan and I should be on our way. We've had a busy day and we were just off to find a bite to eat."

"Oh, I've got a hand all right." Aodhan winked suggestively.

Daisy could have punched him. But that would have gotten Cavan going, and that would not help matters.

She turned away from Aodhan. "Cavan, how about a bowl of Irish stew and some brown bread from Maeve's? We can get it to go so you can get back to the bike shop."

"You don't own that Recycled Cyclery place on the harbor do you? I saw it on the way down and couldn't imagine why anyone would name a place something that sounds like a second hand shop for bikes that somebody rescued from the dumpster." Aodhan laughed. "No offense."

Cavan's body heat jumped so drastically that it totally offset the chill in the wind to the point where Daisy started to feel hot just from standing next to him.

"None taken," Cavan said, and Daisy thought sure...

Cavan stepped out from behind her oozing alpha male and said, "I take great pride in the fact that I built a business from nothing by refurbishing and repairing bicycles that everyone else thought worthless. I now have a fleet of three dozen bikes for rent and a thriving sales and repair business."

"It may not seem like much to you, but Cavan's a wonderful businessman and I'm very fortunate to have him leasing my building." Well, it wasn't exactly her building. Technically, it was the bank's. But Cavan's monthly payment did cover her mortgage, utilities and property taxes, and that was the important thing. It would belong to her someday.

Aodhan raised one eyebrow – definitely not impressed. But then, what did she expect from a man who had millions in deposits and a whole city block to his name?

"If you say so." Aodhan laughed.

What had she ever seen in this man? She'd sold her soul to belong, to feel part of a crowd. And look where it had gotten her in the long run.

"Thanks for checking on me, Aodhan. I'm sure I can count on you to tell the rest of my friends what I've been up to since I decided to return to my roots in Dingle."

Cavan gave her a look that said, 'Like you had any choice in the matter.' She couldn't even look at Aodhan, so she quickly got in Cavan's car and locked the door. What possessed her to do that, she didn't know.

Cavan climbed in beside her a second later, glaring and acting all bent out of shape.

"Sorry about all that."

"I don't want to talk about it." Cavan clamped his jaw shut and peeled out of the hills while the Atlantic faded from view behind them and then disappeared.

#

Cavan had a sick feeling in his stomach. The only thing that kept him from throwing up was the fact that he didn't want to ruin his car.

This Aodhan was the father of Daisy's baby. The thought of her being with the arrogant jerk made him want to rip his hair out. Dealing with the concept of Daisy being pregnant with another man's baby had been difficult enough when Aodhan had been a hazy, obscure image in his mind, but now that he had seen the man and heard his voice, the thought of he and Daisy naked and making love was more than he could stomach.

"Sorry about Aodhan's rude comments," Daisy mumbled, sounding more accepting than truly apologetic.

Cavan gripped the steering wheel and didn't reply.

"He's always been that way. It's not you. He treats everyone that way."

Oh. Well. That might have made him feel better if Daisy hadn't chosen to reward the man's oafish behavior by having sex with him.

Daisy evidently took his silence as an invitation to rub more salt in the wound. "He was nice to me when we first met. I thought he was such a sweetheart, and so kind. I was already starting to see the real Aodhan by the time I found out I had to give the gold back, so it came as no surprise when he ended things the second he found out I was destitute."

Cavan tried to muster up some sympathy for Daisy. She'd been lonely and craving attention. She'd said before how much she wanted to feel like she belonged. He got that. But he couldn't imagine that she hadn't seen what kind of man Aodhan was from the get go. Didn't she know how beautiful she was? How talented? How sweet and loving? Why, oh, why had she given a jerk like Aodhan even one second of her time?

Daisy spoke in a soft voice. "I like to think I would have told him to get lost even if I hadn't lost all of my money. In fact, I'm sure I would have. I know I must appear to have been desperate and needy, but relationships can be tricky sometimes."

Sometimes? For the first time, he acknowledged the fact that Rory could be right about Daisy. Was she with Cavan because she valued their friendship and respected his advice, or because she was desperate and needy? Was she cozying up to him so he would cave and let her turn the bike shop back into an art gallery for her bits and bobs? Or was it because she needed someone gullible enough to pay her bills and help her raise Aodhan's child?

He gave a quick glance in the rear view mirror and slammed on the breaks as hard as he dared. Daisy didn't say a word more. She looked absolutely petrified. He was sorry for that, but he had to get away from her before the police had to add a second murder investigation to their list of mysteries to solve.

He said, "I'm going to walk the rest of the way home. I would appreciate it if you'd park the car in my spot and leave the keys on the kitchen table when you get back to Dingle Town."

She just sat there looking stunned while he got out of the car. So be it. He'd had enough for one day.

#

Daisy listened to Cavan's footsteps clattering down the stairs that led to the shop. The tension between them was so thick it was like trying to slice a slab of Irish cheddar with a feather.

And all because she'd been a wee bit happy to see Aodhan. Good grief! She knew full well how abominably Aodhan treated people, and how egotistical and conceited he was. She was fully aware that Aodhan was totally stuck on himself to the detriment of everyone else in the world. He'd dumped her the second he found out she wasn't one of the elite of Ireland. He plainly thought he was better than Cavan by a long stroke. Did that mean she should have clamped her mouth shut and pretended not to know the man? It was a wee bit hard to ignore someone when there were only three of you as far as the eye could see! What had Cavan expected her to do?

She put on a heavy hoodie and wrapped a blue, green and turquoise tartan coat, also with a hood, around herself and tightened the belt. It had a million pockets and a silk lining and all kinds of details perfectly stitched. The tartan had cost an amount that was now unfathomable. She treasured every second that she got to snuggle in its soft, supple fibers. It was one of the few things she'd bought with the gold money that the authorities hadn't made her give back - something about outer wear being a necessity during Ireland's brisk winters.

She walked down the outside stairs as quietly as she could, knowing that Cavan wouldn't want her to go down to the beach without him. But the tide would be high by the time he got off work, and she really wanted to have another look see now that she was more rested and alert. Her brain had been completely jumbled the day before, but she had a strong feeling that they were really close to finding the gold. Maybe today would be the day!

She owed it to herself to spend every spare second searching while Darcie was still in custody, and she couldn't ask Cavan to take another day off work or close the shop down during high season. Besides, she'd walked that beach alone thousands of times – what was the big deal about going by herself one more time? She'd even packed a lunch to make sure she didn't have a repeat of the lightheadedness she'd felt the day before.

She eased onto her bicycle and glided away from the sidewalk. If the mood Cavan was in said anything about his frame of mind, he'd probably be glad she was out of his way today.

She pedaled down the road at a leisurely pace until she reached the shanty and laid her bike down on the grass.

She followed the trail down to the spot where Darcie had been digging and then stood perfectly still while she tried to visualize the first corner piece that was on the top right of center. Next, the lower right corner, then the lower left and the upper left. The wind teased her cheeks and the sun beat down on her hood, filling her with warmth. The midges weren't biting, but she could hear manx shearwaters, razorbills, and guillemots flapping their wings, cackling and calling out to their mates. A wild hare scampered through the grass. She'd learned to tune out the constant clatter of the birds and the yipping of foxes at night when she wanted to sleep, but today, her senses were sharp, and she heard every motion, every movement.

Her cares and concerns stripped away – everything was laid bare except for thoughts of Cavan. She should have told him how she felt. Why had she even felt one iota of enthusiasm when she saw Aodhan? How she regretted that Cavan had to witness her folly.

She'd tried to explain to him that what had made Killarney so special to her – so special that in one sense, she still longed for it. She'd been accepted, included, part of a social scene. She'd had friends, and a boyfriend to escort her to events, and people to talk to and go places and do things with.

She'd had a life. A personal life. She thought back to nights spent curled up in a corner booth at one of her favorite pubs listening to the ancient cadence of the bodrain while guitars were strummed and accordions were pumped and fiddles were coaxed into lilting melodies as old as Granny Siobhan's grandmother. When she'd lived in Killarney, she'd had a family of sorts. She'd belonged.

24

Daisy lifted her face to the sun and tried not to think about her lonely existence at Granny's sea shanty, or her new reality of living as a guest – a somewhat unwanted guest – in Cavan's flat. Was it so surprising that she longed for her own place, her old friends, and the life she'd had, no matter how imperfect?

"Ye can have it all again if ye put yer mind to it." The whisper resounded through her head with a tiny zing of energy. She could almost hear Granny's voice, the memory was so clear. Had she imagined it, or was it an actual memory? Or was it real? She looked around and saw no one.

She searched through her memory banks, trying to remember a time when Granny had said such a thing. She had nothing specific. The voice had definitely been Granny's, but it had been immediately pertinent to what she was thinking, like Granny knew all about the gold she'd found, and then lost. How could it be? Her imagination took over for a second and went wild with possibilities – Granny as some sort of heavenly messenger or personal angel who was watching over her, or a ghost from the other side who was trying to convey an important message that could save her life or keep her from harm. A lot of people believed in the angels hovering round theory – although she had to say she really couldn't envision her old Granny with a halo. More likely a little red pitchfork that she could use to poke people who irritated her.

"Now wait just a minute, Daisy girl! Is it that hard to imagine me looking down on you from heaven, doing nice things for the people I love?"

Daisy stepped over an outcropping of rock and froze. She'd heard the words as clear as day, and what 'Granny' had spoken was in no way an old adage or commonly repeated phrase that her mind could have automatically supplied.

She looked around to make sure no one was listening. "Is that you, Granny?"

"Finally! It's taken you long enough to figure it out!"

She held her breath. Oh my gosh. It had to be Granny – and it wasn't just her voice. It was the words and inflections. She spoke and sounded just like her Granny. Her dead Granny.

"If it is you, Granny, I'm happy to hear from you. But I don't have anything figured out. My mind is racing, my heart's pounding and I'm scared to death. Well, not death like death is to a dead person. Death like, well, you know what I mean. I don't know what to think!"

"Don't bother," Granny's bodiless voice said. "Thinking, that is. Has it gotten ye anywhere so far? Try feeling. Follow yer instincts. The quilt is the key. Ye looked it over good enough when ye had it that ye should be able to find the gold even though the quilt is gone."

Oh. My. Gosh. So there really was more gold?

"Granny, I don't care how broke I am – if the gold belonged to Father O'Leary - if that's why he was killed, then I don't want one haypenny of it. And I mean it!"

"Father O'Leary was killed because of HIS gold. Ye and I – we have our own gold, and if ye start listening to me, ye'll soon have it in a safe place. And no one will have to get killed."

Her mind was firing off warning signals and fireworks all at the same time. She couldn't wait to tell Cavan! Of course, until they'd found the gold, there was nothing to tell him. And who knew what he would think if she started spouting off about hearing Granny's voice and carrying on a conversation with her like she was still alive instead of six feet under.

"We've looked everywhere, Granny. Can you give me a clue? Nudge me in the direction of the gold?"

She felt rather than heard someone behind her. Was it? Could it be? "Granny?" She spun around on her heels like she was on a polished wood disco floor instead of six inches of loose sand. And froze. "Aodhan?"

"Hi." He looked down. "I didn't think I'd find anyone here.

And then I heard you talking." He looked around. "Are you alone?"

Her wrist and forearm began to prickle like someone had taken an ice cube to her skin. "Um, I was just texting Cavan. Sometimes it's easier to use my voice recognition than type everything in."

"Ah." He didn't look convinced, nor did he question her any further.

"What are you doing here?"

Aodhan moved his arm behind his back and took a step closer to her. "When I got home yesterday, my watch was gone. I searched the car very carefully but it was nowhere to be found. I remember checking the time when I was here, so I figured this must be where I lost it." He laughed.

He sounded nervous. Her neck bristled and she tried to mask her cynicism. He was lying. But why? Had he wanted to see her again? If he was sorry about the way they'd left things yesterday and wanted to try again, why hadn't he called to make sure she'd be around? But then, where was she going to go without a car? She brushed off her paranoia. Sure, Aodhan could be a little arrogant and conceited at times, but she trusted him.

She smiled just as a glint of something metallic caught her eye. "What's that?" She shifted to the left so she could see what he was hiding.

Aodhan moved along with her, to his right and then his left.

She was faster. "Is that a metal detector?"

"Yes. I have it with me because of the watch. It's my father's."

"Must be a watch of fair value."

"It's a Cartier gold watch that my Grandfather gave me before he died."

"Oh." She remembered Aodhan having a nice watch, and he wasn't wearing it now. There was a little strip of white skin on his wrist where it normally sat. Aodhan tanned all winter long so he wouldn't burn when he was at his family's mansion in Spain in January and February. He might have asked her to go along this year if she hadn't lost all her gold and disappeared from his life just before Christmas.

She simultaneously felt something bite her ear and the voice that she presumed to be Granny saying, "Ye did nay disappear from his life – he booted ye out the second he found out ye were nay longer rich."

Saints and begorra – had what she'd assumed to be a personal onslaught of midges going after her sweet-smelling blood been Granny pinching her ear, trying to get her attention so she could point her toward the gold? Holy Mother of God! If she'd paid attention – if she'd not been so dense, she'd have found the gold weeks ago!

"Do NAY turn yer back on that man for a second. Trust me when I say, he has an evil aura, that one."

OMG. Now what was she supposed to do? The gold was out there somewhere, and Aodhan was here with a metal detector.

She stepped over a clump of seaside daisies lest she squash them underfoot and tried to look at Aodhan without tipping him off to the fact that she was suspicious of his motives. Granny saying he was bad news – evil – had her more than a little freaked out.

She tried to shake off her feelings. Aodhan wasn't evil – maybe a bit egotistical and somewhat bourgeois, traits which would not endear him to Granny – but basically harmless. Granny probably had him confused with Darcie. They were both tall. Who knew how well ghosts could see? And Granny's vision hadn't been all that great when she was alive.

Aodhan brought the metal detector to the forefront. "I'll be on my way then. I'm eager to get looking before it gets buried in the sand."

What should she do? She really didn't want him rooting around her property without her being around, but she could hardly forbid him to look for his watch. She wished she could call Cavan, but assuming she even had bars, which was highly unlikely, there was no way she could call him, or anyone else without giving away her apprehensions.

She reached up to scratch her earlobe and then remembered that the 'midge' that had been biting her was just Granny. And you couldn't swat away a ghost. Not that she wanted to. Granny loved her so much that she'd come back from the dead to help her. The knowledge filled her with warmth. But then, the wind whipped around her shoulders and she shivered. Was the wind also a sign from Granny?

Aodhan pulled the neck of his jacket closed and tightened his scarf around his neck. "I'd better get looking if I'm going to find any footsteps left to backtrack."

She held out her arm to gauge the wind. "I'm guessing twenty knots minimum, gusts to 26 or 27. I'm afraid you'll not be finding any footsteps. It's been blowing all night."

"I followed your footsteps last night after you and that Cavan fellow took off. Maybe you can help me."

She hesitated. "Sure." She hardly wanted him roaming around on his own with his ginormous metal detector. If she'd had more money, or really believed there was more gold to be found, she should have rented one herself months ago. Now that she knew for sure that the gold was out there, the last thing she needed was for Aodhan to find it before she did. Not that he needed it, but isn't that how rich people were? Always wanting more...

"Hopefully it's somewhere nearby." Aodhan waved his metal detector in a circle.

True. If they located the watch somewhere close by, she could get rid of Aodhan and give Granny a chance to lead her right to the buried treasure. Granny had always said to strike while the iron was hot. Maybe the ability for them to communicate was a short-lived phenomenon.

All she needed was to spend hours looking for Aodhan's watch only to find out that Granny's transition time had come to an end before she could tell her where the gold was. If that was even how it worked. Who knew?

All she knew for certain was that if they didn't find the gold watch soon, and she retraced her and Cavan's actual steps from yesterday's search, she'd probably be leading Aodhan right to the spot where Granny's gold was actually hidden.

"Well, we should start by walking in this direction." Aodhan had seen her and Cavan returning from their walkabout, so he would get suspicious if she headed in the opposite direction right off.

Aodhan seemed to relax a little and took her elbow to help her step over a long outcrop of rocks half buried by sand and tufts of sea grass.

Their conversation was comfortable as they walked along, catching up on what had become of mutual friends since she'd moved back to Dingle, and reminiscing about things they'd done and places they'd gone. Aodhan swung his metal detector in broad sweeps along either side of the trail she led him down.

The sand was miraculous, the way it swept away all signs of

what had happened yesterday, making each step a new adventure. She felt absolutely no attraction toward Aodhan, but there was some sense of starting out fresh that she certainly hadn't gotten the day before, when he and Cavan had been ready to pounce on each other.

She stopped. "Let me get my bearings." She thought for a moment and turned slightly to the left. She felt someone – Granny? – yank on her right earlobe so hard that she almost lost her balance and tipped over.

"No. Wait." She tried to ignore the pain radiating from her ear piercing and sound convincing. She turned to the right. "This way."

"Are you sure?" Aodhan looked skeptically in the direction she wanted to head. "There are more sea caves down that way." He pointed to the left. "Not that I think we're going to find my watch inside a cave, but it's a lot rockier in that direction and I remember tripping on a few rocks and bending over to grab on to some boulders while I picked my way up and down the hilly terrain. Any of those movements could have jostled the watch off my wrist."

"Or, if the clasp broke, it could have slipped off unnoticed while you were walking along in the sea grasses."

"Wouldn't the grasses be flattened down a little if you and Cavan and then I walked down to the sea and back following this route? It looks like no one has passed this way in months."

"Not the way the wind blows down here," she said, hoping he wouldn't notice that the wind was blowing directly against the grass, pressing it flat instead of ruffling it up the way it would have if what she'd said was true. Darn. It was pretty obvious no one had walked this way just yesterday.

"Well, if we don't find it soon, I'm going to try the other way." Aodhan looked over his shoulder every few minutes. "I'm sure I recognize some of those outcroppings from yesterday."

She silently prayed to God or Grammy or the deceased priest or whoever else might be listening that the detector would start to beep. But short of a miracle, she knew it wouldn't. Not where they were going.

Begorra and the saints. What was she supposed to do? It wasn't that she didn't trust Aodhan, but her gold was really none of his business. He'd wanted her when she had money, and dumped her when she didn't. Money mattered to him, therefore he was the last person to whom she wanted to advertise the fact that she might be rich again.

"I'm turning around," Aodhan stated flatly.

"Okay. Um, maybe I'm remembering wrong."

They retraced their steps through the flattened sea grasses with Aodhan taking the lead this time. Zings of pain shot through her ear.

Stop it, Granny, she thought as intensely as she could to make sure Granny could sense her intentions. Did Granny have the ability to read her mind? In this instance, she hoped she did. But from here on forward, she most certainly hoped she could not.

Aodhan slowed his pace and climbed down a rocky embankment, then another, sidling down to sea level, where numerous caves gaped openmouthed at the incoming waves.

"If you lost your watch down here, it's long gone by now. The tides have come in and out since you were here. It's been washed out to sea."

"But the tide is coming in again. If by some chance it's still here, I need to find it now, before it really does disappear." Aodhan swung his detector back and forth with the momentum and energy of a Newton's Cradle.

She had to get him away from the caves. "There are some tide pools down by the shoreline. We should check there to see if it snagged on a rock. I find starfish caught in the tide pools all the time."

"The force of the waves coming in could have carried it deep into a sea cave." Aodhan swung the metal detector toward a sea cave and watched as the pendulum dipped into the opening and came out again.

They heard nothing but the clattering of sea gulls and the crash of the waves. Thank the Lord for that.

There were sea caves on either side of them now. She held her breath while Aodhan checked each one out. If she'd been able to concentrate, to see the maps from the quilt in her mind, she might have known if they were in an area where she had cause for worry. But she couldn't. Aodhan was moving so fast she could hardly keep up with him. She felt frantic, and at odds, and Granny's incessant ear pinching wasn't helping matters. How was she supposed to interpret them anyway? Was there some sort of Morse code behind the jabs of pain that she was supposed to be getting?

"I'm famished all of the sudden," she claimed. "Why don't we take a break and ride up to the seafood hut on the road to Dingle? There's plenty of daybreak left."

Aodhan ignored her but Granny whispered in her ear. "Watch yer step, Daisy. There is no watch. It's all a ruse." Or was it the pinprick of her own instincts? Aodhan did love to play the hero. Perhaps she should make good use of the fact that he'd shown up, a knight with a shiny metal detector, and hope they found the gold. He would have his moment of glory and she would have her treasure, and life would go on, only this time, assuming Aodhan had plans to help her spend the money, it would be her that dumped him.

Aodhan wandered from sea cave to sea cave like a man possessed. She was in such a frenzy, she'd lost complete track of where they were until they came upon the cave Darcie had assaulted with his pick ax and shovel. Aodhan could see it had been recently disturbed just as well as she could and took special care to scan it thoroughly.

Watch, smatch.

"Aodhan, I really think we've done enough for today. No sense starving, and you're starting to look red. I have some aloe growing back at the shanty that you can use to tame the effects of the burn. Please. The tide is coming in fast now. We don't want to get caught down here."

The caves in this part of Granny's land backed up to a steep bluff, worn craggy from Atlantic storms, that rose sharply from the sand. There were certain spots where it could be climbed, but if the tide got high enough to cut you off from the navigable trails to the top, you'd be trapped on the lower tier.

She heard the crash of a wave against a rock. The tide waited for no one.

"You don't understand, Aodhan. We need to get to higher ground – now."

Had he even heard her? "Aodhan..."

"Just a few more minutes."

"I grew up along the sea. You're a landlubber and a city boy if there ever was one. Trust me. The tide is going to cut us off from any route of escape."

He turned and continued to swing the metal detector. The thing was coming right at her! She took a step back to get out of its path and hit an uneven rock. A jolt of pain shot through her ankle and she felt herself starting to fall.

Her life didn't exactly pass in front of her as she fell backwards, but maybe it should have. She might have liked to have one last look at the good times. She heard a loud cracking noise as her head hit the sharp edge of a rock and then the cackling of the metal detector as it made its first discovery. Had Aodhan found his watch, or was there gold inside the sea cave, or was the noise she heard the sound of her own brain exploding against the sides of her skull? As she passed in and out of conscious thought, it did occur to her that this was exactly the kind of thing that Cavan always worried about happening when she was out here by herself. He had every right to be concerned, except that this – whatever was about to happen next – would never have happened if she'd been by herself. Her last thought was that in this instance, Aodhan was both a curse and a blessing – the inadvertent cause of her stumble, but the one who would save her from drowning.

Her grasp on reality faded – she didn't know for how long. It seemed like seconds, but she felt very woozy. She listened for Aodhan's voice, expecting to hear some reassuring words or to feel his arms around her, lifting her to safety. But all she could hear was the waves lapping gently against the shore. A whoosh, followed by a rumble or a rustling noise, then a murmur – almost like a faint growl in which she could literally hear rocks and shells being pulverized into sand, and lastly, a resigned whisper. The susurrus of the surf lulled her back into unconsciousness. When she woke up again, she was wet. Her beautiful, very expensive wool tartan was sopping wet. Everything was wet. She was icy cold and soaked to the bone. Why was she wet? She tried to get up, but the world was spinning and she couldn't seem to... and then she was out again.

25

Cavan rapped his fingers on the counter and waited for the last rentals of the day to be returned. He picked up a newspaper left by an earlier customer and flipped open the first page. The Killarney Today. He'd been considering trying to open a second bicycle shop in Killarney for some time. It couldn't hurt to get a feel for what was happening in the city. The first headline – Display of Pedal Power: Ring of Kerry Charity Cycle – promised the presence of an active bicycling community. The next story – Making Plans for the Beat on the Street – indicated an active network of community events.

A third headline caught his eye – Adrian Byrne Arrested for Embezzling. At first, he'd thought it read Aodhan Byrne. Byrne wasn't a common name in County Kerry. He kept reading, thinking he might find a connection. Could this Adrian be Aodhan's father? He'd assumed Aodhan's family had plenty of money. Why embezzle if you already had enough money to give your kid a Jaguar E-PACE?

Hmm. The article cited gambling losses in Europe for the possible motivation for the crime. Oh well. He certainly hadn't been impressed by the younger Byrne he'd met and the apple didn't usually fall far from the tree. However, if this was the same family, it didn't bode well for Daisy's baby. Not that he wanted to see her involved with the baby's father anyway, but knowing they were scumbags and thieves didn't ease his mind any.

The chimes on the door jingled and the couple he'd been waiting for came through with their bicycles. He chatted with them briefly but he was in a hurry to close up and find Daisy. She hadn't been down all day, and if he was inclined to bet, he'd put money on her being down by the sea, trying to remember the layout of Granny's quilt.

He took the stairs two at a time and found a note from Daisy. No surprise.

He opted to take his car for no particular reason. Just a feeling that Daisy might be tired from tromping all over the coastline in the sunshine and wind all day long and appreciate a lift home.

He sped along the Wild Atlantic roadway as fast as the trail of tourists would allow, then turned off onto the narrow, single track road that led to Daisy's sea shanty. A half kilometer down, Aodhan's Jaguar E-PACE came roaring toward him. Thank goodness there was a passing place he could duck into or he probably would have ended up in the lagoon along side the road. What on earth? He'd seen Aodhan very clearly but he'd appeared to be alone in the car. He was grateful Daisy wasn't with Aodhan since the jerk was driving like a lunatic, but he also wondered where she was and what had transpired to bring about Aodhan's burst of speed. Or maybe he always drove that way.

He was soon at the shanty. He could see Daisy's bike lying in the grass by the side of the road. He got out of the car and checked the house. The door was unlocked but no one was home. He started walking down the path to the sea, or what he could see of it. The winds had been strong all day. By the look of the clouds, a storm was brewing. Thankfully, they'd finally calmed down now that the sun was setting. He could see and hear a group of birds circling over the coastline just off to his left and wondered what all of the ruckus was about.

Panic gripped his gut and he took off running. How many times had he told Daisy she shouldn't be traipsing around the shoreline by herself? But then, by the look of it, she hadn't been by herself.

He pumped his legs, and as his adrenalin kicked in, he ran faster and faster. "Daisy?" He yelled out. "Daisy?"

If Aodhan had done something to hurt her, he was going to strangle the man.

#

Daisy felt as light as a flower petal floating in a pool of water.

Her mind was fuzzy, but in a pleasant sort of way. Every so often, she could feel something hard and craggy scratching her back, but even that was okay. The sensation of being wet filtered through the haze, and she shivered. What felt like a wave splashed her face. She sputtered and tried to spit out the water that had gone in her mouth, but she was flat on her back and she ended up swallowing instead. She started to choke. The sting of salt water irritated her throat and she tried to roll over to cough up the water that had gone down her windpipe.

No! She flailed in the water until she was able to roll over on her back again. What was she doing? Floating out to sea? It made no sense. She opened her eyes. The sky was pink and purple and peach colored and the sun setting on the watery horizon hurt her eyes. Her head started to throb and she would have gone back to sleep to put an end to her dream if she hadn't been so cold.

She reached for the covers and tried to pull them tighter against her neck to keep the cold out. She tried to turn onto her side so she could snuggle up to Cavan but all she got was another face full of water. Ugh! She hated salt water.

That's when she heard him calling her name. "Daisy? Dai-sy? Daisy! Where are you?"

She tried to answer, but she couldn't seem to form the words.

"Aodhan? Where are you, Aodhan?" Her voice was weak. It sounded lost in the universe.

There was no answer. She drifted off again. She was so sleepy.

#

There were suddenly so many storm clouds hugging the horizon that Cavan couldn't tell if the sun had set yet or not. Lightning pierced the skyline in more frequent bursts of color, the strikes offshore reflecting in the black waters of the Atlantic. The storm was getting nearer and nearer. Even the sheltered bay beyond Daisy's sea shanty was dotted with white caps. He had to find Daisy.

He'd already searched her shanty, and the high ground surrounding the cottage. He should have started down below. He knew the tide was coming in. He just hadn't believed she would be down exploring sea caves at this time of night, when the tide was already lapping at the heels of the cliff and cutting off most of the trails to the beach.

He considered the possibility that there had been an accident and that Aodhan had been transporting Daisy to hospital when he met him on the road. He wouldn't have seen Daisy in the car if she'd been lying in the back seat, or even in a fully reclined front seat. He felt sure the E-PACE had all the perks.

He glanced down at his mobile. No bars. He rang Daisy anyway. No answer. If he gambled on the fact that Daisy might have been in Aodhan's auto, he could miss his only chance to save her.

"Trust yer instincts, lad."

What? The voice called out to him to keep looking. And that, he did. Funny that he trusted a disembodied voice coming out of nowhere more than he trusted Aodhan Byrne.

And then, he saw something floating in the water. Was it Daisy? He could see the shape clearly from his vantage point on top of the cliffs. It was long and oval shaped, like a person. He could see long strands of hair trailing behind her as the waves bounced her over the surface and up from the troughs.

It had to be Daisy! He found a break in the sea grasses and bounded down the side of the cliff, half stumbling and half sliding. When he got to the water, he ran out a few feet and flayed himself into the water, swimming as hard as he could against the incoming waves.

It was much harder to see against the dark water at surface level and the residual light from the sunset was fading fast now that the sun was buried in storm clouds.

He pumped and kicked, pumped and kicked. He was almost there. The water shimmered with the reflections of lightning. He didn't even want to think about how dangerous it was to be out swimming in an electrical storm, but at least the bursts of light were helping him to target his destination.

There she was! "Daisy!" He reached out and grabbed a hold of what he thought were her legs – and felt the solid, stiff, waxy edges of a surfboard. No! He looked right and left over the tops of the waves. He was sure he had seen Daisy. He had obviously gotten disoriented, missed her, and latched on to the surfboard instead of her. At least he had something to hang on to. Fighting the waves was exhausting and the water was freezing cold.

He hoisted himself a little higher to get his face out of the waves. Stuck to the fin at the bottom end of the surfboard's deck was a clump of long, straggly seaweed. The 'hair' he'd been so sure was Daisy's. His heart cramped with disappointment. He was exhausted. He turned to go back and a rough wave washed over him. The water was getting choppier and choppier. The lightning was getting closer and the rumble of sharp claps of thunder mixed with the sound of the waves crashing against the rocks to make a deafening roar.

He was ready to give up, make a beeline for the shore, and hope he found Daisy somewhere else. In a way, he was glad the surfboard hadn't turned out to be Daisy's body. But it crushed him to know he was no closer to finding her than he had been when he first set out.

If the surf came in any higher, if it got any darker, he'd never find her. And if she was in trouble, she'd never make it through the night, especially if a storm hit.

He was close to shore, his arms burning with cramps, when he thought he heard a voice calling out to him.

"Aodhan? Aodhan?" It was Daisy! "Aodhan? Why did you leave me here? Please! You have to save me, Aodhan." Her voice trailed off miserably, so weak, he could hardly hear her. The water was too shallow to swim now, so he stood and picked his way around one rock after another to shore in the direction of her voice.

"Daisy? Daisy, can you hear me?"

There was no response. She was probably slipping in and out of consciousness. He couldn't even think of the alternative, that he might have missed his chance to save her by five minutes time. He pushed forward and slogged through the wet sand and waves. "Daisy? Hang on just a minute more! I'm almost there!"

A burst of energy lit up the beach and he saw the heap that was her body and the tangled mass that really was her hair. He ran to her side and dropped to his knees.

"Daisy! Can you hear me? It's Cavan." He felt for her pulse and found one, but she was unconscious and half drowned by the look of it. He turned her on her side and opened her mouth so she wouldn't swallow any more water.

The tide surged deeper with every wave that crept on to shore. His worst nightmares assailed him as he worked over her. No one had known where Daisy was. With the tide coming in and the storm growing fiercer by the minute, she would have drowned if he hadn't found her when he did. Water was already covering her feet and legs as high as her hips. Waves were splashing at her chest and sometimes over her head. The water was almost deep enough to float her, and as each wave came in from the sea, it picked up her body just enough to slam it into a jagged outcrop of rocks at the back of her head.

She coughed up a lungful of salt water. "What did you say, Granny? I know. I know. I can trust Cavan. I'll tell him where the gold is. But not Darcie, and not Aodhan. Definitely not Aodhan."

"Daisy. Listen to me. It's Cavan, and you're hurt. We have to get you back to the shanty." He kept her rolled on her side and tried to raise her into a sitting position. That's when he saw the blood on the back of her head. Had someone done this to her or had she fallen and hit a rock when she met with the ground?

"Don't worry, Granny. I'll be fine. Yes, Captain Donaghue, I know I can trust Cavan. He's a good boy. I can trust him."

"Daisy? It's Cavan. I'm going to take you to the emergency room."

"No. I'll be fine. I have to find the gold before Aodhan steals it all."

Aodhan again. This whole mess reeked of Aodhan's conceit and lies, of his pompous, condescending attitude. Cavan didn't know how, but he knew he was right. Aodhan had left Daisy to drown.

#

Daisy struggled to sit up. She couldn't remember ever feeling so weak. "I have to find the gold." She pushed at Cavan's chest and tried to swat him away. "I promised Granny Siobhan."

"No, Daisy. The gold can wait. We have to get you to hospital. Someone in your condition shouldn't be taking chances."

"My condition?" Her head started to throb. Her hair felt matted and sticky in the back.

Cavan saw her groping her head. "You bumped your head on a rock – probably several rocks - when the waves were bouncing you back and forth."

"I'm young and I'm healthy. Granny always kept a first aid kit at the shanty. All I need is a warm shower and some dry clothes."

Cavan scooped her up in his arms and started to walk. Probably to climb back to the topside of the bluff. She tried to get away from him. She was too heavy for him to carry her up the hill.

"I don't have enough time or money to pay for a visit to the ER." She squirmed in his arms. "I have to find the gold. I promise you, if I don't feel better by morning, I'll call and make an appointment."

"It's completely dark out there, and there's a bad storm coming in besides. Money – not even gold - should not be an issue at a time like this. I won't allow you to refuse care because you don't have the money. It will be taken care of one way or the other. And if you're meant to find more gold, it will happen in its own time."

"And if not?" Her head sagged to one side, then rolled to the other. A second later, she jerked her head upward and looked around. "Granny told me where the gold was. My gold. I have to find it before anyone else does."

She could feel her head falling back onto the thick of Aodhan's arm and listing back where it wasn't supported. Or was it Cavan's arm? And then she was out cold.

26

"Daisy? Stay with me, Daisy!" The wind stole Cavan's words so quickly and efficiently that it felt like they were being blown halfway to North Ireland. He hunched his back and leaned closer to her. "Stay with me, Daisy. You can't die. I love you."

A few minutes later, the rain came – walls of heavy rain that stung when they hit his face and hands - blowing in a straight line, parallel to the earth, from west to east.

He still had to climb the bluffs to get to the top of the cliffs, and he had to do it fast, before the tide rose any further or the waves got any higher. The Wild Atlantic was already lapping at his feet and it was so dark he had to struggle to see where the rocks were. The path he'd taken down to the shore should be close, but he could see no break in the rocks, or even the tufts of sea grass that grew out of the bluffs.

"Lord, help me find a way!" His words were snatched away by the wind as soon as he uttered them. But he had to try. If ever there was a time when divine intervention was needed, it was now. Cursed gold be damned. Their lives were at stake.

The wind died down for a mere second and the sea calmed with it – he recognized the cadence well and knew exactly what it foretold. In a few seconds, a wave larger and stronger than all the others would come crashing onto the shoreline. The proverbial calm before the storm, except in this instance, it was no comforting bit of wisdom, but a threat – a crushing realization.

He tightened his grip on Daisy and fumbled to find a foothold where he could stand strong against the surge.

The wind rumbled with silent laughter, mocking him, assuming the waves had already won.

Was that his father's voice calling through the gale? As far as he knew, his da's yacht was docked in Belfast, as far away from Dingle as a person could get and still be in Ireland. A wave slammed into his thighs and almost knocked him over.

"You can try all you like, son, but you'll never be strong enough to hold onto her and keep your footing, too. Let go of her so you can scramble to high ground. Save yerself!" He tried his best to shut his father's negative, self-centered perspective out of his head. He'd been but a wee lad when his father left him and his mother for his true love, Mistress Money, but evidently some damage had already been done. Or was it in his genes? The rest of the Donaghue men from whom he came were known for their gallantry, their bravery, their heroism.

"Which is why they're all dead!" His father's cynical voice mocked him.

He tried to find a foothold on the rocky beach and started to slip. The waves were sucking the sand out from under him. He was going down. He struggled to hold on to Daisy.

And then, he heard a voice that he somehow knew belonged to his great-grandda. "Two steps to the left, lad, and ye'll find yer path." How was this possible? His great-grandda had been lost at sea long before he'd even been born. How could he possibly know that this was the illustrious Captain Scully Donaghue speaking to him?

"There. Now climb, and fast like. Lickety-split. Up ye go. I know she's heavy, but ye need to get a move on. Now!"

He scrambled half way up the slope, clutching Daisy to his chest and readjusting his inner fulcrum with each step to keep from tumbling backwards into the sea.

He both heard and felt the crash of the rogue wave as it sucked the sand from the shore and pounded into the bluff. He felt the rumble of the earth, and the froth lapping at his heals, and icy claws of water reaching out for them. But he was safe! They were safe! A faint light appeared in the distance, just enough to light the pathway to the shanty. They were saved! By God's grace, and possibly a wee bit of assistance from his great-grandda, they were saved!

#

Daisy opened her eyes and looked upward to all white. Had she died and gone to heaven? And if so, would they let her stay? She was certainly guilty of the sin of greed, among many others infractions too numerous to recount. Not only had she not been to confession in years, she was suspected of murdering a priest. Certainly God knew she hadn't done it, but what if word of her innocence had not yet filtered up to the keeper of heaven's gates?

She tried to sit up, intent on defending herself, but fell back into a prone position on whatever she was lying on. It was too hard to be a cloud.

"Oh, thank God, she's coming around."

Silence.

Someone squeezed her hand. "As long as she's awake, can I ask her a few questions?"

Cavan? What was he doing here? Oh, no! Had they both died and gone to the great ever after? Cavan would certainly be allowed through the pearly gates. Such a good man, and she knew he was acquainted with Jesus because they'd gone to Joy Club together when they were wee ones. She was so sad he was gone. He would have made such a wonderful da, such a brilliant husband, such a superb lover, such a...

"Daisy? Can you hear me?" A voice she didn't recognize spoke to her from what sounded like a million miles away.

She turned her head with great difficulty and moaned as pain shot from her shoulder to her head. She saw a series of monitors with colorful, other-worldly lights like she used to see when she watched Star Trek reruns, back in the Killarney days, before her telly had been repossessed. She could almost imagine herself on the bridge of the Starship Enterprise. The colorful lights pulsed, and the room started to spin. She felt so bad she'd probably be in the sick bay instead of at Captain Jean-Luc Picard's side where she belonged.

A nurse looked down at her clipboard and up at the fancy lights. "I think that would be fine as long as she doesn't get too tired out."

Maybe she was in the sick bay. Cavan leaned over her and squeezed her hand. Cavan? He did look a little like Jean-Luc, but with hair. She felt a wave of dizziness, then nausea. One or both of them smelled like wet wool and the fisherman's warf at low tide.

"I'm so glad you're okay."

Wet wool. "Oh, no! My tartan! My cape! It's to be dry-cleaned only and I think I had it on last night when..." her memory went blank on her.

"Calm down, Daisy. You're fine. We can get you another tartan. The only thing that matters is that you're alright. I can't even think about what might have happened if I'd waited any longer before I came looking for you."

"Me either." She gulped. But she thought, looking for me? Where was I? Her throat felt like it was severely dry and chapped, like she'd gargled a bucket of salt water and forgotten to spit it out.

A burst of light and the rumble of nearby thunder sent vibrations through her already sore body. The sound of clattering glass and rattling windows echoed like a badly balanced stereo in her head.

"What happened out there, Daisy? Was Aodhan with you when this happened?"

"Aodhan?" She began to shake her head "no" but the room started going in circles again.

"Are you okay?"

She must look pretty bad judging by the look on Cavan's face.

"Give me a minute. The room started swimming again."

Cavan turned a little green.

Probably a bad choice of words.

Cavan rubbed her arm. "Was Aodhan with you down by the sea?"

"Why would Aodhan have been with me?"

"You tell me. Maybe because you had things to talk about. Maybe because you needed a little privacy to tell him, um, what's been going on with you."

Her head cleared, except that it didn't. Not really. "I have no idea. What are you talking about? Before you and I saw Aodhan, I hadn't been in touch with him for weeks. And in case you didn't notice, things didn't go all that well when we saw him the other day."

"You were calling out to him."

"What?"

"When you were floating out to sea. You were calling his name."

"I was?" Her head throbbed. "I was floating out to sea?"

"Partial amnesia," the nurse said, and scribbled something on her clipboard. "Probably just temporary. Try not to rush her or lead her to draw conclusions she may not be ready to hear."

"I'm sorry, Daisy. I just want to find out what happened to you. And if Aodhan is responsible."

"I don't know. I remember being on the beach. I just don't remember seeing Aodhan. But I did just see him. And from all accounts, I was probably half delirious. Who knows what was going through my head."

"Well, it's just if he was there when you fell, and didn't try to save you, or call for help, or if he was the one who pushed you, then..."

"Aodhan wouldn't do anything like that! I know he and I split ways, but he would never do anything to hurt me."

Cavan's face looked stormier than a northwester brewing out on the ocean.

The nurse was scowling, too. "I think that's enough questions for now."

#

Cavan left Daisy's side for the first time since he'd checked her in to hospital and found Daisy's nurse. Flashes of lightning lit the night sky and made eerie shadows around the dimly lit station.

"You must be exhausted, Mr. Donaghue," the nurse said. "I've been listening to the news and I must say, it's an absolute miracle that you were able to rescue Miss Fitzpatrick from the ocean with this storm moving in. It's a doozey all right. I can only imagine how high the waves must be and the damage it's doing to the beach. Of course, the silver lining is that high tides always leave all sorts of treasures behind."

Cavan's mind drifted to the gold for a second. Maybe it would finally be unearthed. Of course, there was nothing he could do about it anyway. Not until daybreak – more importantly, not until Daisy was well.

While the nurse rambled on about the probable aftereffects of the storm, his thoughts went back to Daisy. He'd give anything to know what had happened to her. Her memories might be a jumble now, but his gut told him that she'd been of sound mind when she called out Aodhan's name, and that Aodhan was somehow mixed up in all of this. Why else would he have been at the beach or trying to get away in such a hurry?

He turned to the nurse. "Could I please speak to a doctor?"

"The doctor should be coming up from emergency to check on his patients as soon as he has a break. If you'd like to leave me your mobile number, I can have him page you when he arrives."

"I just need to make sure that the doctor is informed that Daisy is pregnant. I never got a chance to say anything in the ER. Daisy may not mention it herself. She's not told anyone officially, probably because the father of the baby dumped her. She's also afraid of incurring a big hospital bill. If you can just tell the doctor for now, I promise you I'll make sure she starts coming in to the clinic for regular prenatal care just as soon as things settle down. I just don't want the doctor to do any x-rays or anything that might harm the baby."

The nurse's eyes stretched wide. "Do you know how far along she is?"

"All I know is that she's expecting. I'm not the father, but I know who is, and for now, I don't want him involved. It's possible he's the one responsible for her injuries."

The nurse's eyes widened and looked up at him with both shock and sympathy.

He hated having to butt into Daisy's private business, but what choice did he have? "If the doctor could just check her out, and be careful not to do any procedures that will harm the baby, it would be much appreciated."

#

What on God's green earth was Cavan blathering on about now? Was the man daft?

Daisy knew she had a concussion. She'd heard them say that, too. So she was a little out of it, and a few of her memories seemed fuzzy. But surely she'd remember getting pregnant, wouldn't she? Was she really so far gone that she didn't remember having sex? Lord, she hoped not. She'd been looking forward to it for a long time and she'd feel awful if she hadn't even gotten to enjoy her first time.

She tried to still her thoughts so she could hear what Cavan and the doctors were talking about.

A deep voice that she didn't recognize said, "Are you sure she was pregnant?"

Cavan hesitated and then said, "As sure as I can be. My source was reliable as far as I know."

"I've double and triple checked her blood work. My guess is that she never was. If she was – and I've found no evidence of that – then it appears she's lost the baby."

Cavan made a frustrated noise. "If she miscarried because of what Aodhan put her through tonight–"

Aodhan? What was Cavan talking about? She couldn't quite put two and two together, but she did not remember having sex with Aodhan – or anyone else. How could she be preggers when she was still a virgin? The more she tried to remember, the more her head hurt. She felt sure she and Aodhan hadn't had sex. Or had they? They might have gotten close. She remembered kissing him, and some groping going on, and that they had been drinking, probably pretty heavily, at least on one occasion. Had something happened that she'd been too drunk to remember? She certainly hoped not. She didn't remember ever drinking so much that she'd blacked out.

She could still hear voices but they were growing faint. The room was swimming again, and she felt sleepy. A few minutes later she was back in la la land, dreaming of her babies. Such cuties. The wee lad looked just like Cavan except that he had her button nose. The lass was the spitting image of Granny. And they both loved to snuggle, just like their daddy.

27

Aodhan crept around the corner of the tiny, ramshackle shed where he'd hidden his car away and scanned the horizon surrounding Father O'Leary's shanty to make sure no one was watching. He reached above the window frame to the right and around the corner from the entrance and ran his hand through the drift of sand topping the window until he felt a key.

It wasn't the first time he'd used the key to gain entry to the old shanty. The police had assumed the Good Father had left his door unlocked the night he'd been killed, trusting soul that he was. A glowing ember of pride sizzled in his stomach. The police hadn't found the key after they'd discovered the body – probably hadn't even looked. Not that they'd had much to go on. That was the good thing about the wind that raked the Wild Atlantic Way – it was great at covering tracks. For that very reason, he'd made sure to come to see his uncle on a windy night.

He slipped into the sea shanty and closed the door. Now that he knew where Daisy's granny's gold was stashed, he wasn't going anywhere until he'd secured at least some of the gold bars. He didn't especially relish the thought of spending the night in the priest's old haunts, but he wanted to be able to get up at daybreak and begin his search first thing in the morning – before the police started combing the area for signs of Daisy.

He made sure all the curtains were pulled shut and then dusted off the kitchen table to the left of the fireplace, taking care to avoid the stain in the rug where the priest's blood and whatever other bodily fluids had leaked out of him when he died. Messy business, death was, and not something he relished being a participant in. Sometimes, a person needed to stand up for what was right and do what needed to be done.

He tried to think of all the contingencies that could occur to make sure there were no flaws in his plan. If for some reason he wasn't successful in recovering the gold in the morning, he'd have to wait a good long time before it would be safe to approach the beach to retrieve it. If Daisy's body had been washed out to sea and devoured by the local sea life as he hoped, she'd eventually be listed as a missing person and any searches would be called off. But that could take weeks. If the tide washed her body back on shore, a full scale investigation would be launched and he wouldn't dare be found anywhere in the vicinity.

If he was going to recover the gold, it had to be tomorrow at first light. Anything after that and all bets were off. The police would very likely find the gold if they were combing the beach for evidence, assuming the pirate, Darcie whatever his name was, or Daisy's little lap dog, Cavan - didn't discover it first. No, he had to stay close by and make his move first thing in the morning.

He was still shook up about what had happened to Daisy. Thank goodness his head had been on straight enough to think to drive back to Killarney and fill his car with gas after he'd left her. He'd even gone in the kiosk to pay, and made sure to have a memorable conversation with the clerk. He'd mentioned that he'd just returned from a festival that was being held at Blarney Castle, to the north and east of Killarney. After he'd left the gas station, he'd popped his head into a pub, where he'd had a pint and chatted with several people, where again, he talked at length about being at the festival in the rose garden at Blarney Castle. Only then had he driven back to Dingle and very discreetly driven to his uncle's shanty.

He looked around at the four, bare, whitewashed walls that were closing him in. Stupid priest. What was the point of having a secret hideaway if you had no telly, no radio, and no internet? He hated not having anything to distract him from his thoughts.

What if Daisy had survived by some chance miracle? It made it all the more imperative that he get to the gold before she did. And if she tried to tell anyone that he was with her on the beach when she had her accident, or that he'd left her to die, he would say she was clearly delusional and just thinking of him because he'd seen her the day before.

Everything that had happened at the beach was a blur. Daisy had called out to him numerous times as he'd run from the place she'd fallen. If she hadn't been so whiny, he would have stayed long enough to make sure he'd found the gold, that the metal detector hadn't responded to a lost belt buckle or an old iron anchor washed ashore in a storm. Now, he had to wait until morning to find out.

One other thing kept niggling at his brain. For a second, when he'd been barreling away from the beach, on the dirt path that led back to the blacktop, he'd thought he'd seen a car. The sun had been in his eyes, and the car certainly hadn't been in the middle of the one track road. If it had been, they'd have collided head on. But there might have been a vehicle tucked into a passing place at some point. He'd seen the glint of a mirror. Or had it been the sun reflecting off a bird, a leaf, or one of the seaside daisies that grew on the beach.

It made him all the more glad he'd gone back to Killarney to fabricate an alibi. If there had been an auto, it was probably just some goers by in a car hire. If anyone claimed to have seen him, he'd say they were misguided and point out how low the sun was at that time of day. Even if they pointed out that it had been mostly cloudy at the time, no one would be able to prove anything. The weather conditions on the Wild Atlantic Way varied by the second.

He was getting tired. It had been a very eventful day after all. Aodhan used the flashlight on his mobile to illuminate the bed where the priest had lain when he died and found a splatter of dried blood. He kicked at the raveled edge of the rag rug. It reeked of urine. The old man had probably peed himself when he realized he was going to die.

He looked around the room and opted to try to get some rest in the old, wood rocking chair in the opposite corner of the room. If he could fall asleep sitting up in front of his computer screen, he could certainly doze off in the rocker.

He slept fitfully for what seemed like a few minutes, but when he awoke, he saw that it had been over an hour. What the hell was going on? The roar of the wind and the waves crashing against the rocks was louder than being on the underbelly of a jet plane on take-off. The storm pounded the shanty's thick walls with a rage he'd rarely experienced. His father's temper had always had a sharp edge, but this was different. He'd never been so close to the open ocean during a storm. The whole shanty shook and quivered with every thrust of the wind. Great strikes of lightning danced against the walls. Rumbles of thunder punctuated the roar of the ocean.

When he finally managed to doze off once again, he had a nightmare. The priest was in his pulpit, high above the ground, preaching hellfire and damnation to those guilty of breaking the Ten Commandments. Thou shalt not kill. Thou shalt not kill. Thou shalt not covet anything that is thy neighbor's. Thou shalt not steal. Thou shalt not bear false witness against thy neighbor. Thou shalt not kill. Bolts of lightning shot out from the priest's eyes. He held a scythe in his hands. He was using it to cut down the wicked. He woke up in a cold sweat to see sunshine streaming through the window.

Damn! What time was it? He glanced at his mobile. Nine in the morning – and his battery was almost dead.

No! He peered out the window to make sure he was alone and found a regular traffic jam down on the beach. He'd heard local artists and collectors of sea glass, driftwood, shells, and rocks talk about the prizes to be found after a good, rousing, Wild Atlantic Way storm.

Now what was he supposed to do? He could hardly go strutting along the beach as long as all these people were here. Despite his best efforts to cover his tracks by staging appearances in Killarney, he didn't want anyone to report seeing him coming out of the priest's shanty, especially not now, when the police were bound to be investigating Daisy's accident. He just hoped one of these goers by hadn't found his treasure chest of gold.

He continued to alternately pace the packed dirt and slate floor and survey the foot traffic outside the shanty. When more than an hour had passed, he decided it was now or never. He had to secure the gold and get far, far away from the area before the police arrived, or worse yet, found his hiding place.

He peeked out the deep window of the sod shanty one last time and didn't see anyone coming. He waited a few minutes more, checked again, and then stepped outside, looking in both directions to make sure no one saw him.

Stupid tourists. Both Daisy's land and his uncle's were private property. Whoever came up with the idea that the beachfront rimming the Wild Atlantic way had to be open to hikers and bicycles where there was a path was crazy. What good was property ownership if the government could order you to share your land with every random person who wanted to do a little sightseeing? And it wasn't just your neighbors either. People from all over the world came to hike the Wild Atlantic Way. It was idiotic, that's what it was. They were off their heads down in Dublin, pure and simple.

He made another quick scan of the horizon to make sure he didn't have company. The air was clean and crisp and the sky was blue, the complete opposite of the heavy air and oppressive humidity of the night before. He hadn't seen or felt such a thing – the feel of the air both before and after the storm – since he was a lad. He loved his life in the city, but he supposed there was something to be said about being in communion with the earth. Daisy had known what it meant to commune with the land. She'd never fit the Killarney mold. Sure, people had included her and even fawned over her when she'd first moved to town, but it was because of the gold and the novelty of her situation. She was new money to their old. They might have been temporarily fascinated by her, but she would never have fit in. She'd been the latest fad. Even if she hadn't lost the gold, she'd have been old news in no time.

He crept around the edge of the priest's shanty and looked down the beach in either direction, then scanned the sand bluffs and the rippling waves of sea grass behind him. He was alone. Now that everyone was finally gone from the beach, he could find his way back to the sea cave and recover at least some of the gold.

Anger seeped into his bones as he skulked his way toward Daisy's land. If his stupid excuse for an uncle hadn't cut him out of his will and decided to give all of his money to the charities, he would already have the gold that rightfully belonged to the O'Leary family. Nor would he be in the position of having to search for more. All he wanted was enough gold for he and his father to get back on their feet after his father's embezzlement scheme failed. Was that so much to ask? With the price of gold what it was, there would have been plenty to cover he and his father's needs and fund a few charities as well.

He stopped and tried to get his bearings. For some reason, the beach looked different. Where was he? Had he taken a wrong turn, or was he just rattled because he was nearing the spot where he'd left Daisy to die?

He hated that he'd had to leave Daisy to drown, but what happened had been her own fault. If she hadn't been so clingy, she'd still be alive. Not only had she refused to leave him alone long enough to do what he needed to do, he felt sure she had been trying to scam him. She'd done her best to steer him in the opposite direction from any of the sea caves where the gold might have been hidden.

He'd almost lost it when the metal detector had started dinging. What was he supposed to have done? Let Daisy ruin everything he'd worked so hard to accomplish? There was no way he was going to move out of his father's mansion in Killarney and get some menial nine to five job just because his dad had been stupid enough to get caught siphoning off money from his company.

28

Cavan was sitting by Daisy's bedside when she woke up again. He watched as she slowly opened her eyes. Relief poured through his body.

"Where am I?"

"You're in hospital." He didn't try to remind her about their conversation when she'd first arrived. If she didn't remember she was in hospital, she most likely didn't remember what they'd talked about. Now that he knew better, he didn't want to say anything about pulling her out of the ocean in a lightning storm. He didn't want to guide her memories. The doctor had advised him to say as little about what had happened in hopes that she would remember on her own.

"What time is it?"

"It's six o'clock."

"In the morning, or at night?"

"Night." He'd give her that. This time of year, it was daylight at four in the morning and the sun didn't set until ten at night give or take a bit.

"Why aren't you at the bike shop?"

"Rory's been taking over for me at day's end and closing up so I can be with you."

She got a funny look on her face. "How long have I been here?"

"You've been in and out of it for more than a day."

"You're joking."

"No. You had a pretty bad concussion. The doctor said it

would take some time to get you back to normal."

"What happened to me?"

He smiled and spoke in his most gentle voice. "You tell me. What do you remember?"

Her face took on a faraway look. "I was looking for the gold. Granny was with me. And a man. I think he was a sea captain." Her expression turned from mystified to excited. "They told me where the gold is hidden!"

He smiled. He didn't know what to say. She'd probably dreamed the whole thing. Unless the same ghost who had been whispering in his ear had spoken to her, too. At this point, he couldn't rule out anything.

"You do believe me, don't you?" She looked crestfallen.

"I'm very happy that the pieces are starting to come together. Tell me what else you remember."

"I think there was someone else there. Maybe not at the beginning, but at the end." She looked up at him. "Was it you?"

He hesitated. "I came just as it was getting dark and brought you here, but I wasn't there when you were looking for the gold. Could it have been someone else?"

She looked thoughtful. "I'm sure it was. But I can't remember who it was or why they were there. Darcie's still in jail, and you said it wasn't you. Who else could it be?" She shrugged and then grimaced, like the motion had hurt her. "Maybe some trekkers who veered off the beaten path?"

"Could be," he said, weighing his words. "Anyone else coming to mind?"

Her face lit up like she'd had a true a-ha moment. "I remember being in hospital and hearing someone talking about me being preggers." Her face fell from excited to confused.

She paused, and he held his breath. He could almost feel her brain sorting through the files in each recess of her mind.

She looked up at him, her eyes wide and mystified. "I think it was you. But I can't for the life of me imagine how you would get such an idea into your head."

It was time to come clean.

"I heard it from the bartender at the pub Rory goes to – a woman I know named Mandy heard it from a friend who heard it directly from your Great Aunts Ailene and Sheelagh."

"Oh, good grief." Daisy huffed and then winced. "Not them

again."

By this time, he knew full well Daisy wasn't preggers, but he still wanted to let her tell the story. Maybe it would jiggle something loose from her memories of Aodhan if she thought back on the times they'd been intimate. A wave of discomfort passed through his core just thinking about the two of them together.

"Who would have gotten me preggers? I haven't had sex with you, although the old biddies are probably up to their ears imagining the wild times we're having up in my apartment."

"My apartment." He frowned.

"Whose apartment it is isn't the point." She huffed again. "The point is, I haven't had sex with you or anyone else, so how could I be preggers? This is all because they started snooping into my business when I saw them at the grocery. I should have denied it all, but I didn't feel the need to participate in their meddling poppycock. So I let them think what they would."

She looked like she was about to cry. "It makes no difference to me what they think of me." She started to sniffle. "I – I never thought word would get back to you, or that you'd believe such nonsense. I mean, you know me better than that, don't you? I mean, who did you think I was shagging anyway?"

Her face blanched, and his fell. Neither of them said a word.

"You thought I was pregnant with Aodhan's baby."

"Well, you were dating."

Her face turned stony. "And you assumed I was sleeping with him. You're as bad as my aunties."

"I'm sorry, Daisy. I suppose it's none of my business either, but sadly, when word got around town that you were preggers, people assumed I was the father, and that does affect me."

She didn't say anything and refused to meet his glance.

He shuffled his feet and finally found the courage to speak. "I understand that you don't like it when your aunts meddle in your business, but next time... I guess I don't understand why, if you knew you hadn't had sex with anyone, you didn't deny it when they first said something."

"Because they would have twisted it around to like, 'Figures. What man would want Daisy?' And because even though I say I don't care what people think of me, I must care a little because I really don't want people thinking there's something wrong with me."

"I understand."

"I just never met the right man, and I want it to be special, and I don't need people talking about my private life behind my back, and when they do, I don't want to glorify their behavior or even to give them one iota of information that they can use against me." She stopped on a dime. "My head hurts."

"Oh, Daisy." He wanted to hug her but he didn't know what she would do. "I'll call the nurse." He stood and pressed the call button.

The nurse came a few minutes later, took her blood pressure and adjusted the pillows behind her head. "We can be thankful there's still no sign of infection. The sea water used to be so clear and clean, but it's the 21st century. Depending on the currents, it can be full of nasty toxins now. You must have a strong immune system."

Cavan stood at her bedside for several minutes after the nurse left. She still had her eyes closed when he knelt beside her bed and took her hand.

"Anything else you want to talk about, Daisy?"

She sniffled again. "I've been thinking."

"Yes?"

"There's something about Aodhan that I need to tell you about, but I can't remember what it is."

His emotions surged up and then crashed down again. "Um, I'm sure it will come to you. Just try to relax and let things float to the surface."

"Poor choice of words." Daisy rolled her eyes and then looked like she was about to puke.

"Yeah. Sorry about that."

"Maybe if you leave for awhile, I could get some rest."

"Okay. If you're sure you want me to-"

"I'm sure." She tried to smile and winced. "See you later, Alligator."

He really didn't want to go. But then, it wasn't up to him. "After while, Crocodile."

#

Aodhan looked to the north and then to the south. Or was it the east and west? The only way he could even be sure about what direction he was headed was that the beach was to his left. The storm had changed the landscape of the shore so much that he couldn't spot a single familiar feature.

How could the wind and the waves have done this much damage, and so quickly? He felt sure that the beach he was on had been completely covered with a colorful mixture of smooth, penny-sized pebbles. Now, jagged, sharp-edged, ten to twelve centimeter rocks – quartzite, orange granite, dolerite, sandstone, schist and an occasional chunk of basalt – lay in piles, dotting the smooth sand in an abstract design.

What if the storm had buried the gold under thousands of tons of rock, or worse yet, washed it out to sea? How would he ever find it when the very lay of the land had changed so much that he didn't recognize anything?

His hands started to shake. He knew the police would show up sooner or later, looking for Daisy – unless they'd already found her body? That was the only thing he could think of to explain their absence. Either way, he didn't dare bring out his metal detector, at least until dusk.

A chill ran down his spine at the thought of the sea gods conspiring to keep the gold from him, to hide it until a more worthy recipient came along. Or maybe it wasn't Neptune or Poseidon playing with him at all! Could it be the one true God, the real God, punishing him for taking one of his own flock? He shuddered, then started to shake so hard that he didn't see the teenaged boy coming around the corner until they ran into each other head on.

"Sorry to startle you, sir."

The lad had something shiny in his hand.

"No worries," Aodhan said. "I'm just looking for a gold coin I seem to have lost last night. Don't know why I'm so attached to it – it's not real gold, of course, just a lucky charm sort of thing. My mother gave it to me just before she died, and I always keep it in my pocket, no matter where I am."

The lad looked like he was moved, yet a skeptical expression lingered on his face.

Aodhan smiled. "I'm down here because of the storm. I'm an artist. First thing after a high tide, I come looking for sea glass to use in my jewelry creations."

The lad's face relaxed. He hesitated. "Is this it? I found it a few minutes ago in a pile of sea weed. Awful high tide last night. It's a miracle it was washed back ashore. You did say you lost it last night, correct?"

Had he said last night? He thought he'd said this morning. Was the lad trying to trip him up? He couldn't have him going home and blabbing to his parents or his girlfriend about the gold coins he'd found or the man who'd claimed he'd lost it last night. Why hadn't he put on a costume before he'd gone beachcombing? Was he going to have to kill the boy to keep him from identifying him as a suspect in Daisy's murder?

But then, no one would have any reason to suspect Daisy had been murdered. Still, it wouldn't do for anyone to know Aodhan had been with her the same night she died. Suspicions could arise, which could link him to the priest.

The lad opened his fingers and the light shone on the gold coin lying on his open palm. A token from Token. Token was a new retro-arcade restaurant, bar, pinball parlour, movie theater – Dublin's slickest hangout spot. They'd devised a 'token' system whereby patrons could gain entry instead of having to pay a cover charge. Fake gold – a useless piece of junk.

"Thanks, but that's not it." A shame the lad had to die because of a useless piece of rubbish. The two people he'd already killed weighed heavily enough on his mind without adding another to the list.

Daisy's friend, Cavan, was another loose cannon. Cavan knew Aodhan had been down to the sea, and recently. Cavan would be hot on the trail to finding out what had happened to Daisy. It was all too risky. When would it end?

He bent down and picked up a rock. The lad's eyes followed his hand down to the sand and back up again.

"Hey, Charlie! You ready to go?" A dark-haired lad, another teenager, clamored over the rock face of a sea bluff, dropped down to the sand, and started walking toward them.

"Sure. Let's get out of here." The boys took off running. There was no way he could have caught up with them even if he'd wanted to. And he hadn't wanted to. It was one thing to kill an old man who had lived out his life, or almost, who was a self-proclaimed hermit, who had no children who depended on him, no wife to mourn him, who was almost certain to go to heaven. All he'd done was send the priest to a better place. Sure, he'd jumped the gun and sent him off a little ahead of schedule, but not by much.

Daisy had been more difficult. He couldn't think about that without feeling some regret. But he'd done what he had to do. He had no desire to do it again.

All he could do was hope the boys didn't say anything to anyone about a suspicious gent poking around the shoreline looking for gold. All he knew was that he had to get a move on, find the gold, and get out of the vicinity of the priest's and Daisy's shanties, fast.

He took another look around. Nothing looked right! He wandered further to the west, keeping close to the outcroppings of rocks so he could duck behind them if he saw someone coming.

Was that the spot? He approached a sea cave that looked slightly familiar, crouched down and rooted around in the sand at the base of the opening. It was packed full. If the gold were there, it would take hours, and probably some heavy equipment, to free it from its tomb.

This was madness! He'd worked so hard to find the gold and now this! If Daisy hadn't intercepted him the night before when he'd been free to use his metal detector, he'd have been able to recover at least some of the gold before the storm hit. He thought about going back to the priest's shanty and getting the metal detector, but even with it in hand, he wouldn't know where to start. It would take hours of combing the area to find the spot now that all the familiar points of reference were washed away.

If only Daisy weren't dead. She knew the area much better than he. He could force her to help him – to retrace their steps from the night before. He should have thought of that before he left her to die. But then, he'd had no idea the storm was coming, or that it was even possible for a storm to do this much damage. It was as though half the beach had eroded away or been picked up by the waves and redistributed elsewhere.

He was just going to have to lay low until Daisy's body was discovered and her death ruled accidental. At least the timing of the storm would lend credibility to her drowning.

29

Cavan stood beside Daisy's hospital bed and listened as she tried to convince him that she shouldn't be in hospital.

"I need to get out of here, Cavan. I don't understand why the doctors won't release me. I've never felt better! I have to get back to the sea shanty and look for the gold before someone else finds it."

Someone else. Chances were, Aodhan had already found the gold and transported it to a place where no one would find it. Why couldn't she see Aodhan for who he really was? The man had almost killed her to get at the gold.

"I'm sorry, Daisy, but as I've told you over and over again, I trust the doctor's opinion and I'm going to continue to follow his advice. I'm sure he'll sign your release papers in a day or two just like he promised – maybe even sooner."

"Fine. If you're not going to help me, I'll call Aodhan and ask him to take me." She fumbled around for her phone. "Where is my purse?"

"I brought it to hospital last night and put it in the closet, just like you asked me to." Her phone was in clear sight, within easy reach on the tray just beside her bed but he wasn't going to tell her.

He sighed and looked out the window. He knew Daisy had a concussion, but honestly, it was just sad the way she refused to admit that Aodhan had anything to do with landing her in hospital. The man had almost killed her, probably intentionally, yet she still seemed to think he was going to help her find the gold. Right. The only thing her wonderful ex-boyfriend was going to help her find was another concussion, this one very probably fatal. He looked at Daisy and wanted to pound his fist into Aodhan's gut. He'd tried to help Daisy see that Aodhan was not her friend, but she seemed to think he was some sort of big hero who was going to come to her rescue and save the day.

She was lying back on her pillow with her eyes closed. He moved a few inches and she opened them.

"So tell me this, Daisy. Who do you think is responsible for this whole mess – a dead priest, and you, left for dead?"

She didn't even hesitate. "Do you need to ask? We both know it's Darcie Sneem. He's the great-great grandson of the pirate who stole the gold in the first place. We both know that Darcie believes the gold is his since he's the only living descendant. I think Darcie stalked the priest until he figured out where he had the gold hidden, then ditched the priest and went looking for it, only to find out it was already gone. Of course, the priest had no idea I had found the gold and taken it. When he refused to tell Darcie where the gold had been taken, Darcie killed him. Now, he's after me. After he lost the quilt, he probably intended to torture me until I told him where the gold was. Except, I don't know!"

"But Darcie's in jail."

Daisy's shoulders stiffened. "He's out."

"Who told you that? The police?"

"No." She shuddered. "I just know, okay?"

"Fine." The doctor had urged him to humor Daisy until she got her memory back, but this was ridiculous. "I'll call the police station right now." Why have Daisy worrying about something that wasn't even possible? Why not reassure her that he was right, and that there was no way Darcie was responsible for what had happened to her? Maybe then, she would start to accept that Aodhan was the one who had tried to kill her, or at least, left her for dead.

He grabbed his mobile and dialed the station. "I'm looking for Darcie Sneem. Can you please tell me if he's still in custody?" He tried to wipe the I-told-you-so look from his face. He knew Daisy wasn't trying to be irritating. She just-

"Is this Cavan Donaghue?"

"Yes."

"Thank goodness you called. Um, I'm sorry to have to tell you this but Darcie was released two days ago. I walked over to the bike shop to tell you myself, but you weren't there and when I tried to call, it always went right to voicemail."

Cavan turned and looked at Daisy, his hand still holding his mobile. How could she have known? Could Darcie really have been down at the sea caves the night when Daisy almost drowned?

He swallowed hard and ended the call. He didn't know what to tell Daisy. Her eyes were half closed – a good thing. He doubted he could have straight out lied to her, even by omission, if she'd been looking right at him.

He took her hand and whispered, "I promise you I'll get to the bottom of this, Daisy. But you have to give me your word that you'll listen to the doctors and stay here until they say it's safe for you to go."

"I will. I promise."

He kissed her on the forehead and clasped her hand for a minute. When he left, she was so drowsy she didn't even stir.

#

Aodhan leaned back on his haunches to stand. A gentle breeze tickled the hairs on his forehead. He actually hoped the wind would pick up enough to cover the tracks his E-PACE would leave when he pulled it out of the shed at the priest's shanty and left for Killarney.

He rocked on his heels and let his knees bounce once or twice to get enough momentum to stand in the shifting sand. The sand was still wet. His shoes lost their grip and he started to slide.

"What the-?" Something slammed into his back so hard that it knocked the breath out of him.

He twisted around and used his feet to push back with as much force as he could muster. If he hadn't known better, he'd have thought he was caught on the set of Pirates of Caribbean. A swarthy character with numerous tattoos, an eye patch and a scruffy black scarf tied around his head was pummeling him with his fists.

Were there pirates in Star Wars? A recent episode had been filmed nearby – maybe they were doing a scene for the next installment. The beach did have an alien, other-worldly appearance to it – especially after the storm.

Had an actor mistaken him for an extra? His mind whirled in a million directions. Who was this man? An avenging angel? What was going on?

"That gold is mine!" The pirate cursed and attempted to kick him in the gonads. His heavy-soled boots slammed into his inner thigh. Too close for his tastes.

Aodhan backed up like a crab, drew his legs back, and slammed his shoes into the pirate's legs. The buccaneer was thin and scrawny, but strong. Whoever he was and whatever he was up to, the guy meant business. And, it would seem they shared something in common. The gold.

The pirate groaned, lurched toward him and grabbed for his balls. What was with this man? Slam. Crunch. Duck. Roll. The pirate was down. Now on level ground, Aodhan found he had the upper hand. He had weight, height, and bulk in his favor. He said a silent thank you to the rugby coach he'd had as a youth and shifted enough to grab a loose rock that was jabbing his back. With every ounce of strength he had in him, he drove the rock into the pirate. The man was moving so fast it did little good to aim. He hoped the pure force of the impact would down the man no matter where he hit him.

Success! The pirate crumpled to the ground, overpowered at last.

He looked around to make sure there had been no witnesses to the scene and took off running toward the priest's shanty. Good lord. What next?

#

Cavan picked up his step as much as he could walking on sand. The beach was still mostly wet from last night's storm, but the wind was already drying out the surface. He could feel the loose sand shifting and sliding under his feet, sucking up his momentum and making his heart pump with exertion.

He slowed as he neared the sea caves even though the sand around the protruding rocks was freshly packed. He didn't know what he thought he would find – if he were lucky, some sign of the gold, or any sort of proof that Aodhan had been here last night. Any clues that would testify to the fact that Aodhan had tried to kill Daisy would have been washed away. If it had been Aodhan. The fact that Darcie had been released from his jail cell changed everything. He wouldn't put it past either of them to try to hurt Daisy to get at the gold. One thing was certain, after a storm of this magnitude, the gold would likely either be exposed, or buried under tons of rock and sand brought in by the waves.

He picked his way between two large boulders and shimmied down a hill. If he'd truly believed the gold had been exposed as a result of the storm, he should have been here yesterday at daybreak, but he'd had more important things on his mind. Even today, when he could have gone, he'd waited at hospital in hopes that Daisy might be released.

Daisy was chomping at the bit to get out and the nurses had told them the doctor made his rounds during the late morning. Cavan would have liked to have heard what he had to say so he could make sure Daisy followed his instructions to the letter.

When they'd heard the sirens wailing and a helicopter landing, they hadn't been surprised when they'd been told the doctor would be detained because of an emergency.

He looked up and saw another outcropping of rocks that looked halfway familiar. The storm had changed the nature of the beach so much that it was very disorienting.

"Ouch!" He stopped short and looked down, expecting to see a chunk of driftwood or a rock. Nothing. He looked back at the tracks he'd left getting from his car to his present location. Nothing. He looked from side to side and saw no one. But something had hit him in the shins. He'd felt something rear up and slap against the front of his leg. It was almost as though someone had kicked him, except that no one was around.

He took a few more steps and felt someone or something pushing him firmly to the left. Either that, or for some reason he was lurching like a drunken sailor. He hadn't had a drink since the last time he'd seen Mandy at the pub.

What was going on? He turned to the right to head down to the shoreline.

"Nay!"

He heard the voice as clear as day. A deep rumble of a voice had definitely told him not to go to the right. At least, that's how he was prone to interpret it since he'd just been shoved to the left. He looked around for someone who might be hiding behind a rock or crouching behind a stand of sea grass. Nothing.

He would happily have gone left if he hadn't been told he

couldn't. But now that the gauntlet had been laid – he looked both directions and ran to the right, rounded the first outcropping of rocks, and almost stepped on Darcie.

"What the heck?"

Darcie moaned. He looked like someone had beat him up. His lip was split and bleeding, his chin was bruised, and his signature man bun a tangled mass of loose, greasy curls.

Cavan wrinkled his nose. And he stank. He didn't want to know like what.

He paused for a few seconds before Darcie moaned again, more loudly this time, and his instincts took over. "Darcie? Are you okay, man?"

No answer. He reached down and nudged the pirate's shoulder.

Darcie grunted and started flailing his arms, then tried to grab hold of Cavan's hair.

"Will you stop it? It's me! Cavan. I'm not the one who did this to you! I'm trying to help you."

"Get off me!" Darcie slashed at his face with his fingers.

"Stand down, blokes. Now." A deep, booming voice echoed off the rocks on either side of them.

Cavan looked up and tried to disengage himself from Darcie, who had latched onto his shirt and was still trying to scratch his eyes out. Thank God, the police were here.

"Help!" Cavan ducked and rolled.

Darcie had a rock in his hand. The only thing that was keeping Cavan from getting his head bashed in was the fact that Darcie was still half out of it. Cavan used an old wrestling move and pinned Darcie down.

"Do ye see what he's up to?" Darcie screamed. "He's trying to kill me!"

"I was trying to help him get up!" Cavan protested. "When I found him, he was out cold, and it looked like someone had beat him up. I was just trying to make sure he was okay. I didn't lay a finger on him except to try to defend myself when he came to and started attacking me."

The deep voice boomed, "I can see what's up all right and I want you to lay off each other right now."

"Look at me," Darcie yelled like a madman. "It was him that did this to me. He beat me up."

"I just got here, you eejit," Cavan said. "Him, not you," he told the policemen. "Darcie's the eejit. I don't even think he knows who I am."

"I know full well who did this to me, and it were you, Cavan." Darcie glared up at him with eyes full of hatred.

"I swear I'm telling the truth." Cavan let go of one of Darcie's arms and tried to wipe the sandy grit from his eyes.

"From what I can see, you're both rabble-rousers. I'm taking you both in."

"Why should I be charged?" Darcie flailed his arms and feet, sending sand flying everywhere. "I'm the victim here and I've done nothing wrong."

"Except hanging around Daisy's property when you know you're not welcome here, and harassing both of us," Cavan shot back.

"It's public land," Darcie said. "I've got as much right to be here as the rest of ye, probably more. If it weren't for my ancestors-"

"Your ancestors were dirty, rotten, thieving-"

"The pirates were the keepers of the land and the commanders of the wind and waves long before your kin came anywhere near the Dingle Peninsula."

"Shut up, both of you!" The deep voice meant business. That much was clear. "I'm taking both of you in. Up! Now! Brush the sand off your pants or you'll be cleaning out my car before I throw you in jail. I don't want to hear another word out of either of you! And you'd better start making up and trying to get along because you're going to be riding in the backseat of the same squad car. Unless you want me to be making funeral arrangements instead of booking you into a cell. Come to think of it, if you kill each other before we get back to Dingle, it's less paperwork all around for me. So have at it."

"But-" Cavan's protest was echoed by Darcie.

Cavan stood, moved as far away from Darcie as he could without making the policeman more perturbed than he already was and started shaking the sand out of his hair, his shirt and jean pockets, and everywhere else it was hiding.

Of all the...

"If you think you're going to get away with this, you've got another think coming," Darcie ranted.

Why on earth was Darcie claiming it was Cavan who had beaten him up when he had to know full well it wasn't? Cavan looked helplessly at the police, Darcie, and then the policeman again. Did Darcie really hate him that much?

Evidently so.

30

Daisy perched on the side of her hospital bed and tried to reach Cavan on his mobile. She'd promised she would ring him the second she was released. The doctor had finally come about a half hour earlier, and she couldn't wait to get home.

She supposed she could start walking, but the hospital was on the complete opposite side of Dingle from her shop. Well, Cavan's shop. The thing was, despite what she'd told Cavan about feeling better than she had in months, she still felt a little woozy. Plus, it bothered her that she was still so foggy on the events that had landed her in the hospital. If someone – probably Darcie – really had tried to hurt her, then she could still be in danger.

She got up and walked to the window. The sun was poking between two clouds that were mushrooming high into the sky. The nurse had told her that more clouds were moving in and another storm was expected sometime later in the day. Walking was sounding less and less like a good idea.

She tried to reach Cavan on the phone one more time but there was still no answer. Where could he be? Should she be worried? He knew she didn't have a car or even her bicycle. It wasn't like him to disappear and leave her in the lurch.

She dug around in her purse until she found a few Euros. She tried Cavan again, and when he still didn't answer, asked the nurse to call her a cab. Where Cavan was keeping himself was a definite concern. And who was minding the shop if Cavan had been spirited off by the fairies?

A half hour later, the cabbie dropped her off at Recycled

Cyclery and she went in from the front to find Rory behind the counter.

"Where's Cavan?" A shiver of fear ran down her spine while she waited for Rory's words.

"He was hoping he'd be back here by the time you were released so he could spare you worrying about him or even getting dragged into the situation, but that ship has obviously sailed."

"What's up now? The only one guilty of dragging people into situations lately has been me, not Cavan, so you'd best tell me what's going on, especially if the current predicament has anything to do with what's been happening."

Rory looked around the room, avoiding her eyes. She got the distinct impression he wanted to disappear into the floorboards.

"Um, Cavan isn't here right now because he, um, went out to the shanty to check on how things fared after the storm."

"Really. He hasn't been picking up his mobile since this morning. Shouldn't he be back by now?"

"Well, he met up with someone he knew on the beach."

She had a quick flash of Cavan walking on the beach, hand in hand, with a beautiful woman from his past, or even this Mandy person. It would make perfect sense that Rory would be covering for them – the girl was some relation to his girlfriend, wasn't she? And then she thought about how devoted Cavan had been, and she knew better. He wouldn't have left her in the lurch no matter how beautiful it was down at the beach or who he had happened upon unless – her heart skipped a beat as realization – or intuition – assaulted her.

"He found Darcie, didn't he? Is he okay? Darcie is a desperate man-" She had to watch her words. She didn't think Cavan would have told Rory about her quilt, or the gold, or even the search for the sea cave it was probably hidden in.

"Now when Cavan lambasts me for telling you, you will say you figured it out on your own, aye?"

"Darcie." She could feel her eyes glazing over with anger. She'd given him a toehold and he'd repaid her with trouble and angst times ten.

"Is Cavan okay?" Just her luck if he'd been in the very hospital she'd just left.

"He's been falsely jailed for beating up Darcie. They took Darcie in, too. All I can say is I hope they're not in the same cell."

"I know Cavan was angry with Darcie, but I can't imagine him beating up anyone."

"Cavan says he found him passed out on the beach and tried to help him up. He said he supposes it's possible that Darcie really believes it was Cavan who gave him his bruises, but he suspects Darcie's only claiming it was him to get Cavan in trouble."

"I'll go over and clear things up for them. You'd think the police would look at who's involved and know that Cavan's innocent."

"No. Cavan specifically said he'll handle this on his own. He didn't even want you to know. And I'm sure he'll be back soon. Why don't you have a rest, and I'll tell him you're upstairs as soon as he walks in the door."

She was a little tired. She knew it would just upset Cavan even more if she showed up at the police station or got herself all worked up. Rory was right. She would go upstairs, have a cuppa and rest for awhile.

"Thanks, Rory. I appreciate you filling in for Cavan so many times this past week."

She trudged up the stairs to her old apartment. She was even more exhausted than she'd thought. She wondered if Cavan had a chance to check on Granny's shanty before he got into it with Darcie. The storm had been awful by the sound of it, and it would be good to check on things to make sure everything was alright. If the storm had broken a window, there could be water damage. The last thing she needed was for Mama Fox to move her family back into the shanty and ruin something else, especially when she'd finally just about gotten rid of the smell.

She thought she had enough energy to get out to the shanty, especially knowing she could rest once she got there. On second thought, she decided to call back the cab driver who'd just let her off. May as well conserve what strength she had in case she found a mess out at the shanty. He'd been so kind as to give her a card with his personal number for future reference.

She placed the call and asked him to pick her up at the back door. She wrote a quick note telling Cavan where she was going, and hoped that Cavan wouldn't mind her taking some coins from his stash of pocket change by the counter. No sense getting Rory more involved than he already was.

The truth was, she wouldn't mind having a look around to see how the beach had fared during the storm. The Wild Atlantic Way could wreak all kinds of havoc on the coastline. A storm was very probably the way the gold had disappeared and remained missing for so many years. The waves could have unearthed the treasure, washed it away, or buried it again for the foreseeable future.

She grabbed a sweater, stuffed a few things in a large fanny pack, and picked up a bottle of water before heading down the back stairs to the alley to meet the cab.

She had just reached the bottom of the stairs when her ear started to throb like someone was digging their fingernails into her lobe and pinching her for all they were worth. Stupid midge bites. She'd probably been a tasty feast for a whole host of midges that night she'd lain unconscious on the beach. And that was just how midge bites worked. Two or three days after you'd been bitten was when they really started to burn. She had some Calamine lotion at Granny's shanty. Hopefully it would help.

And if not – well, she might not like it, but she could deal with a few midge bites. At least she didn't need to worry about being safe now that Darcie was back in jail. Nor would Cavan have any reason to fret now that Darcie was back where he belonged.

#

Granny Siobhan tugged on Daisy's ear with every ounce of strength she had and huffed when Daisy tried to swat her away – again.

What was it going to take to get through to the girl? After all the progress they'd made in their attempts to communicate with her, it was heartbreaking to go back to ground zero. She watched Daisy closely for a minute and tried to concentrate enough to decipher her thoughts.

The two of them – she and Daisy – made quite a pair. Daisy was still half out of it from being conked on the head and left to die thanks to that lout Aodhan, and Granny, well, she was dead after all. Personally speaking, she thought it was pretty amazing that she could accomplish as much as she could in her present state of being. Or non-being.

The cabby careened around a corner. Granny grabbed the armrest and held on for dear life. Not that it mattered since she was already dead. She sighed and refocused her attention on Daisy, who was chatting with the cabby about the weather. It was on everyone's minds after the storm, but good grief. Didn't Daisy realize that her life was in danger? Her granddaughter had far bigger worries than one more Atlantic storm.

She poked Daisy in the arm and said "Listen to me," as loudly as she could. Daisy rubbed her arm absentmindedly but didn't even look at her. She sighed. There were times when she could almost swear that Daisy could hear her, but the foolish girl kept denying it to herself and chalking it up to the after effects of being unconscious... She needed to get through to her somehow! She had to warn her about Aodhan.

Daisy had dropped the subject of the weather and she didn't say anything for another minute or two. They were well outside of Dingle now, and Granny could hear the surf calling out to her. "Daisy," she crooned like she had when Daisy was a wee young thing. "You are my sunshine, my only sunshine..."

Daisy leaned forward in her seat. "I've been having the weirdest dreams lately. It's probably the concussion I suffered, but you wouldn't believe the things I've been dreaming about. Everything is so vivid and colorful – I know it probably sounds weird, but there are these two people who are always there, talking to me. One sounds just like my Granny Siobhan and the other one has the deepest, most melodic voice I've ever heard. My friend Cavan has a deep, dreamy voice, too, but I think the Captain's is even deeper. Don't ask me how I know his name. I told you – the dreams are so real that it's mind blowing."

Granny sucked in her breath. It was a start anyway! But unless she could get Daisy to believe that what she was seeing in her "dreams" was in fact reality, she couldn't help the girl.

The cab driver pulled over to the side of the road just upland from her shanty and Daisy opened the door to get out. Her granddaughter took a deep breath and whispered a Gaelic prayer she'd taught her years ago.

Granny stayed close by Daisy's side and motioned for the Captain to join them. They both knew what was at stake.

The Captain cleared his throat. "Daisy, listen to me. Aodhan is evil. He killed the priest, not Darcie. He nigh killed you. I know ye think he's yer friend, sweet lass, but he's not. He's intent on only one thing, and that's finding the gold to get himself out of the mess he's in. If he has to hurt ye to accomplish his goal, he'll nay let that stop him. He's already tried to kill ye once. For God's sake, reach back into yer memories, lass. Ye have to remember what Aodhan tried to do to ye."

Daisy looked perturbed. She didn't try to talk back to them like she had the last time they'd walked the shore together. Could it be that she somehow sensed their presence and was reacting to the words they were speaking to her?

"Lord God," Granny prayed aloud. "Please make it so."

Granny watched as Daisy finished checking the shanty to make sure there were no broken windows. The door was latched tight. Her heart swelled with pride. Daisy was such a good girl.

Daisy looked at the featherbed tucked against the wall.

"You could use a good nap," Granny whispered. Again, she had the feeling Daisy had heard her words. She repeated them like a Gregorian chant, over and over, but Daisy was a stubborn one, that she was.

Daisy headed toward the beach. Toward Aodhan. She appeared a bit skittish, nervous, and off-balance. Granny looked at the Captain and nodded. Granny firmly believed that Daisy knew the truth about Aodhan on some level. Now, they just needed to get her to admit it - before it was too late.

The Captain stepped up and walked beside Daisy as she picked her way along the beach. She almost stumbled over a piece of driftwood covered in seaweed.

"Good grief," Daisy sputtered. "Cavan seems so sure someone hit me on the head and left me to drown. I probably just tripped and knocked myself out. I'm such a klutz."

Granny looked at the Captain and shook her head, then whispered, "It was Aodhan, sweetheart. Aodhan was the one who tried to kill you. He wants the gold. He'll do anything to get his hands on it, including killing you."

She felt Daisy stiffen. She had a bad feeling as she raised her eyes and saw Aodhan approaching. He was squinting his eyes. Granny didn't think he'd seen Daisy. And then, the direction of the trail shifted and it appeared that Aodhan got a full picture of Daisy walking toward him. She watched as Aodhan blanched a white as pure as a newly fallen snow. Aodhan thought he was having himself a vision.

Aodhan was quaking in his boots, all right. She could tell the captain was getting a kick out of the lad's distress. It might have been humorous if Aodhan wasn't a priest killer and very nearly a Daisy killer.

Granny wrapped her arms around Daisy as though her will alone could shield her from all the bad things in the world, and most particularly the bad things Aodhan was about to do to her. And then the world went dark. Granny felt herself spinning through a never never land of sparkling lights and twinkling stars. Daisy was no where to be seen. She'd lost her grip on her granddaughter. She could only pray that what she'd told Daisy had had time to sink in. Daisy was on her own now.

31

Cavan walked beside the police sergeant to the end of the long, dark hall.

"So I'm free to go?"

"Not yet. We have one or two items of business to take care of first."

"Paperwork, I suppose." Cavan strained his eyes to see in the dim light.

"Not exactly." The sergeant kept walking.

"I already gave the detective my statement, but I'd be happy to repeat it if it would help. Especially if it helps keep Darcie behind bars." Unlike last time. He'd thought the theft of Daisy's quilt would have been a serious enough offense to hold Darcie for a lot longer than a few days, but evidently not.

"Mr. Sneem is also being released."

"But he's guilty of all kinds of things. If you'd just let me tell you what happened-"

"Oh, I have a pretty good idea of what happened out there." The sergeant paused in front of a wide, wood door and put his hand on the knob. He opened the door. Light spilled into the dark hallway. "Go through, please."

The blue of the ocean, the brightness of the sun glinting against the waves in the harbor filled Cavan with hope and joy. Daisy would be out of hospital soon and they would find their way – hopefully together – with or without the gold. And then he saw the silhouette of a man sporting a man bun. He also appeared to be looking out at the view. Darcie.

"What is he doing here?" Cavan tensed. "Do we have to go through this again? I'm sure Darcie's told you his own version of what happened. I'm telling you, it's all lies."

"Now, now," the policeman said.

Cavan tried to flex the tightness out of his neck. "I don't mind telling you that I find it very insulting that I have to keep defending my position when I am telling you the complete truth."

Darcie turned to face him. His black eyes bored into Cavan's. "All I'm trying to do is set the record straight."

The policeman held out his arm as though he expected Cavan to lunge at the man. Not that he wasn't tempted. But good grief – the police were trying to protect Darcie from him? Were Darcie's lies that persuasive?

The sergeant pulled out the chair across the table from Darcie and motioned for Cavan to have a seat. "The two of you are going to sit here and have a little chat. When you've reached an amicable agreement, you can both go. Do you understand?"

"You're kidding," Cavan said. "He-"

The policeman slapped his hand against the table. "I don't want to hear anything more about it. Say it to each other if you must, but I'd wager you'll both be out of here a lot sooner if you concentrate on what's going to happen from here on forward instead of rehashing what's already done."

Darcie shrugged and tucked a stray wad of hair back into his man bun. "I told you he wouldn't accept my apology - no matter how heartfelt it may be."

"Heartfelt? That's the biggest load of blarney ever. All you've got in your heart is a big black hole that's filled with greed."

The policeman cleared his throat. "However you want to play this – your choice. You can keep going at it like two jackals and be here all day, or you can skip the insults and start talking, in which case you should be out of here in a snap."

Cavan thought about Daisy and the fact that Aodhan was still out there. What choice did he have but to take the policeman's advice? He supposed he could make nice to Darcie if he had to.

Darcie said nothing.

The policeman said, "Darcie has confessed that it wasn't you who beat him up and that he pointed the finger at you to try to get back at you for some things you said and did during your previous altercation."

"You mean when he stole Daisy's quilt and tried to drown me in the bay?"

Darcie suddenly found his voice. "If you want to speak ill of someone, I'd be looking at the man who used to date Daisy. It was he who beat me up this morning."

Cavan looked at Darcie. Darcie looked at him. They both knew what this was about.

"I think we can take it from here, Sergeant," Cavan said.

The policeman exited the room and closed the door.

"So let's be honest, Darcie. What is it you want from Daisy? What do we have to do to get you out of our lives?"

"We all want the gold. We should work together to recover it before the old boyfriend gets his hands on it. It's safer that way."

Cavan didn't want the gold and never had, but he didn't have the time or inclination to explain his feelings about the destruction wealth wreaked on the lives of those who had it - especially to Darcie. Besides, Daisy did want the gold, and he had to respect her wishes. If Daisy's theory about her Granny's involvement with the gold was accurate, then it was her legacy – the only thing she had to show for her heritage unless you counted her grumpy aunts, Sheelagh and Ailene.

Cavan frowned. "What's in it for you – assuming we do find the gold?"

Darcie's eyes snapped to attention. He paused and for a second, Cavan wondered what kind of story he was going to cook up.

"There's an orphanage on the other side of the bay for underprivileged boys. A lot of them are descendants of the travelers and pirates who used to roam the seas and camp on the shore. I'd like to see some of the gold go to them."

Cavan sucked in his breath. Never would he have guessed he would get such a response from Darcie. "I've always thought part of the gold should go to those in the shipping community that are in need - retired sea captains, or the families of men who are lost at sea. I'm agreeable to the idea. If Daisy will go along with it, I'd say we have a deal."

"You may not agree with my methods, but I do have good intentions."

Darcie offered up one of his creepy smiles and Cavan guessed he had no choice but to believe him.

"If I find the gold, you and Daisy will be the first ones to know

about it and I'll guard every bit of it until we can arrive at a fair way
to distribute the goods."

They shook on their deal. Cavan just hoped he could convince
Daisy it was the right thing to do. He certainly hoped she'd given
up the idea of moving back to Killarney, buying another mansion
and living the high life again.

"Just one more thing," Cavan said. "Were you on the beach
looking for the gold the night you first got out of prison, and if so,
did you have any contact with Daisy?"

"No. I was afraid the police would follow me to make sure I
didn't head back to the beach, so I went to check on one of the
kids at the orphanage. He's thirteen now – been waiting to be
placed since he was five. I'm not in a position to adopt the lad but I
try to see him as often as I can."

Cavan weighed Darcie's words carefully. He wouldn't put it past
the man to lie, or even to fabricate a story to evoke his or the
police's sympathy. But it seemed like Darcie was being sincere.

His muscles clenched. If it wasn't Darcie that had attacked
Daisy and or left her to drown on the beach, then his first instincts
had been right. Aodhan was still out there and a grave danger to
Daisy.

He dashed across the street to check into the bike shop and
then set off to hospital to pick up Daisy.

#

Daisy squinted to keep the sunshine from blinding her and
watched as Aodhan walked toward her. She'd felt a chill from the
second she'd realized it was him. Why, she didn't understand.
Aodhan wasn't her favorite person in the world. It had been
humiliating when he'd dumped her, and for no other reason than
her losing her fortune. No surprise that she might feel leery of him,
or experience a prick of irritation when in his presence. But this
was stark fear. With every step he came closer, she felt more
terrified. She couldn't explain any of this, so her reaction of
absolute panic mystified her.

Aodhan was close enough that she could see his face, and it
dawned on her that he looked as perplexed as she did. Another big
question mark. Was he surprised to see her? And if so, why? She
was just a few steps from her Granny's shanty. This was where she

belonged.

"Hi. Daisy?" Aodhan spoke quietly and he hesitated after he said her name, like he was unsure it was really her. He was acting weird, like he didn't know what kind of reception he'd get. What was with him?

"I didn't think I'd see you here. Aodhan. Why such frequent visits now, when you haven't paid me any attention since I left Killarney?"

She stumbled over the word Killarney, and she'd seen his face when she did. She'd gotten hung up on the first syllable. Aodhan had looked like he might faint.

"About the other night," Aodhan started to say, and then very obviously stopped as though he were gauging her reaction.

"What night?" She had no idea what he was talking about, yet fear raced through her veins, as though her body knew something her mind didn't.

"I'm sorry about what happened. The dark just came on so suddenly and then I couldn't find you." He laughed a sick-sounding, nervous laugh.

What was he talking about?

Aodhan inched closer to her and raised his arm.

Her insides clenched. Was he going to strike her? She took a step back and almost stumbled on a rock.

Aodhan grabbed her wrists. She jerked her right hand back but he caught the left.

32

Daisy's head felt like it was going to explode. Her wrist ached from Aodhan's grip. Was he trying to help her or was he going to hurt her?

"Here you are! We've been looking all over for you! We thought for sure we'd find you napping at your Granny's after all the excitement you've had these past few days!"

What on earth? She jerked her hand away from Aodhan. He looked as startled as she felt. Where had Auntie Sheelagh and Auntie Ailene come from?

"What are you doing here?" Not much of a greeting, but it was all that came to her. The two of them had ignored her and acted like they didn't know her for weeks on end. Now, she was in the middle of a crisis and they showed up out of the blue. For some reason, they were the straw that broke the camel's back. Tears started to stream down her face.

Aodhan wrenched her hand from her side and squeezed it so hard that it hurt.

Auntie Ailene's irritated voice struck a blow just as painful. "Why Daisy Fitzpatrick! For shame. There's no need to cry. We were just thinking about your Granny Siobhan and we decided that since she isn't around to talk some sense into you, it was up to us to set you straight."

Auntie Sheelagh started in next. "I suppose this is one of your boyfriends. Does he know you're preggers?"

A look of shock passed over Aodhan's face.

"Don't tell me he's the father? I mean, we just assumed it was that Cavan lad, but-"

"I'll bet she doesn't know!" Aunt Ailene's face was wreathed in a smug, self-righteous glow. "Don't you see, Sheelagh? She's no doubt slept with so many men that she doesn't have a clue who the father is! Lord almighty. It's worse than we imagined. Oh, Daisy. How could you? Am I right? Are Cavan and this lad the only two candidates, or are there others?"

Aodhan's grip was so tight it felt like the bones in her hand were being crushed.

"Well, you'll have to do DNA testing then, won't you?" Sheelagh said condescendingly. "Of course, we all know that even if your Granny were still alive, she would probably just pat you on the wrist and send you on your merry way. That's the whole reason you're in this mess - not a whit of discipline the whole time you were growing up."

Daisy looked at Aodhan. If it hadn't been for the force of his grip, she'd have thought he might pass out. His skin was a sickly green. If Daisy had felt a little stronger and less woozy herself, she would have made a break and ran for it the first chance she had.

Aodhan still looked like he'd seen a ghost. Well, whatever was going on with Aodhan, the whole little Sheelagh and Ailene show had gone on quite long enough.

Daisy mustered her inner strength, squared her shoulders and turned to face her aunts. "Whether or not I'm preggers or with whom or when I've had sex or not, is none of your business! That's why I'm going to ask you to-"

Daisy had a quick flash of sensation. She was falling off a cliff. Her memories rained around her in a torrential downpour of recollection. She remembered! Aodhan had left her on the beach to die. She'd called and called for him to save her from the tide, and he'd left her there to drown.

Auntie Sheelagh was saying something, and it wasn't good or helpful. Auntie Ailene's face was just as unkind. But they were her Granny's sisters and she had to warn them that Aodhan was evil.

And then, everything went black.

#

Cavan got halfway across the street and decided he shouldn't take the time to stop by the bike shop. If he even poked his head inside the door, Rory would want to know what was going on with Darcie and what had happened out at the beach and at the police station. He knew exactly what would happen if he stepped inside - invariably, a favorite customer would come in or the phone would ring, or Rory would have questions and before he knew it, an hour or more would slip by and he'd still be trapped with no way to escape short of being horribly rude.

If he rushed over to hospital and picked up Daisy first, he could take her home to rest and spend all the time he needed at the bike shop. He had his car keys. He went directly to his parking spot and pulled out before Rory could glance out the window and wave at him to stop.

Fifteen minutes later, he followed an ambulance into the parking area, turned to the visitor's lot, and rushed in to get Daisy. He waited impatiently while the nurses at the information desk dealt with family of the patient brought in by ambulance. There were four more people queued up in front of him and each took three or four minutes to deal with, plus interruptions from the emergency team. There went another fifteen or twenty minutes.

At one point, he left the queue and slipped down the hall to peek into the room Daisy had been in the night before. There was no sign of her, which could mean she'd been taken down for an x-ray, an MRI, or even more blood work. Or, it could be that she'd been released, in which case he still had to find out where she was. When he returned, there were two new people in the queue. He was tempted to walk away once more and systematically check the waiting rooms to see if he could spot her, but it seemed counter productive.

He finally reached the top of the queue. "I need to know where I can find Daisy Fitzpatrick."

"I'm sorry, but Daisy has already been released."

"Do you know where she was going?"

The nurse gave him a look and leaned in close. "You know I'm not allowed to give out information on patients, but since you were with her when she was admitted, and by her side during most of her stay, I'm assuming she would want you to know."

She looked around furtively. "I called a cabby for her about an hour ago. She said she was going back to her apartment to rest."

"It's my apartment, technically. But that's okay. I'm surprised she took a cab."

"She tried to reach you several times." The nurse looked at him reprovingly.

He reached into his pocket and slid his mobile off silent. "I'm just glad she's safe. I'll head home now and find her."

"Tell her I hope she's feeling better, and to let us know if she has any problems."

Cavan smiled. Daisy had problems all right, but unfortunately, the bulk of them couldn't be healed with the help of a kindly nurse.

#

Aodhan felt like he was going to be sick. He'd had a hard enough time killing Daisy the first time. Now he was going to have to kill her again. Knowing she was pregnant made the task unthinkable. No one who was Daisy's age was a true innocent, but the baby she was carrying – whoever it belonged to – didn't deserve to die because of Daisy's foolish choices.

Daisy might not remember that he had left her on the beach to die, but eventually, she would, and he'd be hunted down like a cold-blooded killer, which he was not. Oh, she would remember all right - unless she was already dead.

He felt Daisy go limp and her weight dragging his arm down.

"Help her!" One of the aunts screamed.

Good grief. Not again... which brought him to an entirely different issue. What the heck was he supposed to do with Aunties Sheelagh and Ailene? Maybe some people had a taste for killing, but not him. He just wanted the gold. He wanted to be rich, to be able to buy what he wanted to buy and enjoy what he wanted to enjoy and live the life of leisure he was meant to live. Was that so awful? He wasn't a killer, but he was willing to do whatever he had to do to accomplish his goal.

He looked down at the heap that was Daisy and debated whether to kill her first, and then her aunts, or to try to get rid of the aunts so he could kill Daisy. He didn't know if he had the guts to kill her while the hysterical old biddies watched.

He tried to jerk Daisy back to her feet but she was out cold. As long as Daisy was around, the gold would never be his. If Daisy was found dead, if the aunts were still alive, they would be able to identify him. No, they were all going to have to die.

"Aren't you going to do something?" One of them yelled.

It had all happened so fast. He wasn't prepared for this. He'd thought Daisy was already dead.

He scanned the horizon in the three directions he could see without looking behind him and tried to decide what to do and how to do it. He let go of Daisy and lifted his arm to strike but she crumpled and sunk into the soft sand at their feet like a deflated balloon.

What the heck was going on with her anyway? Probably the whole preggers thing.

One of the aunts screamed, "Pick her up, you ill-bred oaf. It's the least you can do – after all, you're the one who got her preggers - probably."

"Be a gentleman and help her. Can't you see what havoc the seed you planted inside her is causing?" The other one chided.

He reached down to pick up Daisy. Why on earth was he bothering to help her when he wanted her dead?

"Let go of her!"

It took him a second to register that this voice was a man's and not one of the aunts'. Good grief. Pick her up. Put her down. Help her...

"Get your hands off her!"

Someone lunged at him from behind and squeezed their hands around his neck.

What the...

Whomever was on top of him was trying their best to gouge his eyes out, or at least that's what it felt like.

"That's not Cavan."

"No. It looks like a pirate."

"A pirate with a man-bun."

"They are so revolting."

"Pirates, or man-buns?"

"Man-buns. The new kind, the ones they wear in their hair. Now, a man's buns – the old kind – one never grows too old to appreciate."

"Not that we ever get to see them now that men wear those baggy, formless pants that hang halfway down their backsides."

He ignored the aunts' clatter and let what they were talking about sink in. The pirate? Again? He'd already beaten him once and he could do it again. The pirate never would have knocked him down in the first place had he not been distracted.

He tried to land a punch and missed.

Sheelagh – at least he thought it was Sheelagh - gasped. "Something just dawned on me. This pirate is another of Daisy's beaus. Why else would he be here? Why, he's obviously another prospective father to Daisy's baby, which means that Daisy has had sex with at least three men – that we know of."

"You've always had an overactive libido, Sheelagh. Mother would roll over in her grave if she could hear you clattering on about sex this and sex that."

Daisy's aunts were going to drive him mad. If he hadn't been so busy defending himself against the pirate, he would have slashed both of their throats right that very minute.

"Well, how would you have me say it?"

"With a little civility, one would hope."

Aodhan ducked but the pirate still landed a blow to his chin while he thought about which aunt would be the first to die.

"Fine. I'm sure Daisy is as untouched as a virgin and that a stork will bring her baby when the time comes."

He couldn't wait to take on her, too. Ouch! The pirate kneed him in the groin. He almost stepped on Daisy.

"What about me?"

Was that Daisy?

The pirate took advantage of his momentary lapse into confusion and rammed a finger down his throat. Crude jerk. He should have bit down on it.

Aodhan gagged but then recovered. "Dirty, filthy-"

"First of all, I'll have you know I'm a virgin," Daisy said weakly. "And the next time either one of you chides me for being a floozy-"

"I'm sorry, dear," one of the aunts said, "but it's impossible for a virgin to be preggers – unless your name is Mary and you've found favor with the Lord God Almighty."

"I have NOT had sex with anyone and I am NOT preggers!" Daisy yelled at her aunts in a loud voice. "And unless you start paying attention, we're all going to die. Darcie stole my quilt and Aodhan tried to kill me! They should both be behind bars!"

Aodhan ducked a blow from Darcie. Crap. Daisy's memory was obviously back. Which meant she had to die. He was not going to prison.

One of the aunts said, "The only reason we think you're a

floozy is because your Granny was, and she's the one who raised you."

"The apple never falls far from the tree." The other aunt chimed in just as Aodhan flipped Darcie onto his back and tried to pin him to the ground.

"We're just saying that Granny wasn't much of an example to you. Why the way she refused to remarry so she could 'do her own thing' and 'keep her own company' with no regard to proper behavior or the expectations of others was downright scandalous."

Daisy fired back just as Darcie toppled him onto his side. "Well, if that's what being like my Granny means, I'm proud to be like her!"

Aodhan could see Daisy watching out of the corner of his eye as he and Darcie flipped from side to side, writhing, contorting their bodies and moaning as they slammed into rocky outcrops and jagged shells.

The aunts had resumed their bickering when he caught a quick glimpse of Daisy picking up a rock.

That was it! Aodhan screamed, "Shut up! All of you — unless you want to end up just like my dear Uncle O'Leary."

He heard the old biddies gasp.

"Father O'Leary was your uncle?" Daisy asked.

"My mother's brother. And he said I was the greedy one. All I needed was enough gold for me and my father to get back on our feet. My father never would have embezzled from the company if he hadn't been desperate. Priests are supposed to be compassionate, aren't they?"

The sound of bones crunching bounced through his head. Was that his jaw? Damn pirate.

Daisy's voice punctuated his fog. "You must have been devastated when your uncle was killed. Were you close?"

"Are you kidding?" He heard his voice screaming the words but he couldn't stop himself. "No one mattered to him but God. I was nothing to him. I should have been his heir, but no. He gave his life — and his gold — all of it — to God. How does that make him a good man? Leaving your own flesh and blood in the lurch so some charity cases who are already a burden on society can drain more money from the church?"

He heard one of the old biddies say to the other, "Well, I certainly hope he's not the father of Daisy's baby."

His anger flared even hotter. "My uncle said he was ashamed of me! He's lucky I killed him quickly instead of sticking the fireplace poker in the peat fire and ramming it through his condescending eyes."

"No," Darcie screamed, and came at him with even more force.

But he was running on adrenalin now. The pirate didn't have a chance. When he'd finished him off, he would kill them all – Daisy, the old biddies, whoever got in his way.

He could feel Daisy's eyes following him as he and the pirate struggled for control. Was she trying to decide which of them was the lesser of two evils?

The pirate must have seen her, too, because he screamed, "I'm trying to protect you, Daisy! I swear it!"

Aodhan had the pirate around the neck. It was just a matter of time. He was bigger and stronger. He had this.

He caught a glimpse of the aunt's faces as he pressed down on the pirate's windpipe. Finally. Fear. Stupid old crones.

Daisy looked like she was in a trance. "He tried to murder me." She sounded scared. Well, she should be.

He saw Daisy totter to her feet and move to slam a rock into his head. If he'd tried to move out of the way, he would have lost his grip on the pirate.

"Ouch! Damn you," he growled.

"Well, now you know what it feels like to have someone try to kill you."

A sense of being dazed hit him a second later. Darcie landed a hard punch to his windpipe and then to his gut. He doubled over with pain and started falling. He tried to regain his footing, but he was falling, falling hard and fast. The noise in his head sounded like he was holding a conch shell close to his ear.

33

Daisy felt like Dorothy in the Wizard of Oz watching the wicked witch melt into nothingness. She felt disbelief and shock, and her head hurt like a vice clamp was gripped around it.

"You almost hit me!" Darcie said.

"I was trying not to! I had to do something. You were moving so fast you were one big blur."

"Well, I'm glad it was him and not me. You pack quite a punch."

"I knew the pirate was the good one," Aunt Sheelagh said with an air of gloating.

"I didn't know who to aim for," Daisy said, being honest and hoping Darcie wouldn't turn on her once she revealed her lack of confidence in him.

"Have you spoken to Cavan?" Darcie knelt down and checked Aodhan's pulse. "He's alive."

Aodhan could have been dead? A jolt shook her to her core. It was freaky enough knowing that Aodhan had killed the priest and tried to kill her. She'd been angry and afraid, but she was no murderer. She looked at Darcie and remembered that she'd only missed his head by a fraction of an inch.

"Was I supposed to have spoken to Cavan?"

"We reached a truce, he and I. Subject to your approval of course. We're joining forces." Darcie stopped and glanced at the aunts. He came closer and whispered, "to find the gold."

Personally, she couldn't imagine why Cavan would have made such an agreement, but she did trust him, and her head hurt something fierce, so she went along with it for now and hoped Darcie was telling the truth.

"What do we do now?" Aunt Ailene asked.

"I don't know. He's too heavy to carry to the car." Daisy checked her mobile for reception. No bars. It was so hit and miss at the seashore.

"One of us should go for help and one stay here to make sure he doesn't get away."

"I'd stay back if I had my pistol," Aunt Ailene piped up.

Well, that was a shock. Daisy looked at her with fresh eyes. Would wonders never cease?

Darcie stood tall. "It's too dangerous for any of you ladies to stay. I'll volunteer."

Daisy thought about it for a second. If she hadn't been able to hit Aodhan with a rock, she felt sure that Darcie would have been overpowered and very probably killed. It really wasn't safe for any of them to stay behind.

"Hopefully Aodhan will be out long enough for us to get to a place where there are enough bars to call the police." A nervous feeling gnawed at her stomach. She still wasn't 100% sure she should trust Darcie, but what choice did she have? She wished Cavan was here!

"I wish we had a way to tie him up," Darcie said.

"I have a handkerchief," Auntie Sheelagh said.

"I have a head scarf and a handkerchief," Ailene said, one besting her.

Darcie smirked. "Nothing short of a rope would hold him for long, but tying his hands behind his back might deter him a little and buy us some time if nothing else."

Aunt Ailene began to dig through her purse.

"It will be more sturdy if it's long enough to go round twice," Aunt Sleelagh said. "Here. Tie these two together."

"Good thinking," Darcie said.

Daisy said, "Does anyone know when the tide comes in tonight?"

Darcie tied and retied the hankies together, "Not until later. We've got plenty of time to get help and get back to transport your friend back to the jailhouse."

"Or hospital. And he's not my friend. Not anymore. Friends don't try to kill their friends."

Aunt Sheelagh helped Darcie wrest Aodhan's hands behind his back and held them there while Darcie knotted the makeshift binding around Aodhan's wrists. "Not to gloat, but I am a very good judge of character."

For once, Auntie Ailene didn't try to argue. They were all shaken.

Darcie finished the job and stood up. "We're all going then? If we're in agreement, let's get moving. The sooner we get help and get Aodhan under lock and key, the better I'll feel."

"We can all ride in my car," Aunt Sheelagh offered, still very cheery, probably because she'd been right about the pirate being the good guy.

Daisy started to trudge up the incline that led to the top of the cliffs. The aunts followed a little more slowly and Darcie brought up the rear. Alone with her thoughts at last, she cringed at the thought of the closeness she and Aodhan had shared. She'd not slept with him, but she'd kissed him plenty of times. If she hadn't lost the gold, she probably would have had sex with Aodhan eventually, probably would have ended up really being pregnant or even married to him. The thought that she could have blithely let him use her that way just to get at her riches made her realize for the first time that money really did bring nothing but grief to the people it touched.

Lord, she felt ashamed. Mortified. Absolutely mortified. And foolish. And naïve and gullible. Granny always used to say that the Bible had something in it about all things working together for good, which was short for everything works out the way it's supposed to in the end. She picked her way around a rock and grabbed a handful of sea grass to steady her step as she climbed. It was true that if she hadn't gone through the hardship of losing everything she had in Killarney, she never would have escaped Aodhan's wicked plan, or found Cavan.

She didn't have anything against God, she'd just never paid much attention to him. Maybe that was one more thing about her life that she needed to rethink.

#

Cavan wove his way across Dingle the fastest way he could and pulled into his parking spot at the bike shop. He bounded up the back stairs, still feeling guilty that he hadn't been there when Daisy was released.

At least she'd called for a cab instead of trying to walk the distance, but knowing how Daisy hated to part with even a few Euros of the limited funds she had at present, it also told him how weak she must still feel.

"Daisy? Daisy!" She was probably napping.

He looked inside the porch where her bed was camped. Not there. Perhaps she'd felt too dizzy or stiff to get down on the floor. He walked to his bedroom and gently knocked on the door before entering. No Daisy. He checked the bathroom and the kitchen just to be sure. No sign of anyone. Which meant only one thing. Daisy had gone to the beach. He could only pray she was resting in the shanty and not trolling the shoreline.

His heart rate quickened. If Aodhan found her in this weakened, confused state, it could all be over.

He ran down the back stairs, still saying nothing to Rory, and leaped into his auto. The tires squealed as he backed up, twisted the wheel and took off for the beach.

As soon as he was out of the congested city center, he pressed the speed dial for Daisy's mobile. He put the mobile on speaker mode, careened around another curve and continued on in the direction of the beach. He'd taken a shortcut by the old castle – not the greatest road, but it was a couple of miles shorter.

Still no answer. He'd no doubt have zero reception once he got to the shanty, so he tried Daisy's mobile one more time. No answer.

#

The reception room at the police station was starting to look all too familiar. Daisy hoped someone came soon. They all knew Auntie Sheelagh and Ailene's scarves and handkerchiefs wouldn't hold Aodhan for two seconds if he came to.

Darcie pulled something out of his back pocket and held it up so Daisy could see.

"What?" Daisy still felt like her head was mince.

"It's the photos you took of the quilt."

"But I ripped them into dozens of pieces and threw them into the trash." They were stained with tea and crumpled up but Darcie had taped them together.

"Where there's a will there's a way," Darcie said proudly.

"Yeah," she said. "Desperate men will do-"

"I can see ye still do not completely trust me," Darcie said.

Darcie might not be the most with-it man she'd ever met, but he had street smarts and sharp instincts. "Would you trust me if the situation was reversed?"

"Would I be showing you the photos if I still planned to go behind your back and steal the gold?"

"I guess not."

"Then have a good look while the lay of the land is still fresh in your mind and tell me what you think."

"Fresh in my mind, eh? Nothing is fresh in my mind. My head is throbbing and what I think is that we need to concentrate on making sure Aodhan is caught now that we know he's guilty."

A policeman entered the room and shook his head. "Not you again, Darcie."

Darcie whisked the photos back into his pocket. "It's not what you think, sir."

The policeman looked at Daisy. She shrugged. She didn't know what to make of the new Darcie and since she hadn't had a chance to discuss things with Cavan and find out why Cavan suddenly trusted him – if in fact he did – it was all a mystery to her.

"We called from the road into town to tell someone that Aodhan Byrne was on the beach, passed out, with his hands tied behind his back, He accosted Darcie and tried to kill me. He also confessed to killing Father O'Leary."

"Yes, ma'am. We dispatched a squad car immediately. No one has radioed in, so we're not sure if they've found him or not."

They'd seen the police car whizzing by when they were entering Dingle and had assumed they were on their way to the beach. Darcie had wanted to head back to the shanty but Daisy had insisted they be dropped off at the police station so Sheelagh and Ailene could go home.

Daisy blinked her eyes and tried to focus on the officer. "Sir? I'm really in need of some rest after getting out of hospital just a few hours ago. Will you please call me and let me know if Aodhan's been apprehended?"

"When," Darcie said. "At times like this, it's best to practice positive thinking."

"Fine. When Aodhan is apprehended, will you please contact me?" Daisy rubbed her temples. "Darcie, thank you for your help. I'll be in touch about the other, um, matter we discussed."

"Could I walk you home? I know it's just across the street, but the way the locals and those crazy tourists go roaring down the lane, I want to make sure you get safely home, especially, with you in your present condition."

"I am not preggers!"

"I, um, meant your concussion."

"Oh. Okay." She closed her eyes. She knew full well that Darcie knew where she lived, and had been inside her apartment – Cavan's apartment – but she didn't want to think about it now. Not when she wanted to rest. "I guess you can see me across the street."

A few minutes later, she stepped inside Recycled Cyclery. She could smell a fresh batch of Maeve's Irish stew simmering on the stove next door. Rory smiled and came out from behind the counter to greet her. She was finally home and all was well – or at least it would be when Cavan came home.

34

The sun was low enough in the sky by the time Cavan reached Daisy's beach that its rays were sparkling on the bay like a million diamonds. The wind had gone down and there must have been a shower out at sea because he could see the mist trying to organize itself into a rainbow.

He found no sign of Daisy at the shanty. He had a bad feeling about that. He knew Daisy. She'd most likely gotten a second wind once she reached the beach and decided to forego the nap she needed. The sea had a way of rejuvenating people – especially Daisy. This was her go-to place. He got that. But even the wind could sap a person's energy say nothing about wading through patches of dry sand up to your ankles. The rigors of the shoreline could be exhausting even to someone in prime condition.

Daisy should be resting. He'd bet money that she was down by the water, searching for the sea cave that held the gold. And if Aodhan found her before he did... He quickened his step and made his way downhill as fast as he could, looking for signs that she'd been this way.

He stopped and stared at the ground. It looked like a herd of cattle had come through this way. He followed the mishmash of displaced sand and trampled sea grass until he found his next clue – a strand of handkerchiefs and what looked like a sheer lady's scarf, all knotted together. He'd never seen Daisy carrying a handkerchief or wearing a scarf on her head or around her neck. Whose could they be and what was going on?

He picked up the fabric and looked more closely. The fabric the scarf was made out of was split in two, a jagged tear ripped apart by force. Had Aodhan found Daisy and tied her up? He doubted she would have had enough strength to bust the cloth in two in her weakened state just out of hospital. If Aodhan had been tied up, he would have had the strength to break loose. But how could Daisy have subdued him enough to overpower him and tie him up?

He scanned the horizon and saw a flash of green that was too dark to be sea grass, too bright to be anything along the shore, which had its own muted brands of wildflowers. He started to run, sidestepping a clump of seaside daisies growing at the base of an old fence post.

The blur of green was moving fast, running parallel to the shoreline, into an area of the beach that looked desirable but was hardly ever frequented because of its reputation for sea eddies and rip tides.

He thought about yelling at the person to stop just to make sure he wasn't following some jogger or marathon runner on a wild goose chase, but if it was Aodhan, he would need the element of surprise – assuming he could even catch him.

"Run, son! Aye! That's the ticket! Just follow yer instincts and run!" A deep male voice sounded out of nowhere, rumbling in his head like thunder. Except there were no clouds.

What the devil? He was sure no one else was around. He didn't dare take the time to slow up and have a fresh look around, or even take his eyes off the uneven ground his feet were flying over.

If the voice came from some sort of inner reserve deep inside his gut, or even a guardian angel of some kind, shouldn't he know whether he was supposed to run in the opposite direction and get the hell out of there, or keep following the blur of green?

His leg muscles were already throbbing. Not for the first time, he realized that the muscles used when riding bicycle were entirely different than the ones used for walking.

The green blur was slowing now. There were places the beach didn't go straight through except during the very lowest of tides. It was possible the runner had reached a place where he had to veer into the ocean and wade around boulders or simply navigate rough, rocky terrain to keep running north. Either that, or he or she had stopped for a rest. Who knew how long they'd been at it at such a crisp pace. Even if it was Aodhan, he might not realize he was being followed and assume he had time to collect his breath.

He was gaining on the man now – it was definitely a man, and judging by the coloring and build of the man, he felt more and more confident that it was in fact Aodhan.

He paused for a second to take a better look, plan his approach and strategize. When his breathing quieted and the sound of his feet slapping against the wet sand disappeared, he heard a stealthy, calculated sort of commotion behind him.

He turned and was half blinded by the sun. No wonder the runner hadn't known he was being followed. The angle of the sun nearly blinded him.

It took him a second to realize that whomever was approaching him – the police, he hoped - might think he was Aodhan. They were gaining on his position rapidly. He had to alert them that he was a friend and not a foe. But how to go about it without alerting Aodhan to their presence?

He looked over his shoulder and kept running. Had his pursuers been the ones that called out to him? If so, they wouldn't have been telling him to run unless they knew he wasn't Aodhan.

He raised his arms in the air and started to wave. He could see their uniforms now. The policemen kept barreling toward him. He stepped aside lest they trample him. They obviously knew their man was dressed in green. Thank goodness he'd put on a gray and black striped rugby shirt that morning.

He took off after the second policemen. This, he wanted to see.

The rest happened in a blur of confusion. Aodhan must have seen them coming and decided to take to the sea rather than be caught and hauled off to jail. Who knew? The beach had narrowed significantly. Aodhan was in good shape – probably the proverbial rich kid who had nothing to do all day but work out with his private trainer in his own million dollar gym. The question was, did he have a plan or had he jumped into the ocean as a last resort?

Cavan watched as Aodhan ran further and further into the water, eventually flinging himself into the waves.

"Doesn't he know about the rip tides?" One of the officers yelled.

The Sleeping Giant was too far offshore for even the best swimmer. Did Aodhan have a boat anchored off shore? They finally reached the point perpendicular to Aodhan's position in the sea.

"Should I follow him in?" The second policeman started to strip down, removing his shoes and gun belt. He sounded dubious, but he obviously was willing to answer the call of duty if need be.

"No." The older of the two nixed the idea. "Scum like him isn't worth the risk." He whipped out a pair of binoculars.

"But we can't just let him go. Miss Fitzpatrick said he killed the priest and tried to kill her."

Cavan's heart started to pound. Daisy was safe. And she knew Aodhan was the enemy, not Darcie. At least, he hoped not Darcie. One person trying to kill you was enough.

"I doubt he can survive. I know you're a strong swimmer, but quite frankly, I don't expect you would either." The older one held out his arm to prevent the younger officer from entering the water. "Justice can be served in a variety of ways."

"Did Daisy..." Cavan looked at the telltale signs of a rip tide forming – a line of debris floated atop the water, a textbook gap in the waves appeared, perpendicular to the shore. And he could see a distinct difference in the color of the water. A large curl of brown water indicated a surge of sand, algae and sediment churned up by the current while another patch remained the usual blue-gray of the surf.

"If he knows what to do, he may come up down the beach."

But Aodhan wasn't swimming parallel to the shore, riding it out. In his effort to get as far away from land as possible, he was fighting an impossible battle.

"Not a single lad raised in Dingle would ever do such a stupid thing."

"City folk." The second policeman shook his head. "Killarney may be only an hour away, but they're a whole different breed, they are."

They watched as Aodhan got dragged further into the tow of the riptide.

The senior policeman followed his progress – or lack of it – with his binoculars. "I told you the Lord has his own ways of punishing wrongdoers."

"What?" The first officer handed the binoculars to the second.

"It's a shark. A big one."

"Could be a basking shark. Wouldn't be able to bite him with no teeth, but it could give him a heart attack if he doesn't know the difference."

"There have been sightings of great whites off the coasts of Scotland and Wales. And one probable as near as Kerry. Water's a little warmer this year. They say the conditions are right for them even along the Dingle Coast."

The officer with the binoculars said, "The shark is circling."

What happened next, Cavan could see even without aid. Aodhan simply disappeared. Gone. No bobbing head. No waving arms. No splashing in the water. Simply gone.

The younger policeman, still in his swim trunks, swallowed hard, as if he was choking on a bitter pill. He lowered the binoculars and finally looked at Cavan square on. "Hey. Aren't you the chap I pulled out of Dingle Bay?"

"That's me."

"You ever find your quilt?"

"No."

The older officer laughed. Cavan guessed you had to be able to find humor in situations like this when you worked such a stressful job, but he wondered what was so funny.

"What?" The young one said.

"I was just thinking there's a wee bit of irony in the fact that the Good Lord sent Fungie, the dophin, to the good lad's aid, and a great white shark to the priest killer's."

Cavan's senses heightened and he felt a surge of relief. There was a moment of silence as the truth sunk in. For the first time, he felt like everything was going to be okay.

"The Lord takes care of his own."

"That he does." The older policeman took out his radio and called in a brief synopsis of what had transpired.

Cavan wanted to ask them more about what had happened to Daisy, but for the time, he was fine just knowing she was okay and in communication with the police.

"Notify the Coast Guard to be on the lookout for a body, or body parts, up and down the west coast or any kind of a boat that may have taken on a survivor."

Cavan sensed a chill in the air. Was that a tall ship out on the waters? He caught a quick glimpse of a two-masted brigantine before it disappeared into the mist. He looked at the officers, but if either of them had seen what he saw, they made no mention of it.

He'd heard of ghost ships sailing the high seas. His grandfather had sworn that his father captained one that had been lost at sea years earlier, quite possibly the one that carried the gold Daisy's grandmother had found.

The young officer was putting on his outerwear.

"Now that we know who you are, I expect that you're eager to rendezvous with your Daisy girl," the older said.

Cavan loved the sea, but right now, he wanted to get as far away from it as he could. He could care less about finding the gold, but finding Daisy was just what he needed.

35

Daisy was already gone by the time Cavan got to the police station. He'd checked the shanty before leaving the beach just to make sure she hadn't gone back there to nap. Since he'd already told the police everything he knew – well, everything except the fact that there was likely more gold hidden on Granny's land – he was free to go.

It still seemed odd to him that the Father O'Leary had fallen prey to Aodhan's greed, one of the seven deadly sins, and the very thing God's servants strive to eliminate in the world. And if God had the power to send a riptide and a shark at the exact moment Aodhan decided to go for a swim, why hadn't he sent a waterspout or a mean badger or something to stop Aodhan before he killed the priest?

His mum would say it wasn't for him to understand, and for now, he guessed it would have to do. But while he might never fully comprehend the Lord's ways, he did want to have a better understanding of Daisy, and he wasn't about to give up on that.

He was thinking about her, and what might happen next, when he took out his keys and walked into the door of the bike shop. He found a note from Rory on the counter telling him everything had gone smoothly in his absence, that Daisy was upstairs resting, and that if he and Daisy might benefit from some craic and trad to pick up their spirits, they were welcome to join he and Lisette at O'Flaherty's.

Craic sounded good, but tonight, the only person he really wanted to share a conversation with was Daisy. He was always up for trad, and there was nothing like playing along or even just watching the musicians perform live – the hand tapping the goatskin head of the bodhran, fingers tickling the banjo, hurdy-gurdy or bouzouki, arms stroking the length of a fiddle or wielding a concertina, or the all body movement of a rhythmic tin whistler or Celtic harpist. But tonight, he'd be content to imagine it all in his head while he sat in his and Daisy's apartment listening to a CD by candlelight.

He loped his way up the stairs with a new burst of energy and called out as he neared the top. "Daisy? Daisy? Love?"

"Cavan?" The sound of her voice had never been sweeter.

And then she was in his arms and he was hugging her and kissing the top of her head and hugging her again.

When they finally broke apart, she backed up a step and stood looking up at him, eyes beaming. He didn't know what to do or say. He wanted to tip her chin to just the right angle and kiss her, but he really didn't know how she would feel about that, and he didn't want to do anything to topple the tenuous balance they'd achieved as friends and roommates. Now that Darcie was on their side and Aodhan wasn't creeping around, up to no good, there was nothing to stop Daisy from moving back to her Granny's sea shanty - the last thing he wanted.

"We did it," Daisy said.

"What? Did you and Darcie find the gold?"

"No. We survived! We solved the mystery. We got everything sorted. Isn't that enough?"

"It is for me. I'm not sure about you. You've wanted that gold with a pretty fierce passion ever since you lost the first stash. And I'm guessing Darcie is still determined to find it."

"I'm almost tempted just to let him have it."

"Is that you or has the Daisy I know and love been replaced by an alien from outer space?"

The room grew still, and for a second, it seemed like time had stopped. He felt like they were a couple of stars suspended in the heavens.

"You love me?" Daisy's voice was soft, sweet, and a wee bit shaky.

"Sure I do."

She came closer and tipped her head up until their eyes met. She parted her lips ever so slightly. If that wasn't an invitation, he didn't know what was.

"Hey, Daisy? Cavan? Anybody up there?"

Darn. He'd forgotten to lock the door.

Daisy looked at him.

Rory opened the door a crack and poked his head through when he heard their voices. "Just wanted to make sure you got home okay, Cavan."

"Just a few minutes ago. Thanks again for minding the store. It's been quite a day."

"No problem." Rory glanced at the two of them and backed toward the door.

Cavan appreciated Rory no end, but if he could tell he'd interrupted something and got out of their hair, that was fine by him.

"See you later?"

"We'll see. We're both fairly tired."

They listened while Rory clattered down the stairs. But unless the stairs had suddenly grown another flight, someone else was coming up the stairs. Cavan lunged toward the door, but was a second late in preventing Darcie from stepping in.

"Now that all three of us have enough privacy to talk, I think it's time to set up a plan."

Cavan glanced at Daisy. She did not look happy.

"Um. Maybe another time," Cavan said.

"Tide's coming in anyway. And, the cops are swarming over the place like bees on a honeycomb. They found Aodhan's E-PACE hidden in the priest's shed."

"Another nail in his coffin," Cavan said.

Darcie scratched his man-bun. "He's found a watery grave where no nail will keep him. Or the inside of a great white's belly, if you believe what the police are saying."

Cavan didn't think for a minute that the police had been sharing their theories with Darcie, which meant he'd been spying on them.

"I wanted to let you know that I found Aodhan's metal detector near where we found him on the beach. I nabbed it before the police found it since we don't want them to know about the gold."

Cavan glanced at Daisy, who looked a bit green. He could hardly fault Darcie for keeping the truth from the police about the real reason Aodhan had been hanging around the beach since he'd done the same himself. But he was still wary of Darcie's attitude.

Daisy found her voice. "A man is dead. We may not have liked him, and we certainly don't approve of what he did to Father O'Leary, but he did have some decent qualities mixed in with the awful ones, and..." She gulped and tears started streaming down her face.

"It's not your fault, Daisy." Cavan put his arm around her shoulder.

"But if it wasn't for me, Father O'Leary would still be alive and none of this ever would have happened."

"I think I'll be on my way then," Darcie stammered. "Maybe in a day or two, when the police are done poking around, we can go out to the shanty for some shrimp on the barbie and see what we can find without arousing too much suspicion.

"We'll get back to you as soon as Daisy feels a little better," Cavan promised.

"There's one more thing," Darcie said. He reached for his pocket and pulled out some half crumpled photos. "It's the photos Daisy took of the quilt. I got them out of the trash and taped them together. I showed them to Daisy down at the police station but I wasn't sure she would remember what with all the confusion and her just being out of hospital."

"Thanks, Darcie."

Daisy looked uncomfortable. "Could I possibly keep them for a few days to study them?"

"I guess so," Darcie said. "They are yours."

"Thanks." It grated on Cavan to be put in a position of thanking Darcie for something he'd basically stolen from them, but what could he do? At any rate, he now knew that Darcie had good motives behind his sometimes questionable methods. At least he hoped he did. Cavan wasn't completely sure they weren't being scammed.

Come to think of it, it irked him even more that Darcie thought he could drop by unannounced at his and Daisy's apartment any time of night or day. They might be on the same side so to speak, but they weren't best friends by a long stretch.

"Listen, Darcie. We've had a really long day. If you don't mind, I'd rather we took this up tomorrow. I've ignored the bike shop for the past few days – maybe right at six when I close? Or better yet, half six so I can get a bite to eat when I'm done."

Darcie looked skeptical. "Maybe Daisy and I could head out to the beach at first light and get started without you."

Daisy turned even greener. "I'm really not feeling up to that, Darcie. But thanks. I appreciate your enthusiasm."

Darcie finally took the hint and left.

Cavan and Daisy stayed quiet until they were sure Darcie was gone. He made sure all the doors were closed and locked.

Daisy gripped the edge of the table. "My energy is just gone. I need to go to bed."

Cavan gulped. He was disappointed, but he understood. "I'm sorry we didn't end up having a little more privacy. I'd like to talk about everything that's happened. Just you and me."

Daisy followed his words with sad eyes. What was that all about?

"I'll be in the bathroom for a minute. Sweet dreams." And she was gone. They might be sharing an apartment once again, but it felt to him like she was a million miles away.

#

Daisy tried to push away the negative feelings that were eating away at her. If she hadn't found the first round of gold - the gold she'd thought was hers, but was really Father O'Leary's - the priest would still be alive. Aodhan would still be alive, too. He might be poor, but he wouldn't have been a murderer, and he wouldn't have drowned or been eaten by a shark or been taken captive by a ghost ship or whatever fate had ultimately taken him down.

She watched as her toast popped up from Cavan's toaster, golden brown around the edges, but still a tad soft in the center, and spread it with a thick layer of butter and then Granny's homemade raspberry jam. It was one of three jars she had left, and now that the quilt was gone, one of the few tangible things remaining on this earth that had known Granny's special touch.

She mentally kicked herself. It wasn't fair that she was alive and well, able to enjoy the crisp, buttery sweet taste of toasted bread when the priest lay cold in the ground and Aodhan's body was being devoured by who knew what sea creatures. Even if she'd kept her discovery to herself instead of splurging on an Edwardian mansion in Killarney and new clothes and a new car, things might not have ended so badly. It was her fault that Aodhan knew about the gold, and that the priest had turned up dead. What had possessed her to do that interview on live camera, she still didn't know. All she was certain of was that the guilt of everything that had happened was tormenting her.

She settled herself on a stool and took a drink of hot rosehip tea to wash down her toast.

If she wasn't careful, she would take Cavan down next. He'd neglected his shop, his bicycle repairs, and his customers because of her. The girl Rory had introduced him to had walked away from him because his attentions had been so divided.

She took another slice of toast from the toaster, swiped it with butter, watched it melt into the bread, and then, spread it with brown sugar – another of Granny's special morning treats. What if Cavan never met another girl? What if his business went down the tubes? He could end up homeless, alone, and childless and it would all be her fault.

Oh, they'd been optimistic all right. They'd gone walking on the beach almost every morning and evening since she'd gotten out of hospital and come up empty handed time and time again. Even with the photos of the quilt that Darcie had taped together, and Aodhan's metal detector, they'd not found a thing. It was almost like God was punishing her for mishandling the first round of gold. Not that she could blame him. Just being able to walk freely along the Wild Atlantic Way and take in the sights and sounds of the place she loved so intensely was better than she deserved.

She took the last bit of toast with raspberry jam followed by the final bite of brown sugared toast and wiped her mouth with a napkin. It was high time she moved back out to the shanty and got on with her life. Her own life. She had a fair amount of inventory and if she worked really hard for the next week, she could finish enough driftwood sculptures, pebblescapes, sea glass mobiles, painted rocks, and paintings to have a booth at Féile na Bealtaine art festival on bank holiday. If the luck of the Irish was with her, she might even meet some area shopkeepers who would agree to sell her wares in their shops. The Dingle Regatta had always been a good moneymaker for her when she'd had the store. If she kept at it, she might be able to rent a small storefront somewhere in Dingle before next spring.

"Daisy?"

She'd been so deep in her thoughts and so busy savoring each munch of her toast that she hadn't heard Cavan come up the stairs.

She pulled her robe closed in front and felt another surge of guilt — this one about getting such a late start to her morning when Cavan had been downstairs, hard at work, for more than two hours. "Sorry I'm being such a slug-a-bug."

"No worries. I'm sure you need the rest."

"I was just thinking I ought to be off to the shanty."

"One more look around to see if you can find the gold?"

"Actually, I was thinking to see if I could borrow your car to move my things back out to Granny's."

"For good?" Cavan looked surprised.

"There's really no reason not to."

Cavan gulped. "I've enjoyed having you here. I'd miss our talks in the evenings."

"You're welcome to come out to the shanty anytime you like. I need to bulk up my art inventory and the only way I know how to go at it quickly and efficiently is to spread everything out and totally immerse myself in the projects. It would make a huge mess. I'd drive you crazy."

Cavan looked resigned whereas she'd expected relief or even outright joy at the thought of having his privacy back.

"How about we go out to dinner as soon as I get off work and then I can drive you out to the shanty myself and help you unload everything and get things set up."

She felt another tinge of guilt. "Are you sure?"

"Positive," Cavan said.

There was a glint in his eyes that worried her. She didn't know quite why. If he thought she couldn't take care of moving herself back to Granny's on her own, the man had a second think coming. She'd been there, done this, plenty of times and she could do it again. Granny had raised her to be self-sufficient and to take care of herself.

"Fine," she said. "There's something I've been wanting to speak to you about." She didn't want to do it, but if she couldn't sell enough art to set up shop again, and more importantly, earn a decent living without mooching off Cavan, she was going to have to sell Granny's land.

"Good," Cavan said, with that hopeful glint in his eyes again. "There's something I want to talk to you about, too."

36

"No! No! No!" Granny wailed, her heart full o' such despair that she felt like she could die – again. She probably would die to the earth once her mission of shepherding Daisy was accomplished. That would nay bother her at all. What was driving her absolutely loony was the thought of Daisy selling her land and walking away from Cavan when it was all right there! She was so close to having it all! She could nay give up now!

"I do nay want her to sell the land either." The Captain's low voice startled her. He had a way of just showing up that was still disconcerting after all these weeks.

The loft was too crowded for all of them. The Captain was a big man.

She saw a shimmer of color as he swept his cape to one side. "I also believe that Cavan and Daisy are meant to be together. At first, I thought we were both sent here to direct their paths so that the gold would nay be spent foolishly this time, but distributed to the right people."

Granny stomped her foot into the sand. Finders keepers still worked for her – as long as the new finders were her kin, but she was resigned to the fact that the gold should be divvied up to suit Captain Donaghue since he'd given his life for it long, long ago.

She said, "But that will happen now that yer Cavan and the pirate have decided to work together. Daisy's heart has softened, too. Yer precious sea widows and little lost boys will get their share of the gold. And yet, here we still are."

"Because Cavan and Daisy have nay yet admitted their feelings for each other. Nor have they actually recovered the gold. We've still work to do."

"What more can we do? Daisy is convinced her chat with me was a dream. The storm practically destroyed the beach. I'd like to believe the quilt would still point the way to the gold, were it found, but I'm not sure even about that."

"I promise ye that I'll make the search for the quilt at sea my first priority. I want Cavan and Daisy to be together. And I do nay want Daisy to sell your land. Truth be told, I'd like to see Cavan and Daisy raising their children by the seashore and living happily ever after."

"Aye! I agree with ye one hundred percent, Captain Donaghue. I've developed a certain fondness for ye. I think we make a good team."

"Aye. There's nothing that would make me rest better than to have grandchildren who have a mixture of our traits." He winked. "Feisty like ye, calm and gentlemanly like me, stubborn and capable like ye, firm and no-nonsense like me. Cavan and Daisy will be a good match once they get past this rough spot."

"I hope ye're right." Granny said a wee prayer and then said, "I'm off to the beach to search for gold. You'd best get on the quilt before it's ripped to shreds by the currents."

They both disappeared.

#

Cavan took down a map and spread it on the counter for the customers to see. "You've got two nice routes to choose from depending how far you want to ride." He pointed to a starting off point and ran his fingers in a circle. "This is the most popular route. It takes you 55 kilometers and goes around Slea Head. The longer route is 120 kilometers. It also takes in Slea Head and then continues on to the Conor Pass and Anascaul via Camp and back to Dingle."

"We'll be back first thing in the morning to pick up the bikes. I'm so excited!" the woman said.

"Why don't we get them paid for right now so we can just take off in the morning?"

"Thanks." Cavan quickly totaled their bill and filled out the rental contract. It was five minutes past closing time, but Daisy would understand. At least he hoped she would.

She hadn't been the same since this whole business with Aodhan and the gold. The situation did nothing to dissuade his belief that gold was a divisive force and did great harm to those who held it. Daisy's Granny's gold – if it even existed – was already causing trouble between them, and they hadn't even found it yet. Personally, he hoped they never did.

Ten minutes later, he'd closed out his credit card machine, made a deposit to take to the bank on their way to the restaurant, and locked the front and back doors. He thought he smelled something wonderful cooking when he started up the stairs to his and Daisy's apartment, but assumed it was just Maeve baking more bread pudding and meat pie filling before she went home, in anticipation of a busy day tomorrow.

He realized the delectable odors were coming from his kitchen and not the bakery's when he opened the door to the apartment and saw a table set for two topped with a lace tablecloth. There was a bouquet of seaside daisies to the left and a lit candle in the center of the table along with two wine stems and a bottle of Bunratty Castle Mead. Daisy had moved the table to a spot where they could look out the front window at the sea while they ate.

"Hey, Dais. Are we eating in? It smells wonderful."

"Yes. Everything's almost ready. I hope you don't mind. I wanted it to be a surprise."

"Mind? It's perfect."

This really was very sweet of her. He looked around and tried to imagine the apartment without Daisy. He really didn't want her to leave.

Why hadn't he thought of putting the table in front of the window? Probably because the only eating in he did was to heat something up in the micro and take it back down to the bike shop so he could eat while he finished his paperwork. Daisy had said once that she had the apartment arranged completely differently when she lived there, but he'd never asked her how.

He went to the kitchen and put his arms around Daisy from behind, cradling her to his shape. She stiffened for a second, or maybe it was him who was feeling angular and hard.

After a few seconds, Daisy relaxed and leaned back into his

embrace. She was so close he could both hear and feel her sigh.

"Anything I can do to help?" He asked, hoping she said 'no' because he really didn't want to move.

"I hope you like everything." Daisy leaned forward to stir a pot on the stove.

"What are we having?"

"Well, I'm stirring the sauce for dessert - Irish Apple Crumble Cake with Custard Sauce. For the main, I fixed a Stout and Irish Cheddar Meatloaf and Colcannon."

"It sounds wonderful and smells incredible."

"I know it's dangerous to fix colcannon. Every family has their own recipe. You may hate Granny's version, but I think it's very good. I hope you like it even if it's different than your mother's."

"I'm sure I'll love it."

She pulled away to whisk out a crock of what looked like pub cheese, surrounded by a variety of thins.

"And yes, everything on the dinner menu has cheese in it. Even the scones. I love cheese."

He smiled. "Me, too."

Funny how they could talk of loving cheese and loving dinner and loving the way the wind felt blowing through their hair down at the seashore, but not of loving each other. Aye, that was the hard part. He hoped he was up to the challenge. Daisy had certainly set the mood for romance.

The last thing he wanted was to scare her off, or, worse, yet, ruin a perfectly wonderful friendship. He looked around the room and admired the way she lit up the whole place with her inner light.

Maybe after dinner, when they were both relaxed and had a couple of glasses of wine in them, he would find the courage to tell Daisy he loved her.

She was still just a couple of inches in front of him and his arms still loosely around her waist. He was unprepared when she turned to face him and lifted her eyes to meet his. She looked nervous. He felt like his heart was going to pound its way out of his chest.

He lowered his lips to find her and they kissed, really kissed, very tenderly – the type of kiss that stirs not just your body but your soul. It lasted what seemed like a few minutes and then she stepped back just a smidgen and broke their connection.

"Well, you took a big risk there," Daisy said, looking flushed and a little dazed. But then, she had been standing over a hot stove.

"I know," he said. "If you want me to leave, I'll miss out on what promises to be the best dinner ever."

"Leave?" She smiled. "It's your apartment."

"Well, technically speaking, it's yours."

"What? Evict you after I went to all the work of fixing you dinner? The loss would be mine."

He reached down and slid one of the thins into the crock of pub cheese. "Delicious. Love it." He looked up at her to stress the depth of his feelings.

She still looked scared and her hand was even shaking a wee bit. "Cavan, can we stop saying we love stuff and start saying I love you?"

He tried to hide his surprise but he had a feeling his cheeks were giving him away. Man, they felt hot. "You love me?"

"I love you, Cavan Donaghue. Is that all right with you?"

"It's more than okay. It's exactly what I've been hoping for. Because I love you, too, Daisy Fitzpatrick."

Her face beamed up at him. "Being in love makes me hungry. Shall we eat?"

He took her hand and only let go because it took both of her hands to dish up the meatloaf.

The End

Epilogue

Daisy snuggled up in Granny's old rocking chair with the twins cuddled in her lap. Siobhan was the older of the two by all of five minutes and had always been a wee bit quiet, although stubborn as all get out. Scully was taller and had a wondering mind. The lad was always full of questions and had been since the day he learned to speak.

"Will you tell us the story of Granny and the sea captain?" Scully looked up at her with Cavan's big eyes. He had an uncanny way of melting her heart just like his da did.

She smiled and readied her heart to tell the much loved tale.

"Once upon a time, there was a great flag ship that was wrecked at sea. The captain was very tall and noble and always wanting to help people, as all Donaghue men do, but the waves and the wind that came that day to the Wild Atlantic Way could nay be navigated by any man. And so the ship went down and many men perished at sea.

"Does perished mean that they died, Momma?" Scully asked.

"Like Auntie Ailene?" Siobhan added with a sad, puppy dog look.

"Yes, sweetie. But this happened over a hundred years ago and people only live so long, so they would all be dead by now even if the boat hadn't crashed."

She re-gathered her thoughts. "Now my Granny Siobhan was as industrious a woman as ye'll ever meet, and believed in the old adage that if ye waste not, ye'll want not. So years later, when the wrecked ship had broken apart and the wood started washing ashore, Granny started to collect it from the water's edge and haul it up to the top of the bluffs so she could put it to good use. And with that wood, she built a sea shanty with thick, sturdy walls that would provide shelter for her family for generations.

"Granny's shanty is where we live, right, Momma?"

"Yes, Siobhan, it is." She smiled. "Now, one day, whilst Granny was out searching for a wee bit more driftwood, she found a treasure – a pot of pirate's gold, half buried in a sea cave, that must have been washed up in the same storm decades earlier.

"Granny knew the gold could be a blessing to her family for years if she used it frugally, so she said nothing and only took a coin or two of the gold from the cave when absolutely necessary."

"Even when there was no food in the icebox?" Scully asked.

"Even when there was no food in the icebox. Because Granny always had potatoes in the root cellar and dried cherries and other things she had grown in her garden to feed us. And, she fished in the sea, and hunted rabbits along the bluffs. There was always something to eat."

"I don't like being hungry," Siobhan said.

"Me, neither," Scully concurred.

"Well, Granny told no one about the gold, but she did stitch a quilt that was really a buried treasure map with an 'X' to mark the spot where the treasure was buried. Sadly, Granny died before she told anyone about the gold, or even the quilt, so her secret went with her to her grave.

"One day long after Granny was dead and buried, her granddaughter, Daisy, realized that the quilt was a treasure map and started to search for the gold with her friend, Cavan."

"Is that you, Momma? Are you Daisy?" Siobhan asked like she did every time she told the story.

"And is Cavan really my daddy?" Scully asked.

"Yes, they are, because Daisy and Cavan fell in love and went to live in the sea shanty with their two babies."

"Is that us, Momma?"

"Yes, darlings. It is."

"What happens next? I want to hear the part about the pirate who came to get his share of the gold."

"Well, first, the quilt got lost, and then, a huge storm changed the look of the beach so much that no one could find the gold. Then one day, when Cavan and Daisy were searching for the sea cave where the gold was hidden, they found the quilt, which had mysteriously washed ashore.

"The quilt was covered with sea weed and the fish had nibbled part of it away. It was very faded, but all four corners were present so Cavan and Daisy were finally able to crack the code. The sea cave where the gold was hidden was completely covered with sand, but they started digging frantically until they found a gold coin, and then a few more, and then a whole cache of gold!

"Was it Granny Siobhan's gold?"

"Yes, it was. Daisy and Cavan researched shipwrecks to find out where the gold might have come from and discovered that very likely, the gold was in the safe of a ship that Cavan's Great-Grandfather Donaghue was the captain of. Captain Scully had recovered it from pirates and was on his way home when the pirates attacked in an effort to get it back."

"What happened to the gold?" Scully was always the one to ask this question. Of the twins, he looked more like Cavan, but Daisy suspected he shared a wee bit of her and Granny's lust for gold.

"Well, your Daddy wanted the gold to be returned to its rightful owners but he came to a dead end when he tried to find out who the pirates stole it from in the first place. So they got in touch with their friend, Darcie, the pirate, and gave him a third of the money to help the children at the Orphanage for Lost Boys. Darcie even used some of the money to adopt one of the boys. Your daddy decided to give his part of the gold to a charity that takes care of the families of men who are lost at sea."

"And what did you do with your part of the gold, Momma?"

"What my Granny Siobhan would have wanted me to do. You see, the gold was the legacy she left me because she loved me so much. I used some of it to add on to the sea shanty so we could keep living here even when our family started to grow, and the rest, I tucked away for a rainy day so the two of you can go to college one day."

"I'm going to be a sea captain and find more buried treasure maps when I grow up," Scully said.

"And I'm going to study history so I can find out who the pirates stole the gold from in the first place."

"She's my daughter, all right!" Cavan came into the shanty with a stack of peat bricks filling his arms. They'd installed electric heaters in the shanty when they remodeled, but Cavan loved the smell of an old-fashioned peat fire burning in the hearth – and he liked to save money whenever and however he could.

The kids clamored down from her lap and ran to help him stack the peat bricks in the basket by the fire. Someday, she would tell the children the rest of the story – how her granny and Cavan's great-grandfather, the sea captain, had danced a jig so enthusiastically when they found the gold that it was seen on both heaven and earth.

One day, she'd probably even tell them the scary parts of the story – that she'd almost died for the gold before she realized that she didn't need money to be happy, and that the life she'd thought she wanted when she let herself be charmed by fancy houses and insincere friends was nothing – nothing – compared to the simple, love-filled life she shared with Cavan.

Scully and Siobhan ran back to her side a few minutes later. "How does the story end, Momma? What happened next?"

"Well, Cavan and Daisy got married, and then, they had the two of you – twins - a little boy named Scully Fitzpatrick Donaghue and a little girl named Siobhan Doreen Donaghue."

Scully and Siobhan laughed and clapped like they did every time they heard the story. Cavan came over and kissed her while their precious babes giggled and whooped with silliness.

"Sing the Daisy song, Daddy! Please?" Scully and Siobhan clasped their hands together and prepared to do the wee Irish jig they always danced to Cavan's song.

Cavan smiled and took his baritone ukulele down from the shelf. He started to strum, and then, to sing.

"Sing the Daisy song, Daddy! Please?" Scully and Siobhan clasped their hands together and prepared to do the wee Irish jig they always danced to Cavan's song.

Cavan smiled and took his baritone ukulele down from the shelf. He started to strum, and then, to sing.

Where my Seaside Daisy's shanty's
On the Wild Atlantic Way
There's a treasure at the rainbow's end
In the caves on Dingle Bay. In the caves on Dingle Bay.

In early morn out on the sea,
The fog gives way to sun.
You can hear the seabirds singing
As the waves come crashing in,
As the waves come crashing in.

Where my Seaside Daisy's shanty's
On the Wild Atlantic Way
There's a treasure at the rainbow's end
In the caves on Dingle Bay. In the caves on Dingle Bay.

The Captain's ghost and Granny's quilt
Are there to point the way
But the pirate's gold and storms at sea
Are turning the blue skies gray,
Are turning the blue skies gray.

Where my Seaside Daisy's shanty's
On the Wild Atlantic Way
There's a treasure at the rainbow's end
In the caves on Dingle Bay. In the caves on Dingle Bay.

For gold can be a blessing
And gold can be a curse.
But true love is the greatest gift
Through better and through worse.

Where my Seaside Daisy's shanty's
On the Wild Atlantic Way
There's a treasure at the rainbow's end
In the caves on Dingle Bay. In the caves on Dingle Bay.

"And then what happened?" Scully was always wound up by the end of the song.

Cavan winked. "Momma and Daddy found love, and the buried treasure. And they lived happily ever after. That's what happened! And that's the end of the story."

Or the beginning... Daisy smiled and watched Cavan rough and tumble with the twins. She'd never felt happier. Because ever since she'd found the gold and then lost it and then struck true gold in Cavan Donaghue, she'd been seeing the world in a whole new way.

ABOUT THE AUTHOR

Twenty-eight years ago, Sherrie rescued a dilapidated Victorian house in northern Iowa from the bulldozer's grips and turned it into a bed and breakfast and tea house, the Blue Belle Inn. Sherrie grew up on a farm in southern Minnesota and has lived in Wheaton, IL, Bar Harbor, Maine, Lawton, OK, Augsburg, Germany, and Colorado Springs, CO. After 12 years of writing fiction, Sherrie met and married her real-life hero. Mark and Sherrie divide their time between a cottage next door to their B&B, and the parsonage where Mark serves as pastor. Their two houses are 85 miles apart, and Sherrie writes on the run whenever she has a spare minute. In her "free time", Sherrie paints scenes from her books, plays the piano, writes murder mysteries, travels to far off corners of the world, and posts millions of amazing photos on Facebook and Instagram. Sherrie's books have been called "the thinking woman's romance" and her latest books contain elements of suspense and mystery. While many of Sherrie's books contain issues of faith and family, some also include "steamy" scenes, and some, a candid combination of both. Most are "second chance at romance" stories with primary characters aged 30 to 50. Many of Sherrie's books contain at least one special quilt. Sherrie loves hearing from her readers and appreciates constructive feedback and honest reviews. Thank you for reading Seaside Daisy!

You can follow Sherrie at:
http://www.facebook.com/SherrieHansenAuthor
https://sherriehansen.wordpress.com/
http://www.BlueBelleInn.com
https://twitter.com/SherrieHansen
https://www.pinterest.com/sherriebluebell/

Made in USA - Kendallville, IN
1055436_9781699846025
03 19 2020 0948